AFTER EVERYTHING

AFTER EVERYTHING

MONNA MCDIARMID

HOUSE OF WINTERPORT PRESS

For Damien, for everything.

AUTHOR'S NOTE

Dear Reader,

Before you begin reading, please be aware that this novel begins with Claire, the protagonist, learning that she has died recently. In the face of the loss of her life and her memories, she experiences both anxiety and anger.

Although Claire and her best friend, Nobu, face some big obstacles in this book, I take very good care of them as a novelist, just as I will attend to your needs as a reader.

Ultimately, *After Everything* is a hopeful book filled with tenderness between people. There are also several sweet dogs and lots of Paris yumminess.

If this is not the right time for a story about two young people who have died, please look after yourself by tucking this book away until you are ready.

Sending you love,
Monna McDiarmid

CONTENTS

CHAPTER 1
IN WHICH I AM NOT WHERE I AM SUPPOSED TO BE

I wake up thrown, as if from a delicious dream, with the feeling that there's somewhere else I'm supposed to be. Like in a bed, maybe. But I'm in a field. A wave of nausea and dizziness overwhelms me. It's a green field dotted with dandelions, stretching far beyond my bare feet, to a line of trees in the distance. The world is so spinny and bright that I close my eyes for a moment. My body is exhausted, but my heart is thumping. What's happening to me?

As I sit up, I see a little boy staring at me with a piercing, but not unkind, gaze. He's young, seven at most, and he's dressed for gym class in a white T-shirt, khaki cargo shorts, gleaming white sneakers, and white athletic socks pulled up to his knees. Around his neck hangs a silver whistle on a red cord. I've never seen this boy before.

I stagger to my feet, trip on my long cotton nightgown, and accidentally step on something that wobbles under my foot.

"Ouch!"

I look down and find I've stood on the hand of a boy who looks like he might be a senior in high school. "Sorry," I say.

"Shhhh. I'm sleeping. And I'm having an especially sweet dream." He smiles and rolls over on his side, pulling his knees up towards his chest. It occurs to me slowly that I don't know this boy either, and something crashes in: an absence so vast, I can scarcely comprehend it. I do not know these boys because I don't know anyone. I can't remember the name or face of anyone in my life. Every hair on my body stands on end. The kid with the whistle steps toward me.

"Claire."

I step back as he speaks. Am I Claire?

"Good morning, Claire. I'd like you to call me Coach. Not The Coach, but just Coach. Like a name. Like Bob. But, you know, Coach."

"Coach?" I say. The older boy on the grass is now sitting up, rubbing his eyes.

"Claire, this is Nobu. Nobu, Claire."

"Nobu. That's a cool name," says Nobu. "Where are we?" He looks around the green field.

"My question is more like, who are we?" Nobu chuckles and I realize that came out funnier than I meant it to.

"You are Claire, and he is Nobu. I thought I made it perfectly clear."

"Kid! Why are you messing with us?" My hands are shaking, and I try to jam them in my pockets. No pockets. Stupid nightgown.

"Claire, I assure you that I will never lie to you or take advantage of you in any way." He nods his head at the end of his statement. This tiny person seems entirely sincere. Still.

Nobu stands and we form a lopsided triangle. Two older teenagers and a little kid with a whistle around his neck.

"Why can't I remember who I am or where I live or how

I got here? Or even where here is? What about you?" I turn to Nobu. "Do you know who you are?"

"Nobu. Just like the kid said."

"Right, but do you know what's happening? Like, why are we in the middle of this field … in our pyjamas?" Nobu looks down at his red plaid pyjamas and shakes his head.

"I expect I'm still asleep, and I'll wake up any moment now."

"Okay, what's the situation, kid? What have you done to us?" I say. Now Coach takes a step back as I move towards him. My anxiety is shapeshifting into anger, and I think the kid can smell it.

"I have some news," says Coach, looking up at us. "It's not good or bad news in and of itself … but it is rather big news."

"You have our undivided attention," I say.

"The thing is that you have both died. Rather recently, in fact."

I'm hit again by the sensation of aggressive absence, but this time it presses all the way in, pushing all the air from my lungs. "Wow. I was not expecting that," I hear Nobu say, as I begin to fall. He reaches out and catches me, guiding me gently to a sitting position. He kneels, facing me, and places his hands on my forearms. "Breathe, Claire," he says, but it sounds like he's very far away. Or else I am. "Inhale. In with big breaths. Exhale the bad stuff." Nobu takes big, loud breaths and I follow him, sucking air in and blowing it out. He glances over his shoulder at the kid, "We're going to need a minute here, Coach."

"Take all the time you need." Coach sits down on the grass. The breathing has helped and so has the weight of Nobu's hands on my arms. I nod and Nobu drops back onto his butt and crosses his legs. Whoever I am, I don't think I like people touching me, but there's something about Nobu that feels alright. That actually helps.

"Okay, Coach. Start at the beginning," I say.

And Nobu adds, "Or is it the end?"

CHAPTER 2

IN WHICH WE ESTABLISH THAT THIS IS NOT HEAVEN

"What do you two fancy for breakfast?"

"Wait! This is insane," I say. "Are you going to answer our questions about us being D-E-A-D?"

"Yes. I promise," says Coach. "But you will feel better after you have eaten."

At first glance, the kitchen looks like something out of a design magazine, but as I look around the room, a sense of peace falls over me. Well-being. Being fed and looked after. The style is French, I think. The stove is old and the tiles behind it are blue and white, some of them cracked or missing their corners. Coach repeats his question about what we'd like to eat and Nobu asks what there is. Coach laughs and says, "Everything." Nobu runs through several choices, rejecting each one before finally settling on freshly squeezed orange juice and eggs Benedict. I ask for a cup of mint tea. Coach pulls out a small wooden step stool so he can reach everything with ease and prepares the tea.

"How old are you?" I ask Coach.

"I'm not entirely certain. Quite old. I suppose it depends on what system you employ."

"Coach, the vagueness of your answers is deeply annoying."

"My sincere apologies, Claire. I can assure you that it's not my intention to annoy you."

"Try asking him in a different way," says Nobu.

"Okay. How old were you when you died? In human years?" I ask. Nobu puts his head in his hands.

"I was six. Almost seven," says Coach.

Six. This kid was six and he died, and now he's standing on a wooden step stool making eggs Benedict for a boy wearing pyjamas that I doubt he would have chosen, but I can't really be sure of that, can I, since I've only known him a few minutes, and as it turns out, both the red plaid pyjama boy and I are also dead. The room tilts sideways, and I need to sit down. The closest spot is a chair at the large wooden table in the middle of the room. My butt hits the seat with a thud and I close my eyes and inhale deeply.

As I practice my breathing, Coach moves his stool in front of a wooden cupboard of dishes and chooses an amber coloured glass for Nobu's juice. He hesitates in front of a light pink teacup, but then chooses a green one. He places the cup on its matching saucer in front of me, then retrieves a small pot of tea from the kitchen counter. The cup is green porcelain with full, pink peonies painted on the bottom. My favourite, I know without thinking. Could peonies be my favourite flower?

"Please be careful. The teapot is very hot," Coach says. I notice that Nobu is shaking his head at me.

"What?" I say.

"Dude, I can't believe you just asked a six-year-old about

his death," says Nobu.

"Six, and also not six. I don't mind," says Coach.

"You just called me 'dude,'" I say.

"Is that offensive?" says Nobu. His brow is furrowed.

"No. It's hilarious." I pour the tea into the green cup that Coach chose for me. I laugh and Nobu joins in, while Coach watches us from the island where he's making hollandaise sauce. I cannot, for the life of me, stop laughing. Then I start crying.

Nobu sits down in the chair beside me. "Drink your tea, Claire."

It's delicious. I drink it quickly and pour myself a second cup. Coach places a plate of eggs Benedict in front of Nobu and another in front of me.

"I said I'm not hungry."

"Just in case," Coach tells me. He sits across the table from us. "Alright then. Ask me anything."

"We're really dead?" I say, as Nobu cuts into his eggs Benny.

"Yes, I'm afraid so."

"Like permanently?"

"It's the only kind I know of," says Coach.

"Will I get back the memories from my life?" I ask. He shakes his head. "Never?"

"No. Not ever."

"And is Claire really my name, or is it some lame name you chose for me?"

"It is the one your parents gave you. It is your human name."

"But if you know that, you must know other details. You can tell me about my life, right Coach?" I lean in towards him.

"I'm afraid I've told you all I can, Claire. Becoming a Helper depends on detaching from your previous life." Detach from my previous life? There's no way that's going to happen.

"Can you at least tell us why we arrived at the same time?" asks Nobu.

"It's quite unusual to have two arrivals at the same time. When this happens, we call those people twins," says Coach. "I'm not really meant to tell you this. It's a bit distressing."

"We can handle it," says Nobu. I reflect that one of us can probably handle it, while one of us is not so sure.

"When people arrive at The Station at exactly the same time, they are called Death Twins." Yup. As suspected. Too much.

I cover my ears and say, "lalalalalalalala."

"Woah! Now, that was a surprise," says Nobu. Then he turns to me. "Sorry, Claire." He brushes the top of my hand with his fingers. "Hey, I thought you weren't hungry," he says. I look down at my plate, which is empty except for a small bright yellow drop of egg yolk. The knife and fork are still in my hands and the taste of hollandaise lingers in my mouth.

"I guess I was. Thank you, Coach," I say. Nobu smiles at me. "So, why's it called The Station?" I ask.

"When people fly first class, they get access to the airline's lounge. This is similar." Nobu nods, but I don't know what Coach means. I shake my head and he tries again. "A place where travellers can get a good meal and perhaps a beverage, and relax before the next leg of their journey."

"So, The Station is the first-class lounge for the dead, and you're the airline attendant?" I say.

Coach nods his head and picks up our empty plates. "Look around for a bit, while I wash up the dishes. Come back when you're ready, and I will happily answer more of your questions."

As we step into the hallway of The Station, I pay closer attention to the building than when we arrived, and check my initial impression that there is no end in either direction. The wood panelled hallway rolls on and on into infinity, and I remember what Coach said about this place being like a flight lounge, which must mean there are flights ... or the equivalent. One of these doors must lead back to the real world where there are actual humans. Live ones. Someone who knows me. I race down the hallway, glancing from side to side each time I encounter a new set of doorways.

There are bedrooms and bathrooms, an indoor swimming pool, several libraries, a ballroom with a grand piano, rooms filled with paintings, and winning the award for the most random, a bowling alley. But the windows in every single room, including those on opposite sides of The Station, look out onto the green field where we arrived earlier today. Of course, that's impossible, but impossible feels like the vibe at The Station.

Nobu catches up with me. "Hey, Claire! What's your favourite?" I don't know how to respond so I shrug. "Mine was the room full of puppies."

"Puppies?" I ask.

"Literal puppies." His face shines as he nods. I want to be happy for him, I do. He's ridiculously kind and literally my only friend but what I need is to discover who I was, and it looks like I'm going to have to play along with Coach until I can figure that out.

CHAPTER 3

IN WHICH WE DRINK MINT TEA AND ARE ENCOURAGED TO DO OUR BEST

"Why don't we sit in the garden?" Coach opens the French doors in the kitchen to the ubiquitous green field. I suppose the garden's as good a place as any in this prison. He grabs a quilt from a bench and leads us outdoors.

"What happens to us now?"

"You'll spend some time with me here at The Station. It's much like an orientation, before you begin your work as Helpers on Earth."

"Just like summer camp," I say.

"Not entirely unlike summer camp, Claire, although I detect your sarcasm."

"I am not exactly trying to hide it," I say. Nobu glares at me, while Coach unfolds the large multicoloured quilt and shakes it out flat on the grass. He gestures to the blanket, so Nobu and I sit. Coach stays on his feet. It's the only way he'll ever tower over us.

"So, do we become angels?" says Nobu.

"I am sorry, Nobu, but we don't use that word here," says Coach.

"But you just said we would be helping people on Earth."

"Yes. I realize that this is confusing. Words like 'heaven' and 'angels' evoke particular images and expectations in the newly arrived, but these are seldom aligned with the reality of The Station or returning to Earth as a Helper. Does that make sense?"

"Sort of," says Nobu. He looks at me and I shrug. None of this makes sense to me, but Coach just said we're going back to Earth, so that's what I hold on to.

"Depending on a person's religious tradition, they might expect, oh, I don't know, trumpets. To be greeted by trumpets. But that cloud-place they imagine does not exist. Or if it does, it is not this place. Consequently, we try to manage expectations from the outset."

"So, it's about semantics," I say.

"No. Indeed, it is not simply a matter of word choice. You are in a new part of your existence."

"Good Lord, Coach!" Nobu says, a little louder than I was expecting. "Are you saying that after all of this, all of life, there is no heaven? That this is not heaven?" Coach slips his feet out of his spotless white runners and sits cross-legged on the quilt in front of us.

"Nobu, I am saying that heaven is not a place. Heaven is a feeling. Only you can decide if this is heaven or not." Nobu glances around as though he's looking for answers. It seems that Coach has struck a chord in him, with this not-heaven stuff, that I don't have. I make eye contact with Nobu and hold it.

"Okay, Coach," I say. "Tell us about the helping, and please don't say it's complicated."

"Alright. In the least complicated way possible, when

you return to Earth, you will be a team. Partners." Nobu smiles at me, and I feel my body relax as we finally receive a piece of good news. "You will assist people in need. Mostly people your age, I expect."

Nobu and I talk over each other. "How old is that?" I ask.

"How will we know who to help?" says Nobu.

"They will be able to see you," says Coach. "They will be thinking about their problem and how they need help with it, and that awareness will make you visible, if you happen to be in their vicinity."

"And to other people?" Nobu says.

"You will be invisible," says Coach. Nobu sits up straighter and his eyes widen. "To answer your question, Claire, you are both approximately the Earth equivalent of nineteen years old."

"That's a lot to take in," I say, feeling wobbly. Nobu turns towards me and takes a deep breath. I follow his lead and, immediately, my shoulders drop.

"Perhaps the best approach is to think of yourselves as travelling social workers." Nobu shakes his head. I hear a bird chirping in the distance and I wonder if it's real, and then I wonder what I mean by real, and that second thought makes me shiver.

"In no way am I qualified to be a social worker," says Nobu. "I don't remember my life, but it's clear that I'm a barely post-pubescent boy, and we're not exactly known for our collective wisdom." Coach doesn't comment. "Is there a training manual or something?"

Coach reaches into one of the gigantic pockets of his khaki green shorts and pulls out a card, which he hands to Nobu. It's small, like a business card, and although I can't read it, I can make out that there are only three words on it. Nobu passes it to me. It says,

Do your best.

I laugh. Perhaps a bit too loudly. Nobu looks worried. "Claire, it's not funny. I don't want to screw this up, and make things worse for some innocent person."

"I get it, Nobu. I just think it's hilarious that you have already moved on to being worried about the people we're meant to help. I'm definitely still stuck on the absurdity of two recently dead youths being asked to do their best. That's a low bar, right there. Also, extremely bold on the part of The Station Master."

"Claire, I understand what you are feeling," says Coach. Just as I'm about to shout that he couldn't possibly, I remember that he does, that he, too, arrived abruptly at this Station in his PJs. "As I have said, I will never mislead either of you. You will make some mistakes as Helpers, especially at first, but the humans are depending on you. I know you will do your best," he says.

I sense he's given this motivational speech before, but it's not working on me. To do my best, I need to know who I am, who I was on Earth. I promise myself that I'll do whatever is necessary to find out.

CHAPTER 4
IN WHICH WE CHOOSE OUR COSTUMES

sit up in bed. It's morning, which is to say I see the fake light shining through our fake window at The Station. Where, I remind myself, we are dead. I tell myself to breathe, and then I remember that whatever I'm doing now is not actually breathing, but it helps the part of me that used to be alive, so I take in a long breath through my nose and exhale through my mouth. I do this several times, and as my phantom heartbeat begins to slow, I realize it must still be very early, so I pull the quilt tight around me and as I drift back to sleep, I think I see a shimmering rope of individual threads of light swooping down from Nobu's bunk to mine. Whatever it was, it's gone when Nobu wakes me to say we're going to The Warehouse to pick out our clothes for training. Didn't we just get here? I wonder what a girl needs to do around this place to get some rest. And a toothbrush.

Coach arrives in the kitchen shortly after we do, ties an apron over his white T-shirt and gets to work making pancakes. Nobu boils water for a pot of tea before he sits on the bench beside me. Coach places a pancake on my plate. It's in the shape of a dolphin. Or so he says.

"Highly intelligent, the dolphin. Arguably more intelligent than humans," says Coach.

"Yeah? If they're so smart, why do they allow humans to lock them up in aquariums, where they are made to do tricks for tourists?" I ask.

"Ouch! Claire!" Nobu looks up from his giraffe pancake.

"Nobu, it's okay. Claire has a right to these questions. Her doubts are an essential part of her that will undoubtedly help you on Earth. You are both perfect the way you are."

Nobu and I laugh at exactly the same moment. Big bursts of laughter that fill up the kitchen. Just as one of us stops laughing, the other goes off again, until I'm light-headed. Whatever we are, we're a long way from perfect.

Then I make the mistake of calling the clothes we'll choose at The Warehouse a uniform, and Coach gently reminds me that these are just clothes, those we would most like to wear, that we feel the most ourselves in. When I volunteer the word 'eternity,' Coach frowns slightly and says, "Nothing lasts forever, dear girl."

I suppose not.

The Warehouse is twelve doors down, on the same side of the hall as the kitchen and our bedroom. "Are you excited about choosing our gear?" asks Nobu.

"Yeah. I'll be glad to change out of this nightgown," I say.

On the door, there is a small gold plaque that says, "CLOTHING ETC." I wonder about the etcetera—Avocados? Trombones? —but say nothing. Coach turns the doorknob—nothing in The Station is locked—and the heavy wooden door swings inwards. The Warehouse is enormous, similar in size to the field where Nobu and I woke up. Nobu whistles.

"Now this, this is impressive," he says.

"Not the pancakes?" says Coach. His eyes twinkle.

"Coach, I love your cooking, but that would be like comparing, I don't know, a cup of hot chocolate to a room full of unicorns. They're not even the same language of amazing," says Nobu.

"I concede the point," says Coach.

"Unicorns are real, by the way," I say. They both turn towards me.

"How do you know?" says Nobu.

"I don't know. How do I know anything, given that I am the Helper equivalent of an infant? I just know."

"It's true," says Coach. "Not exactly in the way you might think, but they did exist. You both have all this knowledge inside you. It's always a bit of a mystery how it will get unlocked in new Helpers. Claire has a particularly uncanny knowledge of human life."

"Who? Me?"

"Yes. You are gifted," says Coach. "You are, without question, a highly sensitive and intuitive being." Nobu is smiling for some reason I can't understand.

"Thanks. I guess."

"You are most welcome." Coach leads us inside The Warehouse, which has a domed ceiling and large stained-glass windows.

"It looks like a church," I say.

"It does indeed. There are certain design ideas that survive even death." Coach reaches inside his pocket and pulls out two folded pieces of paper. He unfolds them, smooths them out against his leg, and passes one to each of us. They are maps. "I know it seems a tad excessive, but it is quite easy to get lost in The Warehouse. I once spent forty-eight hours searching for someone."

"Where did you find them?" asks Nobu.

"They were in the tutu section." Nobu and I make eye contact and Nobu grins. "There is something about The Station that makes most Helpers feel freer than they did in their human lives," says Coach. Nobu nods his head. I have not yet had this experience.

Nothing could have prepared me for the size and scope of The Warehouse. A wide central walkway cuts through what seems, at first glance, like an ancient forest of clothing racks. There are shirts and jackets, shorts and trousers, skirts and dresses, kimono, kurtas, saris, burqas, and so many other items I don't yet know the name of, in every style, colour, and size that a newly dead being could imagine. Around the edge are accessories including belts, hats, scarves, socks, shoes, and boots. Feather boas. Silk squares for the pocket of a three-piece suit. Everything a Helper-in-training might desire to make their outfit sassier.

"Coach, what climate are we dressing for?" I say.

"Your destination will be revealed in due time," says Coach. Nobu and I exchange a glance. "To be on the safe side, you should plan for four seasons. It is likely that layers will be appropriate."

I like the sound of that. Layers will be required. I'll look for a jacket, something cool and edgy. Coach has explained that we won't feel the cold or heat because our new body is entirely self-regulating and a sort of projection of our old one. This is an entirely new way of being. The problem is that I suspect he is lying about how we'll experience temper-ature. I don't know whether this is paranoia or good judg-ment, but I have a feeling I often had similar doubts about people.

Except for Nobu.

He whistles a second time, a long, drawn-out trill, then heads in the direction of the outerwear. He walks slowly, like I imagine a super-chill cowboy would, into the jungle of clothing.

I start with the jeans. I'm looking for a dark blue pair with a wide leg. After a few racks of jeans with rips, studs, and other unnecessary adornments, I come to a rack of regular jeans with pockets in the front and back, and I can tell, just by looking at these, that I'm a fan of the pockets. One of the tricky parts of not remembering your life is not knowing what size you wear, but my intuition tells me to walk beside the rack and touch each pair. About halfway down the rack, a pair makes my fingertips tingle and then several small golden sparks fly up. Whoa! What was that?

I release the jeans from the clips, pull them on, and am not surprised that they fit as if they were made for me. I stick the hanger back on the rack and head to the shirt section, where I quickly find a t-shirt via the same, strange spark method. Yup. Definitely not making it up. Something is happening between these items and me. Like a chemical reaction. I pull my nightgown off over my head and try on the black V-neck. It's soft and perfect. The socks that spark up a storm, feature a couple of pink cherubs and the words, "You Rock." In the footwear section, my intuition leads me to a shelf of Doc Marten boots. For a moment, I'm drawn to a pair of glossy yellow ones, the colour of lemons, but when no sparks ignite, I know they're not right. The pair below them is black. Size six. Fireworks. I sit down on a wooden bench, pull on my new socks, slide my feet into the boots and lace them up. These sparks must tell me what I like, or maybe what's meant for me. Nope, I reject that idea. I may be only two-days old by the Helper calendar, but I don't believe in fate. I conclude that these sparks are part of my inner navigational system, a kind of extension of my intuition, and I wonder if humans have them too.

The outfit feels good. Right. What I need to complete my look is a jacket and some kind of bag, although I don't yet know what I might be carrying. The choice of jackets is overwhelming: fitted blazers, jean jackets, winter coats of every possible length and fabric. None of these feels right. I pass rows and rows of coats and feel dizzy as I take my twentieth turn down a new row. Just as I suspect that my internal clothes-finder has taken a well-deserved lunch break, I turn into an aisle of black leather jackets. I sweep by them, touching only the sleeves. When I touch a vintage jacket with a side zipper and a stiff collar, my sparks stop me, so I slide on the jacket and place the hanger back on the rack.

Although there must be an actual mile of bags, an old black leather messenger bag makes my hand vibrate and spark with recognition. I pull the bag over my head and across my jacket and return to the foyer.

"Oh! Don't you look marvellous!" says Coach.

"Do I?"

"You do, indeed." I feel like myself in these clothes even though I don't know who that is, exactly. I ask Coach if he has something I can use to pull my long hair back. He takes a black hair elastic out of his pocket and passes it to me.

"Seriously?" I ask.

"Of course. I am always serious, Claire."

"Did you know that I would ask for this elastic?"

"I do my best to anticipate the needs of the Helpers who pass through The Station."

"So, that's a yes." He nods as I pull my hair into a ponytail. "And you wonder why I'm suspicious."

"I do not wonder. Just a moment," says Coach, disappearing into the hallway. He returns a few moments later with a flat, square box. "I hope you won't think it presumptuous, but I took the liberty of choosing an item for you." Coach passes me the box and when I lift the lid, I find a bright pink silk scarf printed with the white outline of peonies. The flowers look full as if they are ready to drop from their stems.

"Coach, I love this. I was worried when I saw the pink, but it's beautiful."

"May I?" says Coach, pointing to the scarf. I nod. Slowly he lifts it from the box. It's even larger than I thought. He folds the scarf in half and wraps it around my neck three times before tying it off to the side. He makes a few adjustments and steps back.

"La voilà," says Coach.

"Thank you. I think it makes the outfit ..."

"Go ahead. Say it."

"Perfect, Coach. It makes the outfit perfect."

"I thought it might." Coach tries to conceal his pride by looking away for a moment.

Nobu comes ambling up the centre aisle holding his clothes and their hangers in his arms. When he sees me, he chuckles, which then becomes a full-blown howl.

"What's so funny?" I ask.

"Coach, is there a place I can change?"

Coach points to a series of stalls with red velvet curtains, and Nobu disappears into one, still laughing.

"Claire, where did you change?" asks Coach.

"Oh, you know, in the middle of the aisle." Something I'm learning about myself is that I'm not at all shy. I open my messenger bag and pull out my white nightgown. "Coach, I can confirm that this is most decidedly not my style. Let's make sure I never see this piece of clothing again." As I pass it to him, he nods his head and smiles the way he must have when he was actually six. A smile filled with long afternoons, red bicycles, and puppies. Before all of this.

"Claire, you asked what I was laughing about," says Nobu. He emerges from the changeroom wearing a black tee, a pair of dark blue skinny jeans tucked into black Doc Martens, and a short black leather jacket that zips up the side.

CHAPTER 5

IN WHICH WE BEGIN OUR TRAINING

Back in the kitchen, Nobu and I sit on tall stools at the kitchen counter in our identical outfits, resplendent in all our previously unseen, badass glory. After surveying our preferences, Coach prepares a Caesar salad and grilled chicken, and Nobu watches with interest as Coach deftly dices the garlic into tiny cubes, while I sneak glances at Nobu, who seems much cooler and more confident in his jeans and leather jacket. He's cute, too. Is that the word? It feels familiar, but somehow not quite sufficient.

"Hey, Coach," says Nobu, "what's the statistical probability that Claire and I would choose exactly the same outfit?"

Coach looks out the kitchen window into the field that also grows on the other side of the hallway. "Small. Minuscule. Much less than one per cent," says Coach.

"Does that trouble you?" asks Nobu.

"It does not trouble me, exactly. It is an unexpected development. I shall give it some thought," That is a classic

Coach maneuver, if I've ever seen one. A skillful duck-and-weave.

"Nobu," I say. "Your name sounds like a character from Star Wars." He laughs.

"Yeah. I get that," he says. "Whoa! That's weird, right? We've forgotten our lives, but remember Star Wars?" Nobu shakes his head and then stops. "Oh! And Star Trek!" He pauses for a moment. "I can't explain why, but deep in my bones, I know that Star Wars was better." I choose not to point out that whatever we're made of now, it's unlikely to include bones.

"You sound pretty certain for someone who showed up here in pyjamas chosen by his grandmother," I say. Nobu gasps and covers his mouth with his hand. "What? Too soon?"

"Possibly." He grins.

"So, what happens first when we get to Earth?" says Nobu.

"Funny you should ask, Nobu. We're actually going after lunch today."

"Really?" I jump up and my stool tips over, crashing to the tiled floor. Coach removes the frying pan from the stove and turns to face us. He's mistaken my excitement for fear.

"My apologies, dear girl. It's just a training session. A quick trip out and back to help you get your Earth legs back." I grab my stool and sit down at the table. Okay. I'm up for whatever it takes to know who I am. Who I was when I was alive. The extent to which these Claires are the same. I need to face the truth that I need to solve this on my own, so let's go get some Earth legs.

———

After lunch, Nobu stacks the dishes in the sink and Coach leads us down the hall past the puppies to The Training Room, a door with a plaque that says, WHEREVER.

"I'll be with you the entire time," Coach says, "but this is the easiest way for you to start to get the hang of things." This is the most colloquial phrase I've heard Coach use to date, which makes me think he's feeling nervous. "When I open this door, we will enter the town of Lunenburg in Nova Scotia, Canada. Although someone could theoretically see the two of you here, these are a sturdy and self-sufficient people, not often in need of assistance. If someone does ask for your help, we'll figure something out together, but for today, I don't want you to worry about helping. My goal for today is to teach you three basic skills." He turns the doorknob and the huge wooden door swings open into the centre of a village filled with stately old wooden houses painted in bright colours. We're standing in a gazebo looking down towards a body of water so large it can only be an ocean and there is fog rolling in off the water and I can hear a foghorn blowing in the distance. I turn to look behind me, but the door and The Station are gone.

"I chose somewhere very safe for your first training session. Let's walk down to the harbour." The town's grid is built on a steep hill, or series of hills, and as we head down towards the sea, I touch objects along our path. A wooden gate painted white. A rose bush growing at the edge of someone's lawn. The ancient post holding up a street sign. Everything is beautiful, but nothing feels familiar. No sparks. The first people we pass are a woman and her child. They're both wearing raincoats and rubber boots and they're holding hands and the little kid is telling the mother a story. They are so close I could touch them, but I don't. The mother laughs at some funny thing the kid has said, and her laughter floats in the air for a few moments before disintegrating.

"Humans," I say.

"Yes, Claire." I feel both excited and achy to be in such close proximity to people who are alive. Nobu is quiet. When we reach the harbour, Coach leads us to a bench where the three of us sit and look out at the sea.

"How are you both feeling?" asks Coach.

"All these people are going to die," I say. It's not a decision. It just sort of slips out before I can hook the words and reel them back inside of me. Nobu's eyes fly open, but he says nothing. How can he not be thinking this?

"That's a perfectly natural response, Claire. All humans die. This awareness will become less acute with a bit of time. I promise you."

"But they know, right?" says Nobu.

"They do," says Coach. "The adults know. Some of the children." Nobu nods. Coach continues, "Come on, you two. I would like to demonstrate some of the benefits of being a Helper." We walk up two steep blocks to a shop that sells stationary, art supplies, toys, prints and paintings. As we approach the store, a man in a top hat opens the door and a bell on the door jingles as he exits.

"We're going to walk through that door, without opening it. At first your mind will believe this is not possible, but that is a residual memory from your time as a human. For us, this wooden door is no more of an obstacle than walking through the air outdoors. All the particles of this door will greet us and recognize us and move aside for us to pass. Which one of you would like to go first?" I don't wait for further instructions. I simply climb the steps and walk through the door, just as Coach said. Through the window I see the surprised expressions on the faces of Nobu and Coach. I sense that I'm a complicated person, anxious about some things and courageous about others. Maybe all humans feel that way. In a moment Nobu is standing beside me and high fives me before Coach appears on this side of the door.

"Well done, you two. That was a very impressive beginning. The next step in your training might be a little less pleasant." He looks up at me and adds, "But then again, perhaps not. This really depends on the person. The fact that you've just come through that door with such ease makes me feel very optimistic about this next task."

"No disrespect intended, Coach, but you're making it worse," says Nobu. "What's the second thing?"

"Understood," says Coach. "I brought you here because this shop is often quite crowded, and the next task involves you standing still while a human walks through you."

"Nope. You did not just say that." I turn to leave the shop.

"Claire, I know how strange this sounds, but the energy you are made of is the same as the energy that holds together and pushes apart the particles that comprise the door and the air and everything else. It will make way for these humans. Let me show you." Coach notices a young salesperson walking towards the cash register and moves into the centre of the aisle. Just as he had said would happen, his Coach energy makes way for the young woman to stride right through him without a hitch. As she steps out of his tiny kid body, Coach smiles and gives us a thumbs up.

"Yuck," I say. "That looks positively awful."

"The faster you become accustomed to this aspect of moving around on Earth, the easier it will be for you to do your job as a Helper."

"I'll go," says Nobu. "How bad can it be?" I make a splat sound, which makes us both laugh. The kid and her mother we saw earlier have entered the shop and Nobu steps into the aisle just in time for the woman to pass through him at full speed, as she tries to catch up with her daughter. Nobu looks a bit surprised, but not injured or traumatized.

"Well?" I say.

"Yeah. Fine. A little weird, but not bad." As he's talking, the small girl squeals with delight and I turn to see her barrelling down the aisle with a furry, purple puppet on one hand, but before I have time to get out of the way, she runs right through the bottom half of my body. Whoosh! I am made of nothing to the extent that I have become a hallway for a human child.

The tears begin to fall, and in a few long steps, I'm back out on the sidewalk, doubled over with that aggressive absence waking inside me, demanding something I know, but can't remember. As I swallow deep gulps of air, Nobu appears at my side. "Claire. I'm here." He folds me into his arms, and we stand on the sidewalk of this quaint Maritime town, while I try to shake off this terrible feeling.

At some point I'm aware that Coach is standing beside us on the sidewalk. "I am very sorry, Claire. I have never witnessed a Helper have that kind of response before." He's still speaking as the bell on the door jingles and the girl, still carrying her new puppet, leaps through Nobu, while her mother walks right through me. This time, though, it feels different, like a weird internal slurp. I can't imagine ever getting used to this sensation, but this second time didn't make me want to die. Oh, the irony.

"You okay?" says Nobu.

"Slightly discombobulated, but okay. I'm pretty sure I'm going to become very skillful at dodging the humans."

"Fair," says Nobu. "Coach, you said there was a third thing."

"There's no need, Nobu. This has been far more taxing than I had anticipated, so I suggest we head back to The Station."

"I'm every bit as sturdy as the Lunenburgers, Coach." I say. Nobu flashes me a big smile. "What's the third thing?"

"As you wish. Let's go to a café." We walk down the street a few blocks. Nobu allows people with shopping bags and toddlers to breeze right through him while I duck and weave my way along the sidewalk. I try to imagine how odd this must look to anyone who can see us. We're like newborn foals, just learning to stand. Nope. Baby animals get good at animalling very quickly; we are most like baby humans and the person we're dependent on is a six-and-a-half-year-old kid. When we first came here, I thought I might make a break for it. Get away from Coach and The Station and find some answers on my own. But I'm starting to think I need to understand what I am now, before I go find out who I was.

At the café, Coach leads us around to a courtyard at the back where we sit at a round metal table. Coach is about to speak, but Nobu interrupts him.

"Coach, it seems like we don't need to eat or breathe or sleep, but we can if we want to. Is that right?"

"That's correct. From a psychological perspective, you may need or want these comforts for a while."

"Why?" I say.

"The being you were on Earth ..."

"If you mean when we were alive, Coach, just say so. We've received the memo," I say.

"Very well, Claire. When you were alive, you were accustomed to breathing all the time, and to eating and sleeping at certain times and with regularity. Human bodies cannot survive without nourishment and rest, but these rituals are also important in that they bring most people a sense of safety and comfort."

"Puny human bodies!" I say.

"No! Not puny at all, Claire ..."

"She's just messing with you, Coach." I land a soft punch on Nobu's shoulder, and he grins in my direction.

"Noted," Coach says, "There may be aspects of your new life that may bring up feelings of anxiety." I feel two sets of eyes rest on me.

"Okay, yes. I can confirm this," I say.

"Claire, I have observed that you employ several techniques that help you feel calmer. Deep breathing. Placing a hand over your heart. Speaking to yourself kindly." I nod. "These are all excellent mental strategies, a way of keeping a calm and constant rhythm that doesn't rely on ... that is not connected with the fact that ...

"That I no longer breathe?" I offer.

"Yes. Quite right. You may be tempted to think these processes don't make any sense, but please don't be deterred. If an approach works, it works. It is my deepest wish for you, Claire, that you will continue to treat yourself with kindness and to breathe deeply even if that breath does not exist in the most literal sense."

"I promise, Coach." I'm knocked off balance by his concern.

"As I have explained, you are invisible to everyone except a person in need. However, you are wearing clothes and Claire is carrying a bag and these items are only invisible as long as they are touching you." Coach says. "Does that make sense?" We nod our heads. "Good. Now I'm going to give you a simple set of instructions. Please hang your coats on the backs of your chairs." I shrug out of mine while Nobu stands to unzip his jacket. Just as Coach has asked, we hang the coats on the back of our metal chairs.

"What do you think this looks like from inside the café?" he asks. We glance towards the café and Nobu starts to laugh.

"Two free leather coats hanging on the backs of chairs at an empty table," he says.

"Exactly. And at the moment you touch any part of that jacket, it will vanish into midair which will make anyone looking out the window question their sanity."

"So you want us to put our jackets back on then?" I say. I'm not as amused as Nobu is.

"Yes, please."

"Really?" I say. "Or are you just jerking us around?"

"I am not, as you say, jerking you around." We pull on our jackets although I take my sweet time pushing my arms through the sleeves.

"So, is the lesson here that we should never take off our coats?" I say.

"The two of you will live on Earth for some time, and I need to ensure that you know everything you will need to live unseen, except by those who need you. It is a very strange reality to navigate."

"Finally, something we can agree on," I say. My hands are shaking so I fold my arms in front of my body.

"Very well. Shall we discuss food?" says Coach. "If you were feeling hungry now, how would you feed yourself?" There's no way this isn't a trap.

Nobu looks around the square. "If someone left a sand-wich on their plate and left the table, we could walk over, check that no one was watching, and grab it. Then we would move to another location to eat it."

"Excellent, Nobu. You've covered all the basics. Be aware of your surroundings and who might be watching. Stealthily procure the food and move to a second location."

"I'm concerned that there's no difference between this and stealing," says Nobu.

"Nah. We're taking food that no one else wants," I say. "More like a recycling service."

The corners of Coach's mouth turn up just the slightest bit. "Claire, I appreciate your interest in this aspect of your training."

"It's not so much that, as the fact that I'm hungry. That I believe that I'm hungry. As we were arriving a few minutes ago, a family left and there's an entire cinnamon roll sitting untouched on a plate." I point at a table about fifteen feet away.

"Off you go, then," says Coach. This is easy for me. I stride across the café courtyard, check that the server is inside with their back to the courtyard, and then I look around, but we are still the only ones seated outdoors. I pick up the plate with the cinnamon roll and walk back to Nobu and Coach. I drop into my chair and hold up the plate.

"Well done, Claire," says Coach. I bow my head slightly.

"Cinnamon roll for the win," I say and bite into the soft, sweet dough. "Anyone want a bite?" I extend the pastry towards Nobu and Coach, but they both shake their heads. "Novices," I say, and then devour the pastry.

Coach leads us back up the street to the gazebo where he reaches out his hand and a doorknob appears. I look around this town. There's nothing here that sparks a memory, but I wonder if I've ever lived in an old wooden house. They are both solid and charming in a way that appeals to me, and I think I would like to live near the sea. Coach turns the doorknob and suddenly, we're standing in the hallway at The Station. As he pushes the door closed, I can still smell the salt of the ocean.

CHAPTER 6
IN WHICH COACH GIVES ME HAND-KNITTED SLIPPERS

After the drama of our first afternoon on Earth, the kitchen tiles feel soothing against my feet. Not cold, or even cool, but perfectly comfortable. Nobu must be thinking the same thing because he blurts out, "Everything here feels good, Coach. Did you design it that way?"

I pull one of the chairs back from the table and sit down. Coach jumps up into the chair beside me. I glare at him until he moves his chair back an inch or so. The legs make a little hiccup against the tiles.

"Yes," says Coach. "It's our goal to make you as comfortable as we possibly can. How are you doing, Claire?" Coach leans towards me and my first thought is that his manual must recommend this approach for gaining the trust of the newly arrived. I lean towards him, focus on his small face and imagine what Coach might have looked like at fifteen, thirty-eight, seventy-two, all the future ages he will never be. I shake my head. Damn it. He's tricked me into feeling bad for him. I lower my head and rest my right cheek against the smooth wooden surface of the table. I inhale deeply a few times and sit up again. As I'm about to speak, I close my mouth.

I want to say I'm pissed. I want to say I feel like a ping pong ball, moving back and forth from angry to confused to sad to not even believing this is real. Back and forth and back again. Sometimes I think this is just a long, strange dream and I'm going to wake up in my bed in my own house in … wherever … and everything will go back to normal. Like I'll get up and I'll be eating cereal for breakfast and one of my parents will come into the kitchen and remind me that it's almost time for school and I'll have to hurry to get dressed and pack my stuff into my backpack and that will be the biggest challenge of my day. Getting to school on time.

"Claire?" says Coach. Nobu has taken a seat on the bench across the table. "I asked how you are feeling."

"I don't want to talk about it," I say. "How do most people feel about ending up here?"

"Most of them feel sad and confused. Some feel angry," says Coach.

"Why?" I ask and am surprised when Nobu responds, rather than Coach.

"Maybe they feel angry about not getting to finish their life." His voice is quieter than normal and although my eyes well up with tears, I won't cry in front of Coach. I miss my life. I miss who I was … and who I was going to become. I close my eyes and slow my breathing.

"It's going to be okay, Claire. I can assure you," says Coach.

"Please don't try to cheer me up. I hate that crap." Coach nods his head.

34

"This is simply a fact, dear girl. You are Claire. You are the person you feel like. Nothing about you has been changed."

"Just my ability to remember my life."

"Yes."

"And my status as a real live person."

"And that," says Coach, who now looks as though he might cry.

Coach reaches into a basket on the table and pulls out a pair of knitted burgundy slippers. I hesitate. I'm annoyed with him, but they look soft. I slip them on. There's something so familiar about this feeling.

"How are they?" says Coach.

"Like wearing little rabbits on my feet." Coach's eyes light up and we laugh together for the first time. I notice a pair of knitting needles poking up from a ball of dark green yarn. "Did you make these?" He nods and I'm caught between my distrust of him and my gratitude for this kind gesture. "Thank you, Coach."

"I wanted to do something for you. To make you feel better without, you know, cheering you up," he says.

"When did you have time?"

"While you were sleeping last night. I'm quite a good knitter."

A light breeze lifts the ends of my hair and I look up to see Nobu, closing the glass doors that lead outside. Nobu slides back onto the bench across the table and Coach passes him a pair of slippers like mine, except Nobu's are forest green.

Nobu pulls on the slippers and says, "Coach, you are the coolest." He rubs his feet together and sighs. "Hey, I've been wondering ..." Coach nods. "Will we always be Helpers? I mean, as a human person, you know how things are going to work. You get a certain number of years ... but how does this work for Helpers?"

"You will never feel or look any older than you are now. You will become wiser but not appear older. You will not die."

As Nobu and I sit and consider this news, Coach offers us tea and Nobu says he'd love a cup, so Coach hops up on his wooden stool, fills a large kettle, and places it on the stove. When he turns on the heat, the gas hisses and pops, and he apologizes for startling us.

"But if we're being technical, we're already dead, right?" I say.

"You are, Claire. And the energy that was your human self has transformed into this new form. Your Helper form," says Coach.

"And then what?"

"As long as it goes well, you get promoted, and move on to bigger projects."

"Seriously?" My chair scrapes against the tiles when I get up and stand beside Coach on his little wooden stool. "Now we need to worry about whether or not we'll get promoted from a job we should never have had in the first place?" With the help of his stool, Coach is almost as tall as me and he looks back at me with a mixture of fear and concern.

"Yes, well, when you put it that way, it does seem rather an unfair expectation. Would you enjoy a cup of mint tea?"

"It's pretty difficult for me to think about tea right now," I say, stepping closer to Coach. He presses the back of his small body against the kitchen counter.

"Hey, Claire. Why don't you come sit with me and let the man make us a soothing warm beverage," says Nobu. I cross my arms and stare at Coach, who looks back without blinking.

"Fine," I say, and drop back into my chair. Nobu smiles at me, but my expression tells him I'm not having it. He turns back to Coach who drops two tea bags in a large orange tea pot. He pours boiling water into the pot and places it on a red and white striped oven mitt on the table. Coach hops back up on his stool and pulls three cups out of the cupboard, including the green cup with the peonies.

"Coach, how exactly do we get promoted?" says Nobu.

"By establishing a pattern of exemplary behaviour," says Coach.

"You're talking like a teacher again," I say, as I pour a cup of tea for Nobu and myself and then, grudgingly, for Coach. "You must not get many teenagers in these parts because, if you did, you'd know that earning our trust depends on you seeming less like a teacher," I say, louder than is necessary. I take a sip of the tea, which is both delicious and weirdly soothing.

"It's true that very few young people come through The Station."

I open my eyes wide and stare directly at Coach. "Wow! It just keeps getting worse and worse."

Nobu leans in and whispers. "Claire, I know you're angry, but I still have a lot of questions. Could we please stop attacking every single thing he says?"

"You're not attacking him," I say.

"That's true. I'll be more concise. Would *you* stop attacking every single thing he says? Please. For me."

"Fine!" I say. I imagine that final exclamation mark falling and clattering on the tiled floor.

"Coach?" says Nobu.

"You get promoted when you've made a difference to enough people."

"Is there a quota? Like a magic number?" says Nobu.

"No. Not exactly."

"These are some exquisitely vague guidelines," I say.

"Claire, please ..." says Nobu.

"Sorry," I say. I mean it. I don't want to cause Nobu pain. I tell myself to keep quiet, while also wondering how long that will last.

"So why do we want this promotion?" says Nobu.

"Becoming a Seer is the next stage in your evolution. I am concerned that we are getting too far ahead of ourselves, but I can tell you that Seers can travel anywhere, at any time, without a portal."

"Now that's cool," says Nobu.

"Yes. I hear it's amazing," says Coach. He investigates his teacup decorated with purple lupins.

"You're not a Seer, Coach?" says Nobu.

"I am a Station Master. That is all I am permitted to say about the matter."

"I'm sorry," says Nobu. He reaches across the table and pats Coach's arm, and I am struck by how much better a person Nobu is than me.

"Coach, I have just one more question," I say. Nobu shakes his head and mouths the word 'No,' but Coach nods, so I go ahead, "What happens if we don't help enough humans?"

"Theoretically, if a Helper is not sufficiently helpful after a certain timeframe, they would be demoted."

"But what does that mean? Like what exactly happens to those Helpers?" I ask.

"I couldn't say. It has never happened," says Coach.

"Never?" says Nobu.

"Never," says Coach.

I say, "Not yet."

CHAPTER 7

IN WHICH I BEGIN TO SNOOP (AND FEEL NO GUILT)

While Coach and Nobu wash the dishes, I think back to last night's conversation, and the infuriating small card inviting me to do my best. Okay, Coach. Challenge accepted. There must be records somewhere, a manila folder with facts and details and perhaps some photographs of my family. It's not possible that there isn't a file in one of these rooms, containing an explanation of who I was and how I lived and how I ended up here. If I were Coach, where would I keep such information?

As I get up from my chair, Nobu looks over his shoulder and I give him what I hope is a convincing thumbs up and a wave and then I turn right into the hallway. The room beside our bedroom contains two chairs and an old wooden table, and a chess board with a game in progress. I see a clear way for black to win. It seems that I played chess and that I was good at it, and that thought, the way it shows up so naturally, makes me think I must have been unbearable as a competitor. But there's no place to store a file in here.

In the next room there's a piano, a tall built-in bookshelf

with sheet music organized alphabetically, a green velvet sofa and a coffee table. I sit on the shiny black piano bench and hold my fingers over the keys. Nothing. This probably means that I don't play the piano. Didn't play the piano.

Across the hall there's a library where I feel immediately at home. The books are leather bound, and I run my fingers along them. When I touch *Romeo and Juliet*, a few small sparks burst into the air above the book, creating a tiny firework show. So, the sparks aren't just for clothes, but for other things, too. When they subside, I continue caressing the spines of the books with my fingertips. When I touch *The Collected Poems of Emily Dickinson*, another set of sparks erupts. It happens again with a book called *Harriet the Spy*. I return to the collection of Dickinson poems, pull the volume off the shelf, and open it to a poem called, 'I felt a Funeral, in my Brain.' That feels completely on brand. I read the poem twice, and then I close my eyes and feel the meaning of the words, like fingers on my face. With no evidence to back this up, I know I am this poet's reader and I close my eyes and imagine roses, fierce and red, blooming inside me. Flipping to the back of the book, I read that Dickinson died in 1886, which I sense was a long time ago, but I'll have to verify this. Could she be a Helper now? Or a Seer? Something else? I push the book back into its spot.

Where else? Where might this tiny elf have hidden information about me?

Lunenburg. I'm certain it's not a coincidence that Coach took us there. It's not a plan so much as a thrumming inside me, as I sneak past the kitchen and head back to The Training Room door. This is not a great idea, but I can't help myself. As I open the door, I fully expect to see the Lunenburg gazebo under a star-filled night sky, but it's daytime and there's no gazebo and within five seconds of opening the door, I'm forced to step back to avoid an oncoming red double decker bus. On the front of the bus is a sign that says King's Cross Station, and as I think about this name, something gets dislodged in my brain. This is London. How do I know this? I pull the door closed and stand with my back against it. Have I broken the portal?

Before I lose my nerve, I turn the knob and open the door again. A light rain falls and people on the sidewalk try to avoid bumping into each other with their umbrellas. They say, "Pardon me," and "Excuse me," to each other. The buildings across the street are made of stone. Victorian, I think. Somewhere in the distance church bells are ringing, and then I see another red double decker bus on its way to King's Cross Station. The bus driver pulls up at a stop beside me and opens the door. Can she see me? I step back into the hallway and pull the wooden door closed. I can hear Nobu laughing in the kitchen.

What am I looking for? I know it's ridiculous, but I'm hoping someone on the other side of this door will see me and say, 'Claire! We've been looking for you.' 'Claire, come home.' 'Claire, we miss you.' I want to be visible, to be known. I want to understand my whole story. Yet I'm afraid to let go of this stupid door and walk out into the city on the other side, because I might get lost. Because I might never find my way back. What happens if Coach doesn't know where I am? I don't know how all this works. And my big fear, the one I find the scariest, is what if I never see Nobu again? My heart clangs in my chest as I tiptoe down the hall, past the kitchen, and crawl into bed.

CHAPTER 8
IN WHICH I MEET THE PUPPIES

When I wake, the trippy golden rope is there again and I'm so relieved I didn't make it up. I hear Nobu roll over and sigh in his sleep, and the rope of golden threads rustles and sways and then tightens up again. As quietly as I can manage, I stand up beside our beds and the threads respond by bobbing up and down as I move, then shortening again. The strands are attached to Nobu's torso as well.

What are these things? Either Coach doesn't want us to know about this or he isn't aware of them. I crawl back into my bunk, pull up the quilt, and close my eyes. There's nothing about these threads that feels dangerous or malevolent. I need a word for whatever this is, and I run through some possibilities, stopping when I arrive on filaments. That word feels both accurate and true.

As more light pours in through the window and my mind becomes clearer, the filaments become harder to see, until they disappear altogether. The loss of them makes me sad, which feels weird. What if they're always there, but I can only perceive them in certain conditions, like when I'm closest to sleep? Or in certain lights like dawn or twilight? Something stops me from waking Nobu to ask him about the filaments. It feels too soon, although I can't say why.

If I had to get stuck here, and it seems that I did, I'm happy to be here with Nobu. He sleeps like I imagine babies sleep, like smooth heavy stones tucked inside light-yellow blankets in a small white crib. He sleeps like a person who never made a bad decision or hurt another person. I want some of that for myself. I imagine an accounting department along some infinite hallway, and the person responsible for my case sighs as my ledger dips into the red, on account of my general rudeness and various shortcomings.

Or perhaps all Helping partners get these filaments.

I swing my legs out from under the quilt, get dressed beside our bunk and slip out the door and back down the hallway to the rooms I was exploring last night. Across from the library are several rooms filled with art, like a series of tiny, connected museums, and I stand in front of each painting, allowing a conversation to flow between us. There's a small canvas of a round blonde woman and a black pug on a blue sofa in front of a window, and as I touch the gilded frame, a single spark flies up over my head. Okay. Round women and pugs. Possibly blue sofas. That all tracks. The battles, however, make me shiver so I don't linger in those rooms. There's no sign of a desk or a filing cabinet anywhere, although if I were Coach, I wouldn't make this easy for me, either. As I emerge from one of the gallery rooms, I bump into Nobu.

"Good morning!" he says. "I've been looking for you. Everything okay?"

I nod, but he waits for an answer. "Yup. Just looking for

those puppies you were telling me about." I smile, but he raises his eyebrows almost immediately.

"Puppies, huh? I find that surprising, but okay, I'll take you." I prepare to feign interest in small dogs, as Nobu opens the door to a huge, furnished room that is home to about twenty puppies. A few are asleep on sofas and wingback chairs, while others play, tumbling over each other. They are actually very cute. A small brown pup is just waking up from a nap and Nobu carefully picks it up and holds it out to me. I shake my head. Nobu folds it into his arms and sits down in a high-back chair. The puppy climbs up so that its front paws are on Nobu's shoulder. It sniffs him and licks Nobu's neck and face.

"It thinks you're its mama," I say. He laughs and rests his head back against the chair. While he pets the head of the tiny brown dog, I have a terrible thought. "Oh my Goddess, Nobu. What if these dogs are also ..." I can't say it. I draw an invisible line in the air in front of my throat. Nobu makes a strangled sound, which is part laugh and part shriek and the startled puppy jumps down from the chair. What if this is The Station for Young Things? Human and canine. Us. Coach. The puppies. This is dark, even for me.

"Come on," he says. "Let's go to the kitchen." Nobu reaches for my hand, and as I slip my hand inside his, our touch launches a bouquet of tiny sparks that he doesn't seem to notice. Just me then? Okay. Just me.

CHAPTER 9
IN WHICH I LEARN THAT THERE'S NO DORM

After a quick breakfast of scrambled eggs and bacon, the three of us are back in front of The Training Room door, with its embossed WHEREVER plaque.

"So, Coach," I say, "how do you know where the training door will open up to?"

"Ah. Good question, Claire. It leads to the place the opener most wants to go. Nobu, would you like to try it?"

Nobu shrugs and turns the knob, and the door opens on a view of the sea. Icebergs float in the near distance, and a humpback whale breeches right in front of us. "Cool!" says Nobu.

"This is Fogo Island, Newfoundland," says Coach.

Nobu nods. "I was reading about this place before I went to sleep last night." He turns towards me. "Claire, do you want to give it a go?" Coach nods approvingly.

I think as hard as I can about Emily Dickinson's house in New England and push the door open. We're standing at the exit of the public toilets in a riverside park, but then I see a massive Ferris wheel and in the distance beyond it, Big Ben, and the British parliament. Not Massachusetts.

"Have you been reading about London?" Coach asks.

"Yep," I say, "before bed." But I haven't had a thought about London since I opened this door yesterday. I close it quickly, trying not to draw attention to the fact that I've somehow short-circuited The Station's programming.

"Alright, then," says Coach, reaching for the handle. "Shall we? Welcome to Barcelona, Spain."

I'm grateful not to see London again, as we walk through the door into a large plaza with shops and restaurants around the outside of the square. There are several small outdoor cafes with striped awnings, where people sit at small round tables, drinking coffee and having loud, animated conversations, which makes me smile. I like these people. There's an elder playing tag with two children, and the kids slow down enough so that the man almost catches them and then they speed up again, laughing and calling him Abuelo. I know this means grandfather. The sun is hot and the sky cerulean, as Coach leads us to a tall brick clocktower, where he drops to a sitting position with his back against the tower. Nobu sits beside Coach, and I sink down beside Nobu.

"The tables are very charming," Coach says, "but these seats offer a perfect view with a much lower probability that someone will sit in us." My stomach turns a somersault at this reminder.

"Thanks, Coach," says Nobu, and I know they're both thinking about my reaction to that kid running through me yesterday.

"This is Gracia, a neighbourhood of Barcelona. I chose it because it is some distance from the Old Town, where the thieves are particularly skillful, and I would like to avoid that kind of adventure today."

"Okay, Coach. What's today's training about?" Nobu's jaw is tight, as is his voice.

"Let's start with your physical, or rather, non-physical selves. As you are already aware, Helpers don't need to breathe, eat or sleep from a physiological standpoint."

"Right, because we are basically holograms," I say.

"Not exactly. This is a bit complicated, but the easiest way for me to explain it is to say that you and Nobu are now light. You are light and you emit light. This change in your nature has some consequences you will need to adjust to."

"Like walking through doors," I say.

"Yes. Precisely. It also means that you do not need light to see, because, essentially, you are the light you see by."

"So, we can see everything, all the time, even if it's dark," says Nobu.

"Exactly. The only thing you won't see, are actual sources of light."

"Wait, I don't get it," I say.

"When humans see, light carries information to their eyes, and that information goes to their brains and tells them what they see. Not to be insensitive, Claire, but you no longer have eyes." This fact does not stop me from rolling mine at Coach, which he ignores. "You don't receive light-messages because you are the light-message. But you can only see through your own light. Other sources of light will be invisible to you."

"Does that mean we won't be able to see Christmas lights?" I say. Nobu raises his eyebrows at this very specific reference.

"A light bulb that's switched on will not look very different to you than a light bulb that's off. You will be aware when lights are turned on, because everything around those lights will look different. The same will be true of the sun. You and Nobu will feel it, you will see its effect on everything else, but you will not see the sun itself."

"That seems sad," I say.

"It also means you cannot watch television or movies, read computer screens or see anything on digital phones."

"No TV or movies? Now that's tragic. What a terrible rule," says Nobu.

We turn to each other and say in unison, "No Star Wars!" and laugh.

"Don't you miss TV, Coach?" Nobu asks.

"It had not been invented when I died," says Coach. What! Nobu leans forwards and stares at his boots. This kid! I can't decide whether to hug him, or tie him up and make a run for it. "As I was saying, you will not have a reflection on Earth, and you also won't cast much of a shadow."

"Are we vampires?" I ask. Nobu laughs, sits up too quickly and bangs the back of his head against the clocktower. "What?" I turn to Nobu. "It's a fair question."

"You are not vampires," says Coach. "Humans are mostly unaware of Helpers, but occasionally, they see some quality of a Helper they don't comprehend. It's natural that they create a story to make meaning of it."

"So, we're not vampires, but vampires are us!" I laugh and turn to Nobu who smiles half-heartedly. I suspect he's still grieving the loss of Star Wars. "Well, I liked it better when we were holograms," I say.

"Holograms do not have free will," says Coach.

"Hmm. If I had free will, I'm not convinced I'd be sitting on the ground being lectured to by a child on a Wednesday afternoon. Or whatever day it is."

"Claire!" Nobu says. Thankfully he's back from wherever he went in his mind.

"I understand that Helper Training is tedious, Claire. But you do have agency as a being. You will be free to make your own decisions and to shape your experience."

"Agree to disagree, Coach," I say. Nobu crosses his arms and stares at me.

"May I suggest a walk," says Coach. We follow him to something called an Internet Café, where Coach says people can rent time on a computer.

"Aren't we super-exposed here?" I ask.

"If someone needs help, they will see you and Nobu. If not, you will simply continue to be invisible. Whenever you are concerned about being seen, you can simply follow another customer through the open door." A person wearing a deep pink shirt covered in bright yellow pineapples opens the door, and Nobu and I hurry through before it closes. Coach glides through the glass.

"Well timed, you two," says Coach. "Now please wander around and take a look at their screens." This is obviously a trap since he's just told us we won't be able to see anything, but it's infuriating, just the same. There's a woman typing very quickly but I can't see what she's working on. Is she messaging someone, or writing a novel? There are two teenagers sitting at the same computer in the corner, and they are whispering and laughing. I feel grateful that I can't see whatever is on their screen. An older woman is reading her computer screen and crying. Oof! I feel totally overwhelmed by this place and I slip outside, into the blaring hot square. Coach and Nobu follow a couple of minutes later.

"Coach, I don't like the computers," I say.

"The humans must love them, though," says Nobu. "They even have computers in their phones!" Coach nods his head.

"But we won't be able to read the phone screens either because ... still emitters of light, right?" I say smugly.

"Yes. You are very clever," Coach says but I can tell he doesn't mean it sarcastically, which makes me feel a little worse about how easily I fall off the sarcasm truck.

"Okay, Coach. We've got this. Can we talk about where we'll live as Helpers?" says Nobu.

"Right," says Coach, clearing his throat. I've never heard him do that before. What is there to clear? He begins walking across the square and we follow. "When we receive your assignment, I shall escort you to the location, which is more likely to be a large urban centre, somewhere like Barcelona, rather than a small town like Lunenburg."

"It's a number's game," says Nobu.

"Exactly. Large cities are home to more humans, and therefore, there are more people in need of assistance. I will get you settled in and then I will return to The Station."

"Like we're going off to university," I say.

"Yes. That's an excellent analogy," says Coach.

"So, there must be some kind of dorm for Helpers? Like at The Station?" asks Nobu.

"There is no dormitory or other such accommodation. Some teams stay outdoors all the time. Walking, sitting, riding a tourist boat along a river. A place like this square would be perfect." He gestures around us and keeps walking. "Remember, your desire for sleep and nourishment is only an illusion. You no longer need these things," says Coach. A quiet growl rises in my throat. Nobu reaches over and squeezes my hand.

"And the other Helpers? The more indoor un-dead?" I ask.

"Some check hotel reservation records and inhabit empty rooms." He stops in front of a small hotel and points at a clerk talking on the phone. "Some Helpers house-sit while the owners are on vacation or are trying to sell their house. Some frequent favourite museums or stores with sofas, slipping in after closing and departing by morning." Again, he gestures towards the small boutiques on this side street. "At any rate, we ask that you exercise extreme caution in making these arrangements. Please return all objects to their original locations and refrain from using electricity in places where no humans are meant to be at home. We try to minimize this kind of attention. Speculation about robbers and ghosts and such." I stop walking, lean against the building beside us and try to catch my breath. What is he saying?

"Coach, man, this comes as a surprise to us," Nobu says, glancing towards me. "And not the good kind."

"Dear me! I am terribly sorry that the nomadic nature of your new life comes as bad news. Terribly sorry. This is the way it has always been." Coach places his tiny head in his hands. The look on Nobu's face tells me that he wants to say it's not a problem, wants to let Coach off the hook, but when his eyes meet mine, he knows I'm not okay.

"Thank you for your apology, Coach," says Nobu.

"Thank you ever so much," says Coach. They both sneak side glances at me, but it's not my job to make Nobu and this man-child comfortable.

"Any more good news for us, Coach?" I say.

"That is enough training for today, I think," Coach says. Despite the shocking revelation about our housing situation, I'm sad to leave this vibrant square, this city of footie-playing grandparents, loud friends, and thieves.

CHAPTER 10
IN WHICH COACH LEAVES A NOTE

When I hear crashing sounds followed by cheers from the bowling alley down the hall, I know that Nobu and Coach are absorbed enough in their game for me to continue my investigation. I pass the rooms I've already searched: the one with the chessboard, the room with the piano, the library, and the gallery rooms. I wonder if they have been designed specifically for us, for our interests. The puppies are definitely for Nobu.

The first room I enter is a huge woodshop with several machines and a selection of labelled wood: oak, maple, cherry, poplar, hickory, walnut, alder. I don't recognize all of these names. On a table in the centre of the room are instruction manuals for the machines. I flip through them, but they're exactly what they seem to be.

The next room has wooden floors, a mirror along one wall, and a long wooden bar mounted halfway up the mirror. A piano sits across from the mirror. Above it hangs a painting of young ballerinas in white dresses, preparing for a performance. The dance studio feels familiar, but uncomfortable. I close the door on my way out.

I walk along the hall for a while, looking into rooms, but not entering. I pass the swimming pool with its yellow and white striped lounge chairs, several sitting rooms that lead outside to that same green field, and a bedroom with a canopy bed, dressed in pink linens. No way that room was designed for me.

The next room is a study with light blue walls, but all the furniture is child sized. Why? Who is this room for? As I step inside, my heart pounds. Two framed paintings hang over a small wooden cabinet. The first is a portrait of Emily Dickinson, whom I recognize from an image at the back of her book of poetry, and the second is a handsome golden retriever. I open all the drawers and doors, but discover nothing. Not one piece of paper. I slide my hand along the bottom of each drawer, and when I don't feel anything, I remove the drawers from the cabinet entirely so I can be sure. Getting them back on their rails proves too challenging so I leave the empty drawers piled up on the floor. I don't care if Coach knows I was here.

On the other side of the room, a tiny wooden desk and chair sit below a window, and I notice that the drawer has been left slightly ajar. Nothing that happens at The Station is a coincidence; everything is on purpose and has a meaning. When I open the drawer, there's a note written on a small green card. My hands shake as I open it. It's addressed to me.

Claire,
There is no file or folder.
I have told you as much as I am permitted.
Warm regards,
Coach

Warm regards. That guy has really misjudged his audience. I jam the card in the back pocket of my jeans and return to the kitchen, with the evidence that Coach has known what I was looking for the whole time. I sit in the blue and white plaid wingback chair in the corner, and wait for them to return. I lean back, close my eyes, and consider what questions I should pose and whether it even matters what, or how, I ask. It's his job to orient me to my new role as a Helper, and that new life depends on me not remembering my time as a human. We are at an impasse.

When Nobu and Coach arrive, they're discussing lasagna recipes. Nobu is determined to enjoy the infinitely stocked pantry, a luxury we should enjoy now, as we won't have access to a magic pantry on Earth.

Coach brings me a cup of mint tea in the green cup and sets it on top of a book on the small table beside me. "I got your note," I say. He nods.

"I'm aware. I am deeply sorry, Claire." He stands in front of me and does not look away.

"I know, Coach." For once, I believe him.

Coach returns to Nobu and their Great Lasagna Adventure and I tuck my feet under me, sip my tea, and pick up the book beside me. It's called *Heidi* and is a children's book, which is fine with me. The protagonist, as it turns out, is an orphaned girl who lives with her very grumpy grandfather in the Swiss Alps, and I can't help but think that I have some things in common with this grandfather. Also, with the orphaned girl.

"Claire, would you like to join us in the kitchen? I'll get you an apron," says Nobu. I can see he's trying to broker a truce.

"Um. No thanks. I'm god." Nobu and Coach laugh at my weird Freudian slip. "I mean I'm good."

Coach chooses a Chet Baker record and plays it on an old turntable. Coach sings along to the song, *Come Rain or Come Shine*, and Baker's voice is a little wonky, not anything close to perfect, but there's something disarming about his tone, which is honest and wistful. It's amazing that humans can do this, sound like this.

The meal is delicious, and everyone is on their very best behaviour. Then Nobu cooks each of us a perfectly golden marshmallow over the fire. I try my hand at it several times, but my marshmallows always catch fire and are practically charcoal before I notice and pull my stick away from the fire. Nobu says that a little carbon never hurt anyone, and he eats all my failed experiments.

Without me even asking, Coach says I can take this copy of *Heidi* with me, and that, in the future, I don't need to ask, because everything in The Station is here for Nobu and me. I'm actually starting to believe him. While it's been difficult for me to trust him, I also can't say that Coach has lied about anything. Objectively, he's been nothing but kind. Nobu bends down and hugs Coach good night. I nod awkwardly and Coach bows in return.

The covers on the bottom bunk are twisted up at the bottom of the bed. I'm about to hop in when Nobu says, "I wonder if you might sleep better if we take a moment to straighten those out." I raise my eyebrows at him, and he shrugs and climbs up the ladder to his own bed. I sigh loudly, shake out my sheet and blanket, and tuck the ends under the mattress before I hop into bed and pull the covers up to my chin.

Nobu is, of course, right.

CHAPTER 11

IN WHICH NOBU AND I HAVE AN EARLY MORNING HEART-TO-HEART

Nobu is on a carousel. He's seated on a bright pink bench between two white horses. I'm waiting to get on the carousel and behind me, there's a long line of little kids with their parents. Each time he spins by, he extends his hand, but I can't reach him and the carousel spins faster and the music becomes louder, and I hear him laughing as the carousel spins up into the air and disappears.

This dream shakes me awake. Since we arrived, my dreams have been vivid and disorienting and because this place isn't real, or maybe because I'm not real, it's hard to know where my dreams end, and the day begins. Heart still pounding, I swing my legs out of bed, place them on the floor and focus on my breathing. Inhale the light, exhale the darkness. As I breathe, I place my right hand over my heart and then cover it with my left and begin to feel more peaceful.

I smell coffee brewing in the kitchen, and hear Coach and Nobu talking, and as I look towards the bedroom door, I see a thick rope of filaments, golden and sparkling, leading from my belly button, out into the hall. As I stare at the golden threads, Nobu walks directly through them, carrying a wooden tray with two bagels slathered in cream cheese, and a bowl of strawberries. When he stops, the rope of filaments shortens to the distance between us and then begins to fade from view.

"Good morning," he says. "Look what I brought!"

"That's really kind, but I'm not hungry this morning." He shrugs, sets the tray on a red wooden chair, and sits beside me on the lower bunk. His hair is messy, and he smells like coffee and strawberries. As he turns to speak, our shoulders touch. The spot glows and sparks, and I look away so he can't see me blushing.

"Claire, I'm sorry this is so hard for you."

"Thanks. I don't know how to ask this without sounding super-rude, but why is it not harder for you?"

"I've been thinking about that. I should be upset, like that would be perfectly normal, but what I feel is more like ... curiosity maybe. I don't really have angry feelings. I've been searching for them, but I've got nothing."

"How nice for you," I say.

"I don't know. Maybe." He closes his eyes but doesn't say anything else.

"I've been trying to understand why I'm so mad," I say. "For sure, I'm furious about being dead. About not growing up, falling in love, and having kids. I don't know. I don't seem very maternal, but maybe I would have wanted that some-day. There's also a chance that I've always been angry about everything, but maybe, if I'd lived long enough, I might have been able to, you know, sort it out. Get to a better place. Feel better about myself. I feel so pissed that I won't get a chance to stop being mad all the time."

"Claire, there's time. Coach says that Helpers are constantly learning and evolving. We're not stuck wherever our human lives left us."

I sigh. "How do you trust Coach so much," I say.

"I just do," says Nobu.

"And you're really not angry?"

"A little melancholy. Mostly fine."

"You're a freak, Nobu, but you're going to be a great Helper." He frowns. "You will! You're kind and an excellent listener," I say. "I, on the other hand, am probably not bringing much to this partnership."

"I completely disagree," he says. "No one is ever going to push us around when we get back to Earth."

I laugh. "I assume you mean that as a compliment?"

"Definitely," he says, smiling.

"I envy your ease with all of this," I say. "You're like this huge neon arrow pointing to how I'd like to feel, but I'm not there yet."

"You're fine, Claire. When you're ready to be some other kind of way, then you will be, and that Claire will be fine, too."

I test out the idea that maybe I'm okay the way I am. I want to find a way to Velcro myself to this possibility. "Nobu, that's very wise."

"I don't think I've earned that yet, but do you know what we definitely have going for us? These most extraordinary slippers." Nobu wriggles his feet around inside the green slippers Coach made for him. His slipper joy is contagious, and my feet dance alongside his, and as soon as he notices, he laughs out loud. For a moment, we're just two friends having a lovely chat. "Oh," he says, "when you're ready, we have another training session this morning."

As Nobu stands, our shoulders connect again, and my face and shoulders are showered with sparks he doesn't see.

CHAPTER 12
IN WHICH NOBU
LEARNS TO HELP

We stand in front of the Training Room door, with Coach. "When I open the door, I will ask that you just start walking, and stop when I tell you." Nobu nods and I shrug. We step through, into a massive crosswalk with thick white stripes painted on the pavement, and as instructed, we keep moving, swept up by a great surge of well-dressed humans, making their way across a wide street. I stick to the outside of the crossing so I won't have to dodge the fast-walkers, who might charge right through me. There are hundreds of people around us and then my brain reaches for another number. It's thousands. I practice my breathing, and as I exhale, I notice that although my mind expected that all these people and cars in states of passing and waiting would create a cacophony of sound, it's not loud here, wherever here is. When we reach the other side of the street, Coach beckons and we stand beside him with our backs against a large store with a sign that reads, TSUTAYA.

"Intense!" says Nobu.

"Indeed," says Coach. "Welcome to Tokyo, Japan. This

is Shibuya Crossing. It is a very touristy spot, but I can only assume the architects placed the portal here, as this intersection is so busy with shoppers and commuters, that no one would notice three people appearing out of thin air." Now that I've got a bit of distance, I see that it's not just one crossing, but rather five, a large square and a fifth crossing that runs diagonally across the square. I suspect Coach has been working us up to this, starting in Lunenburg. My guess is that if all the people who live in that pretty town were dropped here in Shibuya, they would not equal the number of souls moving through this intersection right now.

"Are you quite alright, Claire?" says Coach.

"Yes. I was just thinking that this seems like a long way from Lunenburg." Coach pulls a small world map out of the pocket of his cargo shorts. Lunenburg, Barcelona, and Tokyo are marked in his handwriting, which I recognize from his plucky, 'Do your best' card, and the note he wrote to let me know that he knew I was snooping around The Station. I pass the map to Nobu who looks at it briefly, before handing it to Coach.

"So, what's the plan here, Coach? What have you got in store for us?" says Nobu.

"Am I that predictable?" asks Coach.

"Yes," we respond in unison.

"Very well. Two things. As you know, people in different parts of the world speak different languages." We nod. This seems like a Grade Two piece of information. While Coach tries to get to the point, I wonder if this is where we've been assigned. Could I live here? Have I visited this city? The majority of the people here have features like Nobu, and I wonder if this is where he lived. Before. "It's one of the great challenges that humans face," Coach continues. "It is already difficult enough to communicate effectively with a person who speaks the same language, but when we introduce different languages and cultures into the mix, understanding each other becomes terrifically complicated. Obviously, language differences would make your work as Helpers untenable, so an elegant solution was devised. When humans speak to you, no matter what language they use, you will understand them perfectly."

"But what about the reverse? How will they understand us?" says Nobu.

"The language filter ... My apologies. That term is not precisely correct, but it is, perhaps, close enough. The language filter works both ways." Nobu nods. "Let's cross over to Shibuya Station. There's no doubt in my mind that someone here will require your help and you can see for yourselves, how well this language filter works."

"What?" I say.

"Ah yes. That is the second order of the day. The time has come for the two of you to begin helping. I'm quite certain that whatever pops up today won't be too challenging."

"Wait. You mean you don't know?" I say.

"This isn't a simulation, Claire. We are in Tokyo which is the most populated city in the world. The chances are high that someone will need your assistance in the next few minutes, but please remember that I will remain invisible to them, and I am here to help you." I glare at Coach and when the light turns green, Nobu places his hand on my shoulder. I step into the crosswalk and move away from Nobu and Coach. There is a red-haired person, a round girl about my height and size, walking directly ahead of me. She wears a pink and green polka-dot linen skirt, and I think how difficult it must be for her to blend in here, against this sea of slim humans with black hair. She wears her hair pulled back, and as she and her friend turn left at the sidewalk, the end of her long, thick ponytail touches my face. The scent of citrus is followed by small sparks that shoot up from the place her hair has touched me. Like the clothes I chose at The Warehouse and the books at The Station. She and her friend hug and then head in separate directions, and I follow the red-headed girl for about a block, before Coach catches up with me.

"Claire," he says. "Where are you going?" His voice is as stern as I've ever heard it.

"That girl. I think maybe I know her," I say pointing towards the person with the red ponytail, who is getting farther and farther away.

"We can't take the risk of you getting lost in Tokyo." The sternness is gone from his voice, but when I look up, the girl has been swallowed up by the crowd.

"She's gone," I say but Coach doesn't respond as he leads me back to where Nobu is standing. Coach hasn't said that I couldn't possibly know the person with the red hair. He hasn't said that it is impossible, that I must be mistaken. What is he not telling us?

"Hey," Nobu says. I nod. He can see I'm not okay and he doesn't ask, for which I'm grateful.

"What now?" says Nobu.

"We wait," says Coach. As it turns out, we don't wait long. An elderly man approaches us, looks at me and then Nobu and says, "Excuse me. Do you speak Japanese?"

"Is that what we're speaking now?" says Nobu, which makes me grin like a maniac. The man looks puzzled, but nods. "Then, yes," says Nobu. "How can we help you?"

The man lifts a very expensive looking camera from around his neck. "My wife and I are visiting from Nagano Prefecture. We would very much like a photo in front of Shibuya Crossing."

"Are you sure you trust me with your camera?" says Nobu. The man nods and shows Nobu how to use it. Nobu eases the strap over his head and gives the couple simple instructions about where they should stand. He has to put his eye up to the viewfinder instead of looking at the camera's digital screen, but it doesn't seem to be a problem. He takes about ten photos and then he says, "Okay. Last shot. Do something crazy!" The woman laughs and covers her mouth with her hand, while the man makes two adorable peace signs. Nobu takes a few more shots and then the three of them step back from the traffic, where Nobu returns the camera and asks them to check that he captured the photograph they were hoping to get. They bow and thank him, what seems like an excessive amount for taking a few photos, but what do I know? They disappear into the crowd, in the same direction that the red-headed girl went.

"Well done." Coach pats Nobu's hand, as he's not tall enough to reach Nobu's shoulder.

"I, um, I wasn't too smooth at the beginning there," Nobu says.

"Not to worry. It worked out splendidly. You took very good care of them," says Coach.

"I did my best," says Nobu looking down at his black boots.

"That's all we can ever do," says Coach.

"But it's going to be harder than that sometimes, right? Like people are going to have bigger problems than wanting a photograph?"

"Yes," Coach pauses. "That's correct, but I don't want us to get too far ahead of ourselves.

"That was a very good morning's work. We'll head back and have a lovely meal. Claire, you can practice being the Helper in our training this afternoon." I glare at the back of Coach's tiny head, as he leads us back to the portal that only he can see.

CHAPTER 13
IN WHICH WE DEPART UNEXPECTEDLY

Coach makes grilled cheese sandwiches, which he claims are the Holy Grail of sandwiches, whatever that means, but I pass on his offer. Partly because I'm mad about losing the red-headed girl and partly because I can't stand the idea of becoming more attached to this place, or him, or his stupid sandwiches, when we will be leaving soon. I know this doesn't make any sense, but I'm unbothered by the contradictions that seem to make up my personality. While they're eating, I curl up in the wingback chair and read *Heidi*.

"Coach, I don't want to be rude here, but you haven't said how soon we leave." says Nobu. I'm relieved to know it's on his mind as well.

"We're slightly behind schedule due to some unforeseen circumstances. I'd like to depart tomorrow after breakfast," says Coach.

Tomorrow. Tomorrow? I can't breathe, and then I'm out of my chair and moving quickly. My boots sound like small bombs detonating as I run from the kitchen, past our sleeping quarters and the bowling alley and then I keep running and running along the hallway with no end.

I pass identical oak doors with glass doorknobs, rage by them without any curiosity about what is stored behind them. My boots, which just a few minutes ago, pleased me enormously, are now a source of annoyance because they're slowing me down. I slow to a jog and rest against a wall where I loosen my laces, kick off my boots, peel off my socks, and leave them in a wicked little pile in the hall. I run on, my bare feet slapping the hardwood floor of the hallway in a painful, but satisfying way.

Things keep getting taken from me. My life. My memories. The ability to say when I'm ready to leave The Station and become a Helper. I haven't found any of the answers I'm looking for, yet.

I run until a stitch in my side makes me slow down to catch my breath, and I notice a bright yellow door to my left with a plaque that reads, THERE. I open it and enter what looks like the back of a restaurant or café. It's dark, and as I arrive, someone in a long black coat exits the front of the café and locks the door, before walking away. I shiver. Where am I? Is this still The Station? There's a bar with wine glasses hanging above the counter, and twelve small round tables with white linen tablecloths. Above each table hangs a glass light fixture, and in the centre of each table sits a small vase with one pink rose, in various shades of perfection.

I face the wooden door that leads outside. On each side of the door, a huge window runs from waist height to the ceiling, allowing the space to be filled with blue moonlight. I sit at a table by the window, and my eyes rest on an enormous church on the other side of the river. The sight of it jiggles my brain as if to say, 'You know me.' The structure is simultaneously solid and graceful, and I'm in awe of the stained-glass windows. I wonder if the windows at The Warehouse were inspired by these. To the right of the church is a small park, a manicured space where all the trees and bushes have been trimmed into obedience, but I imagine this park as longing to jump up and erupt with life, all chaotic and riotous. These trees and bushes want to behave in unexpected ways. A couple is seated on a bench under a light and they are kissing. The kissing is unexpected. How do I even know this word? How frustrating to have vocabulary for things this version of me, Claire 2.0, has no experience of. How unfair. I wonder who they are, and if this is the beginning of something, or the middle, or closer to the end. Perhaps this is one last kiss, the kind you have before you leave. Wow! Why does my mind automatically go to the end? Oh yeah, I remember.

I hear the squeak of the door before I see whoever is there.

"Coach, don't bother. I'm not going yet. I'm not ready."

"Hey," someone says, but it's not Coach. I turn to face the door at the back of the restaurant. From this side, it looks like the door to a closet. Nobu steps into the café, and all the moonlight streaming through the windows, gathers itself and lands gently on his skin.

"Hi." I drop my gaze from his face to the wooden floor.

"You're fast," Nobu says. He goes behind the bar and pours himself a glass of water. "Would you like some?"

I nod. Nobu crosses the café, places both glasses on my table by the window, and pulls up a chair beside me. He drinks his entire glass of water in large noisy gulps and I laugh, shake my head, and take a few sips from my glass.

Nobu shrugs his arms out of his leather jacket and hangs it on the back of his chair. Suddenly warm, I do the same.

"I get it, Claire."

"What's that?"

"Not being ready." I turn towards him. "I like the way things are at The Station. I like living with you and Coach," he says. I snort at the mention of our mentor-captor. "Claire, I know you don't trust him, and I get that, really. But I like him. He's about good things."

I lean towards Nobu. "You mean good things, like throwing us back into a world where, up until very recently, we were actual human beings? Abandoning us before we are ready to go? Good things, like demanding that we help other people without sufficient training or instructions. Not even a freaking manual? Good things, like, 'Oh. By the way, you're going to be homeless, but it's, like, no big deal.' Those good things?"

"You're not wrong," says Nobu.

"I know. The fact that you are not pissed is really pissing me off."

Nobu starts laughing, which makes me laugh, and for a moment, I forget everything that has happened to us, and I'm happy to be laughing with Nobu, just sitting beside him in this magical glass room.

"Maybe I'm defective or something," he says, "like I'm not capable of the full range of human emotions. Um, Helper emotions."

I cover Nobu's hand with mine and squeeze for a moment. "Nobu, I know almost nothing right now but the one thing I know is that you are not defective. You are goodness in jeans and Doc Martens."

"You are too, Claire," says Nobu.

"Oh! My boots. I kicked them off."

"Coach has them."

"Oh. Okay. Thanks."

"We'll be okay, Claire. We'll figure this out together." The small patch of skin on my palm that's touching the top of Nobu's hand tingles, and sparks fly up towards our heads. Nobu is staring right at me, yet he doesn't see the fireworks show our touch has created.

"Yes. I think we will," I say.

"Really?" says Nobu. "Just like that?"

"Oh, I'm still a mess, but I'm allowing myself one tiny glimmer of hope."

"Cool." His smile is a portal that allows his entire being to flow out into the cafe. All of him. Unguarded. This feels like the perfect time to ask Nobu about the filaments and the sparks, but there's a knock at the door.

"Come in," Nobu says. Coach appears in the doorway holding my boots and my bag.

"Do you two need more time?" asks Coach.

"Nah. Come on in, Coach. We're fine," says Nobu. I stick out my tongue at Nobu. Coach places the boots on the floor beside my feet and I notice that my "You Rock" socks have been folded and tucked neatly inside the boots. He hangs my bag on the back of my chair. Although I want to express my gratitude, I can't, so I nod my head at Coach, and he nods back.

"This is a nice view, Coach. Just a little something the architects of The Station threw together?" I say.

"Actually, Claire, this is Paris. That's Notre Dame." He points across the river. There's a buzzing in my head. Notre Dame. Our Lady.

"There's been a bad fire here," I say.

"That's right. It was a structural fire that destroyed most of the roof and caused the spire to collapse. They have been rebuilding it ever since."

"It's beautiful," I say. Coach nods, thoughtfully.

"I am afraid I have some difficult news," he says. I can't imagine that anything he says will top the disclosure that we're being evicted from The Station tomorrow.

"Okay," says Nobu. His hands are shaking. I look at Coach.

"You have been assigned to Paris. That's not the bad news. In fact, I think it is a rather positive revelation, as the city will suit you well, especially Claire. The problem is that when a Helper passes through their departure gate, their Station ceases to exist. The Station is no longer there for you to return to."

"The yellow door?" I ask.

"The door that takes you THERE," he says.

"But what happens to you, Coach?" Nobu says. "Where do you go?"

"I am a Station Master. I move on to the next Station. That is why I brought your bag, Claire. I must take you into the city tonight." Nobu turns towards me, his eyes wide. "I need to be clear that this is not a request. Claire set this in motion the moment she came through that door."

Tonight. I asked for this by saying that departing tomorrow couldn't be topped. I feel tears welling up, but I won't give Coach the satisfaction, so I focus on getting ready. I pull on my socks, lace up my boots, push my arms through the sleeves of my jacket and drop my cross-body bag over my head. Then I nod at Nobu.

"We understand, Coach. We're ready," says Nobu. He takes my hand and one tiny spark shoots straight up into the air between us, frolicking in the darkness. I can't believe that Nobu doesn't see it, but then I realize that Coach is staring directly at the spark, as it rises and shimmers into noth-ingness.

CHAPTER 14
IN WHICH WE ARRIVE

oach opens the café door that leads to Paris. It's not like I'm happy about any of this, but I've decided it's best to get on with the rest of our lives, whatever that means ... plus it's clear that I'm not going to get any more information about my identity from Coach. But someone out there knows who I am. I'm sure of it.

As I descend the steps to the sidewalk, the human world comes rushing at us, and although we are not alive, I feel something like it. I can smell something sweet, like caramel, a recent rainfall, flowers pushing their way through the earth, and the scent of ancient things. The moon is arrogantly bright. Birds chirp and restructure the atoms of the sky with their soaring.

I breathe it all in. Glancing over my shoulder, I see that Nobu and Coach are still standing on the steps of the café. As the door latches, Coach reaches back up through the handle and locks it again, from the inside. Then he turns and looks at Nobu, and then at me.

"What are you waiting for?" I ask Nobu. I suppose that everyone is born in their own way. When Nobu and I arrived at The Station, he was relaxed, while I was anxious, suspicious, heartbroken. Now, I feel bold and curious, ready for anything, and he seems reluctant. But maybe I'm making this up. I stretch out my hand and Nobu takes it. He steps down onto the sidewalk beside me. "Breathe," I say. He nods his head and inhales, then exhales deeply.

"Okay, Coach. Where are we headed?" says Nobu, releasing my hand.

"Our Lady of Notre Dame." Coach points across the river. We walk with restaurants and homes on our left, and the river to our right. We pass a park that smells simultaneously like flowers and urine, followed by a cosy-looking bookstore with a green door and large windows. We cross a bridge spanning the Seine and approach the church.

"Is Paris a happy place?" I ask.

"Sometimes. For some humans. The matter of happiness is a bit complicated. You'll have a better sense of this after you've lived here for a while."

"Are you trying to be obscure?" I ask.

"Not at all. Only as truthful as possible," says Coach, as he approaches the massive wooden doors of the church. "Please follow me inside." He takes a step into the door and disappears, and we follow. Coach stands smiling on the other side.

Everything feels different in here. The air is cooler than outdoors, but when I look up, I see that part of the roof is missing from the fire. The moon is visible through the hole in the roof.

We pass through the scorched sanctuary in silence, until Coach motions for us to sit on a wooden pew, where a couple of hard hats and a lunch box have been left. The bench is hard, but the wood is incredibly smooth. I find the church calming. The quiet and the half-light is exactly right for me.

Coach explains that although religion is on the decline in Paris and elsewhere, many people still come to churches to seek forgiveness, assistance, and comfort. As he's talking, I have a vivid flash of a church with long rows of wooden pews punctuated by people, mostly women, with their heads bowed. Some of the people murmur quietly. Somehow, I understand that the people in this memory are praying.

"Do you feel sad for the humans, Coach? I mean, knowing everything you know?" I ask.

"Not sad, exactly. I feel empathy towards them because life can be difficult, and everyone passes through painful moments. Being here, in the presence of a higher power in whom they believe, is helpful for some people," says Coach.

"Were you this frustratingly open-minded as a child?" I say.

"Although I cannot be certain, I assume that I was. All the Helpers with whom I have worked possessed the same personality they had as humans, as described in their records."

"Wait! You said you didn't have records about us."

"No. I said I would share as much as I could, and I have already done so."

Nobu leans back and closes his eyes. "Hey," I say to Nobu. "You've been quiet since we entered the city. You okay?"

"Yeah. I'm just trying to understand how everything works." It's clear that Nobu doesn't want to chat, so I don't ask him what he would pray for, if he were a person who prayed.

"Claire, it is pleasing to see you embracing your new life as a Helper," says Coach.

"Hate to break it to you, Coach, I'm not embracing anything," I say

"Claire, that's not kind," says Nobu, without opening his eyes.

"You're right. That was unnecessary." I turn to Coach. "What I can tell you about our little mission here, is that when you opened the outside door of that café, every part of my being felt like it was pulled out the door, into the world. It was quite strange, actually. But in a good way."

"Excellent. And you, Nobu?"

"I'm fine, Coach."

"Very good, then. Let us go to the Louvre, so I can show you how to reach me in case of an emergency. It is a lovely walk, and it will help you get a better sense of direction."

On the way, Coach explains that Notre Dame is located at the very centre of Paris, and that this island, Île de la Cité, has been inhabited since the fourth century. The Louvre, where we are headed, is on the Right Bank, which means it's on the north side of the Seine. We can stay at street level or go down some steps and walk along a path directly beside the river.

"I'd like to walk by the water," says Nobu. The path is made of ancient cobblestones and I'm grateful for my Doc Martens, which make the terrain feel as smooth as the wooden floors at The Station. We pass two people in an embrace. An elegant-looking person, wearing a silk blouse and scarf, a skirt that ends just above the knee, and high heels, has their arms wrapped around a person in a grey suit. They are kissing, but this is different from the kissing on the bench near the church. It's like they're drinking each other, like they will die if they stop.

"Wow!" I say. When I look around, I see that Nobu and Coach are already passing under the next bridge. "Hey! Wait up," I yell, and run ahead. "Didn't you see that?" I ask.

"See what?" says Nobu.

"That extraordinary kissing event going on back there. They could sell tickets." Nobu shakes his head.

"Claire, the Parisians are a particularly passionate people," says Coach.

"Are you old enough to be saying this? Actually, are you old enough to be seeing this?" I ask.

"Although you are fully aware that the truth of my advanced years is masked by my youthful appearance, I am delighted at your attempt at levity."

"I don't like those high heels, though. What if you needed to escape a dangerous situation ... or wanted to dance?" I say.

"That's an excellent point," says Coach. He looks up at the massive stone building in front of us. "This is the Louvre."

The grounds are spacious and empty, except for a few people using the large garden as a shortcut. No one sees us. Coach motions for us to sit on a bench near the glass pyramid.

"I'm going to draw you a map," says Coach.

"You're not coming?" I ask.

"No. This is something you must do on your own." Nobu and I sit quietly, while Coach creates a guide to the offices on the back of a napkin. "My plan was to arrive in the early afternoon when the administrative offices would be fully staffed, but that is not the case now. Please note that I am including all the obstacles you are likely to encounter during working hours." He passes me the map.

"Armed guards?" I say glancing at the napkin.

"Of course. The museum, of which the offices are a part, is filled with irreplaceable art. My greatest regret about our change in plans is that you will not set eyes on the type-writer's usual operator, so please listen very carefully. She wears her white hair pulled into a tight bun on top of her head, and she works at lightning speed at an ancient type-writer, while everyone around her works on computers. When taking a break, she will remove her glasses and release them, so they swing from a chain around her neck, then she will stand and leave the office through the doorway beside her desk.

"Wow. She sounds a little scary," says Nobu. Coach nods his head.

"How do you know all this?" I say.

"I have escorted many Helpers to Paris over the years, Claire." I want to ask him how many and over how many years, and did any of them find answers about themselves, but I know Coach will respond that none of them were looking for that kind of information, with a tiny side order of exasperation. He's already upset with me about having entered the departure gate earlier than planned, so I stay quiet.

We sail through the ancient doors, walk down the inac-tive escalator, and follow Coach's map to the basement. When we get to the administration wing, there is a locked door with a sign that says, "Authorized Personnel Only," and without speaking, Nobu and I join hands and step through the door. Briefly, I consider my molecules, the bits of me that will be rearranged as we pass through the door, or the door passes through us.

We stand at the end of a long corridor of offices. A pair of guards walks right through us, without noticing we're there. I imagine that this is how Jell-O must feel when people drop fruit inside it to make a salad. It turns out I don't enjoy being Jell-O. I look at Nobu for signs of how he feels about being Jell-O, but there's no time to talk. We follow the map to Office 1-F which is, as Coach predicted, empty, and I sit at the woman's chair, making sure not to move anything. I glance at the napkin and follow Coach's instructions by typing directly onto the typewriter. "This is a test from Claire and Nobu." I add a sideways smiley face with a colon and a closed parenthesis. I wonder if that symbol was left over from my old life.

We run down the hallway, pass through the door in fits of laughter, and climb several sets of stairs and escalators. We resurface to find Coach asleep on the bench. This seems odd, as I've never seen him sleep before, but we sit beside him and wait for him to wake up. I lean back, close my eyes, and feel the spring breeze on my face. Perhaps I am not alive, but the world is real, and I am in the world and this thought helps me to relax. At this moment, I have everything I need.

CHAPTER 15
IN WHICH WE ARE LEFT ON OUR OWN

No one talks on the way back to the Seine.

When we arrive at the bank of the river, Coach reminds us of our cardinal directions: north, south, east, and west. Nobu says he's got this, which is a relief because I can't keep these directions in my head. Can't yet. Back at The Station, I read a few chapters of *Zen Mind, Beginner's Mind,* in which Shunryu Suzuki wrote that the beginner has an open mind, one that is filled with possibilities. This is the best news I've heard since I died.

Coach recommends that we use the churches and other Paris landmarks to orient ourselves, beginning with Notre Dame. L'Eglise de Saint-Germain-des-Prés sits just across the river in the sixth arrondissement. Coach points down the river towards the Eiffel Tower in the seventh arrondissement, to the south. He then turns to face Sacré-Coeur, and even before he explains it, I already know this means Sacred Heart. This church, he explains, is built on a hill in a neighbourhood called Montmartre. Finally, he turns back towards us.

"You like churches a lot for a guy who doesn't believe in heaven," I say.

"It's true. I find them comforting. Also, there's always someone in need of help. All right, then. It's time for me to depart."

"Wait!" I say. "Don't you want to check our message?"

"I received it," says Coach.

"But how can we be sure?" I say.

He pulls an Indian food take-out menu from his pocket and passes it to me. In the margin, he's scribbled my message along with the sideways smiley face. "As soon as I received your transmission, I put my head back and it seems that I fell asleep."

I pass the menu back to him and he folds it up before popping it back inside his pocket. As we stand under this tree beside the Seine, the sun begins to rise in the east, and a band of pinks and purples emerges at the bottom edge of the night sky.

"Isn't it a wonderful city?" Coach says. Nobu agrees. "Do you have any last questions before I go?" I have about a million, but only one forces its way out.

"How long will we be here, Coach?"

"I am very sorry that this will be an unsatisfactory response, Claire, but there is no way to know how long you and Nobu will be here. You will be here for as long as it takes. Are you quite alright?"

"Yes." I bite my bottom lip to stop myself from crying.

"Nobu, do you have anything you want to ask?" says Coach.

"Nah. I'm good, Coach."

"Very well, then. Claire, I've placed a few things in your bag. A few items I thought you would appreciate. We'll meet again. That is a promise," says Coach. Nobu bends down and hugs Coach for a long time. I stand still with my fists clenched by my sides. Coach bows deeply in my direction, and then he turns and walks down the path along the river. We watch as his tiny self gets smaller and smaller. When he reaches the next bridge over the Seine, he turns and waves. Nobu waves back with a big, broad gesture. Although part of me wants desperately to wave, I choose, instead, to shove my hands inside the pockets of my leather jacket.

"Excuse me." A short woman with white hair stands a few feet away. She's dressed in light blue jacket and navy trousers and clutches a large leather purse firmly under her arm. Nobu and I stare at each other.

"Are you speaking to us?" says Nobu.

"Well, who else is here?"

We look around. We are the only three standing at this intersection.

"How can we help?" says Nobu.

So, it begins.

"I'm afraid I've gotten turned around. I'm meant to meet my tour bus at a place called Richelieu Passage, but now I can't find it." She turns to me and says, "We're off to Versailles this morning to see the gardens." I attempt to smile.

"Do you have a map?" asks Nobu. The woman eases her grip on her bag long enough to pull a map from the side pocket. She passes it to Nobu, who, in one great shake, opens the map to its full size and quickly pinpoints where we are standing. He folds back the bits of the map that aren't needed and flips it around so the woman can see it. "Do you see this point, right here, that's where we are now." The woman nods. "Your meeting spot is just on the other side of the Louvre, right here." He moves his finger over to the other side of the Louvre. "It's easy to get confused with all these entrances."

"Oh my! I hope they haven't left without me," says the woman.

"Would you like us to walk with you?" says Nobu. Then he turns to me and says, "Is that okay with you, Claire?" I flash him the sunniest smile I'm capable of, and just like that the two of us find ourselves escorting an elderly tourist to her bus, just minutes after Coach has left us.

"Yes, please. That's very kind of you. Oh, the light's turning!" says the woman. I can hear the anxiety in her voice. "I'm visiting from Nova Scotia. That's in Canada. I've always dreamed of visiting Paris and I'm finally here." Her face is flushed from walking what is probably quite quickly for her, but her eyes shine with happiness.

"You're not from Lunenburg, by any chance, are you?" asks Nobu.

"No, I'm from Wolfville. Do you know Lunenburg?"

"We've heard good things. What do you think, so far? Of Paris, I mean," says Nobu.

"Oh, it is grand, isn't it? When I saw the Eiffel Tower yesterday, I started to cry. To tell you the truth, I was a bit embarrassed, but our guide, Colette, said it happens all the time. I have jet lag something terrible, but I don't mind a bit. My goodness! Where are my manners? I haven't asked you kids where you're visiting from."

"Actually, we live here," says Nobu.

"Lucky you! Oh! There's my bus. It's the one with the red stripe. And there's Colette. I've probably worried her sick by now. Thank you very much."

"It was nothing. Enjoy Paris!" says Nobu. We wave, but

she has already turned and is jogging towards her bus as quickly as she is able. The tour guide comes out to meet her. When they meet, the elderly woman points back in our direction, but the guide looks right past us. Nobu and I wait until the woman and her guide board the bus before we turn and walk back to the bench where we sat with Coach earlier.

"It turns out that you are good at this," I say. I take off my bag and hold it in my lap.

"I guess," says Nobu.

"You can be that way if you want, but we both know that you are feeling proud of yourself," I say.

"Okay. A little." He straightens his back as he speaks.

"How'd you learn to read a map like that?"

"No idea," says Nobu. "It seems likely that we know how to do a lot of things we're not yet aware of."

"I guess so," I say.

"Why were you so quiet when we were walking with her?" Nobu says.

"Was I?"

"Claire, you didn't say a word, and you are normally a very talkative person."

"I caught that VERY, buddy. I didn't have anything to add because you had it all under control. And she thought you were cute."

"Claire, although our ages are 'approximate,' I'm quite certain that woman is old enough to be my grandmother."

"The heart is not concerned with such matters." I lean against the back of the bench.

"Why are you trying to change the subject?" asks Nobu.

"I'm not. I just don't have anything more to say. You had it. You did a great job and I'm proud of you."

"Hmmm." Nobu pauses and looks like he's about to say something, but decides not to. "Thank you, Claire."

I unzip the front flap of my bag and pull out a map of Paris and two books. The first is the copy of *Heidi* I had considered stealing, before Coach gave it to me. On the front page, Coach has written, "Property of Claire. Do not mess with this book." Nobu laughs when I show him the inscription. The second book is a journal with a black cover and gold lettering along the spine saying, "Claire's Manual." When I open it, I find a letter from Coach.

Dear Claire,

If you are reading this manual, it means that you and Nobu are in Paris, and I have returned to The Station.

I am aware that this transition has been extremely difficult for you. Please know that this is not a criticism, but rather an acknowledgement of your unusual circumstances and the pain that becoming a Helper has caused you. Although I cannot change that, please know that I apologize for all the times that I was not sensitive enough to your needs. It was never my intention to hurt your feelings.

I am aware that you wanted to hug me when I left you and Nobu beside the Seine today. I knew that you wanted to wish me well and I understand why you couldn't. It is all okay.

Do you remember when I explained how things work for Helpers and you asked for a manual and I handed you a small card? I am quite certain you remember. The card said, "Do your best." In a very real sense, that is the best guidance a Station Master could ever give to their Helpers. Yet I could see that you need more information, so I've created this manual for you. It is not a manual in the most conventional sense of the word. There are no scripts of what to say in certain situations or how much time to spend with each person in need. You and Nobu will figure out those details as you go.

What you will find here is a list of the rules we discussed at The Station; please call them guidelines if that is more helpful.

The best part about this manual is that it is also a journal for you to record your observations and questions.

Every day I will be sending you love. Perhaps you will not feel it at first. Then you will. Of that I am quite certain.

Warmest regards from your friend,
Coach

My tears hit the page and splash back up. Nobu leans forward and slides the manual out of my lap, so my tears won't obliterate Coach's words. I pull my tee shirt up and use it to wipe my cheeks.

"Go ahead," I say to Nobu, and as he reads what Coach has written, I contemplate the possibility that my heart might break right here, on a bench in the courtyard of the Louvre. At least the view is excellent.

"Wow," says Nobu. "He sure does love you." He closes the manual.

"He loves you too," I say.

"Yeah. I know," says Nobu. "But I'm nice to him."

"Ouch!" I say.

"It's not shade, Claire. Just a fact. You don't trust him, but that doesn't stop him from caring about you."

"Do you think that's a Helper thing?"

"He's not a Helper. There are also pens in the inside pocket of your bag." I unzip the pocket. There are six medium tipped pens.

"How did you know?" I ask.

"Coach told me before I followed you into the café. He said you might not find them right away and that you'd be cross with him if he gave you a journal but no pens."

"He was not wrong," I say. "Do you think he can read our minds?"

"Maybe. I'm not certain. Sometimes I think you can read my mind," says Nobu.

"Really?" I say.

"Pretty sure," says Nobu.

I may not be in my old life, but I know that I belong on Earth. It's only been a few hours, but I feel myself waking up and taking life from the city.

We spend the day walking and watching and smelling and marvelling. At the end of our first day of round two, I open the manual gifted to me by Coach and write:

A LIST OF SURPRISING THINGS FROM MY FIRST DAY (BACK) ON EARTH

1. The impossibly delicious smell of bread baking.
2. Music wafts out of stores and restaurants and meets up with sounds escaping through other open doors and creates a new thing.
3. Two children danced with two older humans, perhaps their grandparents, on a pedestrian

street. One of the children was wearing a dress and it fluttered as they turned. When the child noticed this, they said, "Watch what happens when I dance" and everyone in the family turned to watch as the child spun around again and again.

4. The way the city dissolved into golden light just before sunset. It was the same exact colour as the filaments.

5. The ringing of church bells in the evening. We overheard someone explain that the bells at seven o'clock in the morning and at night are called 'Angelus,' an ancient pattern of bell-ringing that's a call to prayer for Catholics.

6. The wind makes many different sounds. I want to collect all of them.

7. A lot of people know each other here. They stop on the street and say hello, how are you, I've missed you.

8. So. Much. Kissing.

CHAPTER 16

IN WHICH WE COLLECT FAVOURITE PLACES AND LISTEN TO NINA SIMONE

During our first weeks in Paris, Nobu and I begin collecting favourite places. The city is filled with intriguing corners, lush private gardens, and beautifully decorated interiors. Each time we find a new spot we love, I make a note in my journal, recording the location and the opening hours. I then mark the location on my map.

Little by little, our world expands beyond the corridor between Notre Dame and the Louvre; we add the first, second, third, sixth, and seventh arrondissements to our Paris. Mostly we walk along the Seine and the grand boulevards that divide the centre of the city into a tidy grid, but we also begin taking the metro. Nobu's internal GPS is impressive. He's much better at navigating the city, the sidewalks, and the metro than I am. I frequently forget which side of the stairwell to walk on, and commuters rush right through me creating a strange wind tunnel where my internal organs used to be. Nobu, however, seems to enjoy this Jell-O-ish aspect of our existence. Sometimes, just for fun, he'll speed towards a group of school children and then laugh like a flock of birds, as the kids speed through him, towards their next great adventure, oblivious to his existence. But, for me, the sight of a man in a well-tailored suit entering my chest, briefcase first, never ceases to surprise and disgust me. The happy news is that the tourists move more slowly than the locals, so I can usually dodge out of their path.

At first, we don't mention Coach at all. My heart is filled with nails and other pointy, guilty, angry things. I miss our life at The Station, and I'm surprised to find myself missing Coach and his quaint way of speaking, his hospitality, the way he always picks the perfect teacup for each of us. I'm conflicted because I'm certain he knows more about my life than he's saying. How could he not? Part of me that wishes I could time travel back to the day Coach dropped us off at Perpetual Summer Camp, and ask or beg or demand that he tell me about myself, but I know it wouldn't have mattered. He had already told me everything he's allowed to. Although I want to discuss this with Nobu, I don't want him to think I'm crazy. On second thought, it's probably too late for me to be worried about that.

So, we walk the streets of Paris, ostensibly on the ready to help the humans, and adopt the appearance of a couple of carefree runaways, while I search for clues and connections that might lead me back to my life.

Across the Seine from Notre Dame, snuggled into a little block between a park and the tourist shops and falafel joints of the Latin Quarter, is the bookstore we saw on the night we arrived. It's called Colette and Company. The store is staffed by uber-cool young people, most of them foreigners, living in Paris on practically no money. After eavesdropping during a couple of visits, I've learned that most of them are writers trying to find themselves; in other words, they are my people, and I'm aware that their soul searching might make Nobu and me particularly visible, so we keep a low profile as we slip into the shop at night. I love everything about this place. Books are stacked high in every available space of the two-storey shop. Like tiny satellites, dust molecules move through the air collecting light and bookish bits of conversation. Time moves slowly here. This bookstore has already become my favourite place on Earth, followed by the Tuileries, which I think of as our garden.

The poetry section is close to the door. Even the names on the skinny spines of the chapbooks and poetry collections are beautiful. Works of fiction fill two entire rooms, and as I run my fingertips along the volumes, small sparks fly up from several books. I record the titles in my notebook for future reading. I underline the heading of this list, an action that brings me an inexplicable amount of joy:

A LIST OF SPARKY BOOKS FROM COLETTE AND COMPANY

1. *Anne of Green Gables* by L.M. Montgomery
2. *Sea of Tranquility* by Emily St. John Mandel
3. *Our Lady of the Lost and Found* by Diane Schoemperlen
4. *Unless* by Carol Shields

Below it, I make a second list:

A LIST OF SPARKY BOOKS FROM THE LIBRARY AT THE STATION

1. *Romeo and Juliet* by William Shakespeare

2. *The Collected Poems of Emily Dickinson* (Poem:
   I felt a Funeral, in my Brain)
3. *Harriet the Spy* by Louise Fitzhugh

Since arriving in Paris, the sparks and filaments have been dormant and I wondered if I'd lost them, or if they were Station-specific, but the books have reactivated them. I suspect I've always been a reader. I look at the titles of the books on these lists and decide to read them for clues about who I was and why I loved these stories. The first is shelved in the children's section, which surprises me, and the back cover says it's the story of a strong-willed, red-headed orphan named Anne Shirley. I am not an orphan, though, am I? I am the opposite of an orphan.

Upstairs, I find Nobu asleep on a large window seat, facing Notre Dame. We walked all day and although it's not possible for us to be physically tired, our core selves retain a memory of sleep that makes us want to rest. I seem to need more rest than Nobu. As the sun descends, the sky turns inside-out and the white walls of the shop reflect abstract swirls of gold and pink. I lie down beside Nobu and breathe in the sunset.

When I wake up, it's dark inside the shop except for the golden light of a rope of filaments flowing down the stairs, I assume, to Nobu. I'm relieved that they're back, along with my sparks. Happy even. I think of these strange lights as my superpower, although I don't yet know what that superpower is. I make a note in my journal about their reappearance and the fact that they're thicker than before. I wonder if that's significant. When I look up from my journal, the filaments are disappearing even though it's still dark in the store, which makes me suspect that I'm best able to see them when

I'm closest to sleep and my mind is open to this phenomenon.

I make my way down the stairs and find Nobu standing in the back room where the children's books are shelved.

"How did you sleep?" he says.

"Like you normally do, I think."

"Okay, except I don't know what that means," he says.

"Soundly. Like the sleep of the innocent. What are you reading?"

Nobu holds up a book. "I'm reading poems about dogs by this amazing person named Mary Oliver. But now that you're up, there's something I want to play for you." Back upstairs, he kneels in front of a wooden cabinet with a turntable, like the one Coach had at The Station. A newer model, maybe, but the same idea. Nobu removes a record from its paper sleeve, places it on the turntable, and carefully drops the arm onto the record. The sound of a woman singing in a low voice, flows out through two speakers, one on either side of the machine.

"Her name is Nina Simone. She was a jazz singer."

"Can we meet her?" I ask.

"She's dead so, no," he says.

"That doesn't mean that we can't meet her. Maybe she's down here, too."

"As a Helper?" says Nobu. "I had literally never considered that possibility. That is a cool thought."

Her voice is soulful. Rich and full but kind of busted up too, like she's lived through some hard times. Nobu sits on the floor with his back against the wall and closes his eyes. I drop down beside him, while Nina Simone sings, *I loves you, Porgy.* The sadness of her song tucks itself inside me, inside the hologram where my body used to be, and for a moment, I feel like I'm starting to understand something important about humans.

The bell on the door rings, signalling that someone has entered the store. Nobu jumps up, lifts the arm from the record, slips the record back inside its sleeve, and places the album between its siblings in the cabinet. I'm not sure if I'm imagining this, but it seems like he's getting faster. I grab my bag from the window seat, sling it across my body, and we descend the wooden stairs as quickly as possible.

"Hey Priyanka. Did you leave the sound system on last night?" The two women who work at the store are not much older than us. "Nothing's playing but it sounds like the speakers are on."

"Um. Maybe?" says Priyanka. "Sorry."

"You know we're supposed to turn everything off at night. A lightning storm could totally fry that thing," says her colleague.

Nobu points to the front door, and while Priyanka's colleague continues to tell her off, we slip through the fiction section, past the poetry, then walk right through the front door and run from the store laughing.

Listening to that Nina Simone album has put me in my feels, and the things I've been feeling arrive mostly in the form of questions, so I pull out my manual and write:

A LIST OF QUESTIONS ABOUT MYSELF

1. Who was my favourite singer? No. It would be too difficult to choose. I would never choose just one.
2. Did I wear a lot of black when I was alive?
3. Where did I live? In a house or an apartment?

4. Did I like my hometown, or did I yearn to be somewhere else? Where?

5. What was my middle name? Did I like my name? Did I think it suited me? I feel like a Claire, whatever that means.

6. Was I a good student? Did I care about that?

7. What did I want to do with my life? Like for a job.

8. Did I like making things? Art? Music? Writing? Knitting? Gardening?

9. Did I have an animal companion? Do they miss me?

10. What was important to me? What was I passionate about?

11. Was I too cool to dance in public?

12. Was I a kind person?

13. Who was my best friend? What did they love about me? What did I admire in them?

14. I have questions about my parents, but I can't even write them down yet.

15. Have I always been this angry?

CHAPTER 17

IN WHICH THERE IS DANCING AND A HARD CONVERSATION

Now that we're getting a feel for the city, Nobu comes up with a schedule for where we'll go each day for the rest of the summer. He shows me a map and explains his logic, which is that little by little, we expand our area, while keeping the corridor between Notre Dame and the Louvre as our home base. He thinks this will maximize our opportunities to help both locals and tourists.

"Your plan looks great," I say.

"You don't care, do you?"

"Not really, but I appreciate that you do."

"But it's our job."

"I'm well aware," I say. As Nobu's been honing his helping skills and expanding his territory, I've been scouring the city for threads that might lead to my past. I pay attention to what I'm drawn to and especially what causes sparks. Everything goes into my journal. I scan the city for people I might have known, even though I can't remember them. Every time I see a red-headed woman, my heart skips a beat. I realize that I'm looking for the girl from Shibuya Crossing, but Tokyo is very far from Paris, and it is never her. Although

I want to tell Nobu about the sparks and the filaments, I'm not sure he's ready. No. If I'm being honest, it's that I'm not prepared to admit how weird and wrong I am. I worry that he won't want to be my friend.

Later that day, we head home from rue Cler in the seventh arrondissement, where Nobu has helped eight different people between the ages of eleven and eighty-seven, while I've fallen in love with a house painted in a particularly fetching shade of pink; a bouquet of sparks shot up when I touched it. On the metro, Nobu overhears a man tell a friend about a ballet he has just seen. Nobu has this freakish talent for focussing in on one conversation, one voice at a time, as if this was the only voice in the world, whereas, I feel like a surfer, riding the waves of all the conversations that surround me. People whisper, "I love you," to those they are, and are not, married to; some argue in hushed tones while others loudly register their discontent, causing others to stop and stare; they disclose stock market tips, and gossip about this one's father and that one's best friend. While I'm sometimes nauseous in crowded public spaces, completely overwhelmed by the noise, Nobu is a Zen master, calm and still in the centre of the cacophony. I envy him his chill.

When he tells me about the ballet I say, "Let's go. Tonight." He raises his eyebrows. "How could it hurt? We've already spent the entire day helping people."

Paris is an opulent city. Of course, I haven't visited any other cities for more than a couple of hours yet, so I don't know how Paris compares, but I'm pretty sure Paris is on the opulent end of the spectrum. That word arrived on its own, fluttering down with a tiny parachute on its back. Opulent. Ostentatious and luxurious. Splendid. Lush. I practice the synonyms I know, and it turns out I'm good at this game. I must have been good with words when I was … well, when I was. As we approach the Palais Garnier, just after sunset, the lights of the opera glow from the windows and illuminate the exterior, which Nobu says is in the style of Beaux-Arts. Beautiful arts. An era of architecture. He says it's a very big deal. I tell him it looks like a wedding cake for giants. As we approach, I see statues above the windows, and on either side of the doors, like guards. They let us pass.

We climb the grand staircase and enter the theatre, just as the lights flicker to tell the guests to take their seats. We follow the humans inside, and I do my best to dodge the walk-throughs. There aren't any empty seats, so we sit on the steps of the orchestra section, and I rest my back against Nobu's knees.

The stage lights come on and the stage seems tilted towards us. The floor is black, and a large semi-circular backdrop of individual ropes hangs from the ceiling, falling almost to the ground. The dancers, dressed in various shades of pink, run onto the stage, along the perimeter of the arrangement of ropes, brushing them with their fingertips as they pass, causing the ropes to vibrate and shimmer like rain. The music sounds like the thrumming of the human heart. The man on the train called this modern dance, and although I have nothing to compare it to, I love the way they sway, touch fingers, move away and then back together.

The ballet feels like life in Paris. People lunge towards each other and drift away as if they can't stop themselves from destroying what they've created, and then, filled with guilt or longing or both, they try to repair the damage. Come back, please come back. Sometimes, if it's not too late, and if the loved one has a strong heart that can forgive what's been said or done, they move towards each other again.

The dancers shrug their shoulders and grasp forearms. They hold hands and skip with an incredible lightness of being. They rest their heads on each other's shoulders. I feel everything they are dancing in my stomach.

The ballet is near its end when the dancers begin running around the semi-circle of ropes again. That's when it happens. I slip out of my boots and socks. With six strides I land at the bottom of the stairs, leap over the heads of the musicians in the orchestra, land on the stage with both feet and run towards the troupe, speeding up to fall in step with them. We're led by a small woman with shoulder length black hair that flies out behind her as she runs, and she's moving so quickly, I wonder if she will fly. It is the easiest thing in the world to connect with their shared energy, to speed up and slow down, and I hear their breathing shift as they ask more or less of their bodies. We've been running for two minutes when I notice the arrival of the golden filaments. They're extremely faint, but they've begun moving out from me, like sacred snakes. When I search the crowd for Nobu, I see that one particularly thick rope of filaments has attached itself to him.

As the music ends, I bow with the dancers and experience the applause of the audience; it sounds like rain. People are on their feet clapping, and I hear Nobu yell, "Bravo!" I bow again and return to our seat on the stairs, where I pull on my socks and lace up my boots. People step over us and through us on their way to the exits, but Nobu and I wait for them to pass.

"Come on," he says, "I want to show you something." At the back of the auditorium, we take a side exit leading to a room called the Grand Foyer. It's twice as big as the park near the bookstore, and is lit by enormous chandeliers that hang low from the ceiling and make the room appear like liquid gold.

"I read about this opera house," he says. "At the time it was built, they called it a drawing room for society, but I thought that must be wrong."

"What do you mean?"

"A place where people came to draw?" says Nobu. He raises his eyebrows before he stretches out the wooden floor with his hands behind his neck.

"I think this was like a living room, a place for people to gather, but by the looks of it, only the richest people in Paris. They were known as 'high society,' which was sometimes shortened to just, 'society,'" I say.

Nobu sits up. "How do you know this stuff, Claire? Really."

"No idea. I must have liked history in my last life. Um, my only life," I say.

"But this is a life, isn't it? Don't you feel alive?" says Nobu, his body leaning towards me. My mind flashes back to being on stage earlier.

"I felt alive watching the ballet tonight and ...," and then I'm quiet. I know how impulsive that was, and that Nobu may not be happy with me.

"Go on," he says.

"It wasn't like I made a decision, exactly. Jumping up on the stage was pure instinct. It only took me a moment to find their rhythm and then everything was effortless. I loved every aspect of it. The pale pink costumes and the way the dancers moved so expressively. I loved all the stories within the story, people getting together and relationships falling apart. I liked it when they were like children playing. That felt joyful. Oh, and the running! I loved running around the circle with the dancers, touching the ropes and hearing our feet make the sound of rain." I'm out of breath from talking so quickly.

"It made you happy," says Nobu.

"Yes, but it was more than that. The act of dancing with them was about creating something new and vibrant, you know? I felt connected to everyone. To the dancers, to the audience, to you. Then, at the end, the sparks and the filaments showed up, and you're the only person, or whatever we are, that I've experienced them with."

"The what?"

"The filaments. Look, this is going to sound weird, Nobu." When he clears his throat, I say, "Yes, even under our current circumstances. Don't freak out, but there are these thick threads of golden light that connect us." His eyes grow larger. He looks in the space between us, then back up at me. "I saw them first at The Station. I've only seen them when I'm waking up, so I'm not sure if that's because it's still kind of dark, or because I'm not fully conscious." I wait for a response. He has tilted his head slightly. "Nobu, I am not making this up."

"I believe you. I'm just wondering about the significance of the ..."

"Filaments," I say.

"Did you tell Coach about this?" he asks.

"As if!" I snort, and Nobu frowns. "Oh, you're being serious. No, I definitely did not talk to Coach about them, but I'm pretty sure he saw a spark that shot up between you and me at the café, the night we arrived in Paris."

"What kind of spark?"

"I don't know exactly. I get them sometimes. Like when I touch certain books or objects that maybe I liked when I was alive. My theory is that they're like an internal guidance system or something, but the GPS isn't very effective, obviously, because I don't understand how it works or what it's pointing to."

Nobu shakes his head. "I don't get why you waited so long to tell me."

"I don't know, exactly. I've wanted to tell you since the first time it happened, but it never felt like the right time, and I was scared that Coach would overhear us." Nobu folds his arms and avoids my eyes. I feel my face heating up. "Nobu, are you actually mad at me, right now?" He stares at me. "Are you?!" It's like I can hear the buzzing of the words he's not yet said.

"It's just that I wish you had thought for a moment, before you jumped on stage."

"Why?" I say.

"Didn't it occur to you that somebody would see you?"

"You're the only one who can see me," I say.

"Me and any of the nineteen-hundred people in the crowd who might have needed assistance."

"Oh."

"I cannot believe you forgot," he says.

"It's not so much that I forgot, as I questioned the premise of our little assignment."

"Claire, you can't NOT feel like a helper. That's what we are. That's what we're here to do. It is the reason we exist!" I've never heard him sound so frustrated. It sounds like music warped out of tune.

"No. I don't accept that, Nobu. I didn't sign up for that. I'm here to figure out who I am. Or who I was. And who loved me and why, and what happened to them when I went away." I want to share everything with him, but I feel scolded for dancing on that stage, for not being willing to help the humans. I can't bear that he's disappointed in me. He opens his mouth to say something, but I hold up my hand. "That's enough. I'm done for today."

I get up and walk the length of the foyer, and as I pass a mirror, I am briefly startled by the complete absence of myself. Then I remember Coach saying that mirrors on Earth do not register the image of Helpers. Or vampires, apparently. At the end of the room, I drop my bag and jacket on the floor. A dragon of fire grows in my stomach and the heat of it spreads up through my heart and throat, but I feel something else mixed in with the anger, something of a different intensity. Sadness.

From my bag I pull out my journal. As my stomach churns, I read my most recent list:

A LIST OF THINGS THAT MADE ME FEEL ALIVE TODAY

1. Two small girls in navy and white striped tee-shirts playing tag outside a café on rue Cler.
2. The black cat who lives at Colette and Company. I'm quite sure it can see us.
3. How the city feels at night when all the tourists return to their hotels and the Parisians go home for dinner and we have the streets and the bridges and the ink-black Seine all to ourselves.

I want to rip the pages from my journal. I want to set them on fire with my eyes and watch them burn to ashes in the middle of this large room. I imagine the wooden floor catching fire and then spreading, racing out to the walls where the heavy damask drapes flare up into golden columns of fire. In my mind, the whole room is engulfed in flames.

Breathe. I hear someone say the word clearly. Breathe. But Nobu is asleep. I can see him on the other side of my imaginary inferno. *Claire, you need to breathe. Inhale through your nose. Exhale through your mouth. Go ahead.*

I do what the voice says.

CHAPTER 18

IN WHICH WE ARE TOURISTS BUT NOT REALLY

When I wake, I'm still in the foyer of the opera house, which has not burned down, and my first thought is a memory of Nobu's disappointment in me for risking being seen on the stage, and for not yet becoming a Helper. Ack! I am flattened by the weight of his disapproval. There aren't any filaments this morning, or at least none that I've seen, and for one strange, surreal moment, I wonder if I made them up out of desperation to be close to the only non-living being my age. No, that's absurd. On our first day at The Station, Nobu became my best friend, and I'm certain that I am his. The truth is that it never occurred to me that someone might see me on the stage at the ballet. I acted in a super-impulsive way and Nobu would never have taken that kind of risk because he's always thinking about other people. I should apologize, but I can't make myself. But I don't want to be angry with him either, so I decide to pretend that last night never happened.

Nobu finds me as I'm packing up my bag and our good mornings are quieter than normal. We descend the grand staircase in our matching, chunky Doc Martens, and stop in the square in front of the Palais to look back at it.

"I'm so hungry," I say. The words slip out.

"You know, you're not, really. Hungry."

"Joke all you want, but I'm dying for some roast chicken." As soon as the word, 'dying' pops out of my mouth, I crack up. We laugh for so long, I have to wipe tears from the corners of my eyes.

"Roast chicken, huh?" he says.

"Absolutely. And I know the perfect spot. It's called Le Grand Colbert and it's on Rue Vivienne, really close to the Palais Royal gardens, you know the place with the big, mirrored balls?"

Nobu nods. He's totally humouring me, which is okay with me right now. "How do you know about this place?"

"Last night at the ballet, some people behind us had just eaten there. I swear, my mouth started watering just listening to them describe the meal," I say. As the restaurant won't be open for hours, we walk to a nearby park called Jardin Nelson Mandela. Someone has left a magazine on a bench, and before I reach for it, I remember our training in Barcelona, when Coach taught us how to prevent a situation where a human might see a magazine levitate and then disappear into thin air. Although I like the idea of a little magic show, I look around to make sure no one is looking in my direction, before I pick it up and open it to an article called, "Twenty Cool Things to Do in Paris." Colette and Company, which we've been haunting regularly, is number eight and I'm weirdly proud of us for finding such a great Parisian place so quickly after we got here.

What I really need is a list of 20 Places Where I Can Learn About My Life, but there's no such magazine article.

It doesn't exist. For all intents and purposes, I don't exist. The thing about death is that it's not some small obstacle you bounce back from. I feel myself circling the drain. Stop it, Claire. It's fine to be heartbroken, but you need a plan. I pull out my journal.

A LIST OF WHAT I KNOW AND DON'T KNOW:

- I don't know where I lived.
- I know the sparks and the filaments are significant.
- I don't yet know how they work.
- I know that the more sparks I observe, the more likely it is that patterns will emerge.
- I don't know how long this will take.
- I know it doesn't matter. I need to follow the sparks back to myself.

I think back over my wardrobe choices, the books, the red-headed girl in Tokyo and the dancers. There's a web of meaning here and although it's invisible to me right now, one thing I can do is to expand my world, or at least my Paris, so I open a new page and record the names and addresses of some of the spots in the article including the cross streets. Some are familiar, but most are not. Then I unfold my map and mark these places with Xs.

"What are you reading, Claire?" Nobu is lying on the grass beside me, and he's got one Doc crossed over the other. His eyes are closed.

"I'm making a list of places to visit in Paris."

There's a silence, then Nobu says, "Claire, it kind of feels like you think we're tourists here."

"What?" I feel like I've been punched in the stomach.

He repeats himself, but I heard him correctly the first time. I don't respond.

"Hey, I don't mean to hurt your feelings, and I know you're going through a lot right now, but I feel like I'm the only one who cares about the fact that we're here to help the humans."

"Too late," I say. He raises an eyebrow. "It's too late. You have hurt my feelings. And between last night and this morning, it's starting to feel like you're doing it on purpose." I stand up and stuff the journal, map, magazine, and pen into my bag, but because I'm in such a hurry, I drop my pen and have to get down on the ground and search around in the grass for it. As I storm off, I'm close to tears and I'm not really paying attention to where I'm going, so I end up on a sidewalk crowded with morning commuters walking briskly to and from the metro station. A woman carrying two bags of groceries whooshes through me, and I'm struck by the indignity of being walked through when you are already upset. I hear my name.

"Claire. Wait." I turn and face him. "I'm sorry for hurting your feelings." He does look properly glum, there's no question about it.

"And?" I say.

"And I want you to forgive me, and then I'll help you find this chicken restaurant."

"Le Grand Colbert. It's called Le Grand Colbert." I'm yelling, which seems unwise, so I lower my voice. "And why exactly did you say that thing about us not being tourists?

Where there's no clarity, there can be no forgiveness." I'm proud of my declaration.

"I'm worried about you," he says.

"Nope," I say.

He steps closer. "Yes. I am."

"I don't accept that your way of showing concern is to scold me and pronounce that we are not tourists. As if I don't know that. As if I've had a chance to forget." A small boy in navy shorts, a striped T-shirt, and a red hat runs through Nobu and then me. I stay as still as I can to minimize the discomfort, but it's hard when I know it's coming. As the boy steps out of me, I exhale.

"I am concerned. You are a very kind person. You are always very kind to me and sometimes to Coach, even though you kind of hate him. So why don't you want to help the humans?" Nobu points to a nearby tree and we leave the sidewalk and sit beneath it.

"It's not that I don't want to help them, but that I can't. It's like helping them is a distraction from what I need to do," I say.

"Which is what?" Nobu says. I sigh. He's a very smart person. How does he not get this?

"Find out who I was. Learn the truth."

"Even if you know we could get demoted?"

"Even then," I say. He shakes his head and now I'm full body crying with tears streaming, a runny nose, and a complete loss of control over my face and the noises I'm making. I take a deep breath and consider what I need to convey. "Nobu, you think I'm being selfish, but you might not if you understood how this feels for me. You have no memories of your life." He nods. "But that is not the case for me.

My past life runs just under the surface of everything, like an electrical current. It's like I'm being haunted by myself. I don't know why this is happening to me, Nobu, but it is, and I need to get to the bottom of it, to discover who I was and how things ended so I can have one moment of peace."

Nobu pulls a handkerchief out of the back pocket of his jeans. It's white and it looks like it's just been ironed, although I don't know how that's possible. "Here," he says. I unfold the handkerchief and dry my cheeks. I blow my nose and feel a little better. I fold up the handkerchief and wonder what I'm supposed to do with it now. Do I give it back to him? Do I put it in my bag? What?

"Keep it," Nobu says. "Coach gave me several." I tuck the handkerchief in the side pocket of my bag. He places his hand on my forearm. "Thank you, Claire."

"For what?" I ask.

"For trusting me. For telling me what you're going through. It's true. I did think you were being selfish, but I don't know what it's like to almost-but-not-quite-remember my life. I was being selfish in not trying to understand you better, and I'm really sorry." I place my head on his shoulder and he wraps his arm around me, and while there's no part of me that thinks this kind of apology is normal, I'm so grateful to him for listening to me, so grateful that he's my person. Nobu, who seems comfortable everywhere. Comfortable and completely himself. As if it never occurred to him that this stuff is hard. Dying. The green field. The Station and Coach and all his rules. As we sit together on the grass, I start to think I might be okay someday, that there might be answers to my questions, and that Nobu will help me as I face the truth.

"Claire, would it help if I backed off a bit about the helping?"

"You're going to have to. Or else you'll need to find yourself a new helping partner."

"Ah. Salty as ever. That's a very good sign. I promise to give you more space. Just tell me what you need."

"Thank you," I say.

"Claire, will you please accept my apology now?"

"I forgive you," I say. Nobu grabs my hand and squeezes it, and as he releases my hand, a series of small sparks punctuates the air between us, and I look up at them.

"There," I say pointing.

"Sparks?" he says. I nod. "I can't see them, Claire, but I believe you."

CHAPTER 19

IN WHICH IRÈNE HAS LOST HER MOTHER

We slip unnoticed through the front door. The restaurant dazzles me with its high ceilings, white linen tablecloths, and sparkling wine glasses at every table. I wonder if I ever came here when I was alive, if I was the kind of human who could afford to eat at a restaurant like this. I suspect not, although I'm not sure why. There are no sparks but ultimately, it's just a feeling, and I have a lot of these. Perhaps the technician responsible for wiping my mind after my death had a bad day, and left just a little too much memory in me. Or maybe it was a good day, and it was his intention to give me this little gift. Or maybe I'm an experiment. Maybe that's why I can see the filaments. My thoughts are speeding, and I ask them to slow down. Regardless of whether I am a glitch in the system or an experiment, I have access to some clues about my essential self that Nobu doesn't. I need to keep following the sparks and filaments and see where they lead, because somewhere out there, the story of my life is waiting for me.

"What's this? I ordered duck, not chicken," I hear a diner say. An opportunity.

The waiter says, "Oui, Monsieur," and we follow him as he takes the roast chicken and French fries back to the kitchen. The waiter sets the food on a counter, writes a new order, clips it into the queue of waiting tickets, and returns to the dining room. Nobu and I exchange a meaningful roast chicken glance, and I scan the room before grabbing the plate.

"Back garden," Nobu whispers, as he looks around and then pockets a couple of sets of utensils wrapped in linen napkins. We slip through the back door into a small garden space, which must be where deliveries arrive and employees take their breaks. There's a bench right under the high restaurant window, and inside the restaurant, the window is filled with large leafy plants, so it's a perfect, private place to have a quick smoke, or in the case of two Helpers, to enjoy an illicit chicken dinner without being asked to help a soul.

Nobu rests the large plate with the chicken on his lap and passes me a set of cutlery. I smooth out the linen napkin and cut a piece of chicken. It's crisp on the outside and juicy on the inside and every bit as delicious as advertised. After each bite I make a "yum" noise like the ones that toddlers make when they're enjoying their food. Nobu laughs.

"I'm going to give you this one, Claire. This was worth it," says Nobu. We savour each bite of chicken and French fries in silence. When we finish, Nobu says he'll return the dishes to the kitchen, so no one gets in trouble. I assumed we'd just stash the dishes under the bench. I wonder if he's always been like this, even before he died. I suspect he has. He wears this ability to do the right thing easily, like it doesn't cost him anything.

Beside the bench is a black bucket of large white flowers. They haven't fully opened yet, and I wonder if they're destined for the tables of this restaurant as soon as they're ready to show off their yummy floral goodness. As I reach down and touch one, a spark flies up into the air followed, in quick succession, by a second and third. For a few moments, the three sparks circle around each other, as if they recognize the other sparks, before fading into the sky. Despite the drama of the last twenty-four hours, I experience something deeply pleasurable inside my body. Is this joy? Elation? When we get back to the bookshop, I'll look up what kind of flower this is and add it to my List of Sparky Things.

When Nobu re-emerges from the restaurant, he says the dishwasher didn't even look up from his work, he just nodded when the dishes appeared beside him. Maybe humans are also kind of invisible to each other sometimes. If I had another chance to be alive, I wouldn't waste it by taking others for granted.

"Thanks for coming here with me, Nobu. It meant a lot." He flashes me a classic Nobu grin. "I'd like to head to the Palais Royal next if you're cool with that," I say, and he nods. The day is perfect, with azure skies and decadent white clouds that seem even closer to Earth than usual and as we stroll through the garden, I so much want to forget why we're here. I long for the carefree feeling of being two friends out for a walk after a shared meal, but I have a self to find, and he has humans to aid.

"Hold on," says Nobu. "I hear someone crying." He veers right, off the centre path, into a garden organized around a fountain. There's a small blonde girl, perhaps four years old, sitting in a green chair. Nobu kneels in front of her. "Hello. I'm Nobu. What's your name?" She looks from his face to mine. "This is my friend Claire," he says. I try to smile.

"My name is Irène. My mother told me to wait right here, while she took my brother to the water fountain," she points at the water feature we just passed, "but then they disappeared." Irène takes a deep breath and says, "I am sorry, but I'm not allowed to talk to strangers."

Nobu nods. "It makes complete sense that your mother would ask you not to talk to strangers. Would you like us just to wait here with you until she gets back?" Nobu asks. Irène hesitates for a moment before she says yes. Nobu sits on the grass, facing Irène, and I kneel beside him. She's such a brave little kid. What could have happened to make her mother leave her alone, even for a moment? My stomach feels tight with worry. Nobu is half singing, half speaking a song and as he sings, he acts it out with his hands. Irène knows the song and sings along:

The itsy, bitsy spider climbed up the water-spout.
Down came the rain and washed the spider out.
Out came the sun and dried up all the rain,
So the itsy, bitsy spider went up the spout again.

Irène claps her hands and asks him to sing it again. I raise my eyebrows at him, but he winks at me. The second time he sings it, Irène imitates the hand motions, using her fingers to suggest a climbing spider. When Nobu finishes, we both applaud for her, and she smiles broadly. Then Irène does the thing I least expect, and am not at all prepared for. She stands, steps towards me, and places one small hand on each of my cheeks to bring my face close to hers.

"She likes you," Nobu says.

I reach up and place my hands over her hands and something like a filament, but smaller, begins to sprout from my palms. I'm so surprised that I drop my hands.

"Irène!" we hear a woman yelling. She's running towards us holding a toddler. Irène runs towards her mother.

"Maman!" The woman kneels on the ground, without letting go of the other child.

"I'm so sorry I left you!" Irène's mother is crying. "We went to use the water fountain, but Luc had a nosebleed, and I didn't have anything to stop the bleeding, so I ran to a bathroom to get some tissues. I should have taken you with me, but it all happened so fast. I don't know what I would have done if anything had happened to you." She pulls Irène into a tight hug with her and Irène's little brother.

"It's alright, Maman. Nobu and Claire sat with me. We sang the petite spider song."

"Who, darling?" her mother asks.

"Nobu and Claire," Irène says, turning with a gesture in our direction. Nobu stands, grabs both my hands to pull me up, but the sudden confusion on Irène's face makes it clear that we are no longer visible to her. We head back to the central path and when we look back, we see that Irène's mother has stopped crying, and they're discussing what they should prepare for dinner. For some reason, the fact that Irène can no longer see us makes me sad.

Nobu and I walk through the garden in companionable silence, and when we reach the courtyard with the black and white striped columns, he asks if I am okay.

"Sure," I say. "Why?"

"That was intense back there when Irène touched your face. She was really looking at you." He pauses and looks up for a moment. "No, that's not it. It's that she really saw you."

A LIST OF IMPORTANT THINGS ABOUT IRÈNE

Today
a four-year old
held my face in her hands
like it was the most
natural thing
on Earth.

She smelled like
fresh cut grass
and apples.

In the strange
invisibility
of this time
in which I'm neither
human
nor
Helper
she made me feel real again
and for today,
at least,
that feels like enough.

CHAPTER 20
IN WHICH WE MEET THE MONA LISA

"If I had to wait for ninety minutes to get into the Louvre, I probably wouldn't bother," I say. Nobu chuckles quietly as we slip past the guards, ticket collectors, and hundreds of people who are not-so-patiently waiting to be admitted. Would they enjoy their lives more if they didn't spend so much time complaining about everything? Or does the complaining also provide a strange kind of pleasure? Humans are weird.

I'm here to see what sparks for me. Like artists I might have loved, and possibly things represented in their art. Places, foods, activities that my former self might have had an affinity for. But after months of hearing so many tourists talk about the *Mona Lisa*, we're both curious to check her out. After consulting a map on the wall, we head to the first floor of the Denon Wing, which houses the Italian paintings. As always, Nobu saunters. He moves at his own pace and I'm not sure whether to be annoyed at him, or filled with admiration at the way he does his own thing. Nope. Annoyed. He's taking his sweet time in front of the Botticelli frescoes. The women in Botticelli's paintings are blonde and full-bodied like me, except they're sort of glowing. Nobu stands for a long time in front of a painting called *Venus and the Three Graces Presenting Gifts to a Young Woman*. It looks like it was originally painted on a wall, and the colours have faded over time. There aren't any men in this painting, and although I'm not sure why, I suspect that's significant. A small girl near us speaks to her mother in a ferociously loud whisper, "They look like angels." When they move to the next room, I quickly lean in and touch Venus, but there's no spark. Nothing.

Then I move on to a painting called *Madonna with Child*. There are several paintings of this woman and her baby, each with slightly different names. In this one, the woman is wearing a red dress with a dark blue cape, and the colours are so vibrant that I feel as though she is standing right beside me. The baby doesn't look much like a baby, though. More like a fifty-year-old man with the body of a baby, but his mother is portrayed more realistically. She looks like someone I could have seen on the street this afternoon, minus the cape and the halo. They are looking into the distance, and they seem sad, as if they already know what's coming. I look around the room and then touch the painting and there aren't any sparks here either, but for some reason, I'm transfixed. I haven't heard him arrive, but I look up and see Nobu standing beside me. "You're crying," he says. It's not an accusation, but a gentle observation. I touch my cheek and it's wet.

"Hm. That's strange," I say. It feels unlike me to cry in front of a painting, but the truth is I don't yet have enough data to know if this is unusual.

"Do you need a minute?" he asks but I shake my head and wipe the tears away with my fingers. "Okay. Ready for the *Mona Lisa?*" Nobu asks, as he rolls up onto his toes, grabs my hand, and pulls me towards the next room.

She's not hard to find, as she's surrounded by tourists checking her off their lists of Paris things to do, and art lovers from all over the world. It's easy to tell them apart because the art lovers don't take selfies with the *Mona Lisa*, and they stay longer. Parents hold their kids up to get a better look and the kid who said the Botticelli women look like angels is now perched on her father's shoulders. "She's kind of small, Daddy," the kid says. I turn to Nobu and nod in agreement. This kid knows what she's talking about. Nobu and I slip through the crowd, dodging the humans wherever we can, but sometimes slipping through them. When we get to the front of the crowd, I read the name of the painting: Portrait of Lisa Gherardini, wife of Francesco del Giocondo, known as the Mona Lisa.

"I like her," I whisper.

"Me too," says Nobu. "She knows who she is."

"Exactly," I say. "Like she's got some things sorted, but she doesn't want to be smug about it. She's just sitting here, having her portrait painted, living her best life." Nobu leans through the glass they have mounted her behind, right into the painting.

"She smells like chocolate chip cookies," he says when he leans back out.

"Not possible," I say. Nobu laughs.

"There's only one way to find out," he says. I accept his challenge, take one step towards the painting, and lean into it. Immediately, sparks fly up above the painting. I smile and step back out. While Nobu's joy takes on the scent of baked goods, my happiness expresses itself through sparks.

"Well?" Nobu says.

"Sorry. I can't smell the chocolate chip cookies, but I believe that you do," I say. In an effort to get closer to Mona, two teenage girls step inside us, and I duck to the right as quickly as I can. Nobu and I plan to meet up at closing, when all the humans in need of a Helper will be forced to leave the museum. Is it wrong that I think that's exactly the moment that the museum will get good? Probably. But time apart is essential if I'm going to learn more about who I was.

I speed through two sections, then slow down to study Titian's, *The Woman in the Mirror*. Just like at the *Mona Lisa*, sparks fly up when I touch the painting. There's something here that's important to me, but there's no way to know which life, human or Helper, these sparks belong to. I inhale and then exhale loudly, in an effort to shake off my existential angst.

My heart-not-heart races, my hands shake, and the room tilts slightly. I think this is a panic attack, which I learned about from a memoir recommended by a Colette and Company employee named Sophie, via a small handmade sign. Humans are so charming sometimes. My mind is churning, and the room is spinning, so I lie down on a bench where I try to ride out the storm of my own swirling thoughts and fears. This is where Nobu finds me.

"Claire." He drops to his knees facing me. "All you have to do is breathe," he says.

"Not a human," I say.

"I know we aren't, but you know what I mean. Just breathe." He gently wraps both of his hands around my forearm and squeezes lightly. "I'm right here, Claire."

I close my eyes and work on slowing my breath down. I am okay. I am okay. I am okay.

"You are okay," Nobu says.

"Get out of my head, Nobu."

"Oh," Nobu says. "Someone is about to ..." And then two squishy butts press through my midsection.

"Yuck!" I say, jumping up from the bench, but I'm already feeling better. The breathing helped, as did the distraction. And Nobu. My cheeks are hot as we walk towards the main hallway.

"Do you want to talk about what made you feel ..."

"Flattened?" I say, and he smiles. "Do you remember the sparks I told you about?"

"Did it happen again at the *Mona Lisa?*"

"You saw them?" I say.

"No. I saw your face change for a moment," says Nobu. "Sorry."

"It's okay. It's not your job to see all my weird phenomena. I saw sparks at another painting, too, which got me thinking about whether the sparks indicate things I loved when I was alive or now, and then I just sort of lost it."

"It's a lot, right?"

"Yup. I keep a list of what triggers my sparks. Like specific books and works of art. I'm trying to understand if there are patterns that will help me understand who I am." It all sort of tumbles out of me.

"Thanks for telling me," he says. "Hey, I have a thought, but it might not be that helpful. I'm not sure." I give him a thumbs up. "Um, I wonder what would happen if you decided it didn't matter. Not that it doesn't matter, because I know it does, but that it's all good, either way. The sparks could mean you liked something in your human life, or like in your Helper life, or both. You know?"

"I'll give it some thought," I say, but Nobu avoids looking

at me directly. "Hey, thanks for before," I say. "At the bench. Did you end up helping anyone?"

Nobu laughs. "I helped nine people find the *Mona Lisa*. I barely made it out of the Italian section."

"No one even saw me. Strange, right?"

"Maybe not," he says, as we emerge into the twilight of a crisp fall evening.

"I did see a lot of people in love, though, like holding hands and sneaking a quick kiss."

"Hm," says Nobu shrugging. "I didn't notice."

MY ATLAS OF SPARKS

- When I chose my clothes at The Warehouse: Jeans, Doc Martens and socks, leather jacket, messenger bag.
- After seeing the puppies with Nobu, he pulled me up from a chair which created a spark.
- The morning after Coach gave us the slippers, Nobu brought me a bagel with strawberries, and we talked in bed. Our shoulders touched which made sparks appear, twice.
- All the sparky books from The Station and Colette and Company (see previous list).
- The redheaded girl at Shibuya Crossing in Tokyo.
- When I touched Nobu at the departure gate/cafe at The Station the day we left—I'm pretty sure Coach saw these sparks.
- When I danced at the Ballet, there were filaments for sure, and maybe sparks.

- When Nobu and I fought and made up, he lent
  me his handkerchief and the spark appeared
  when he grabbed my hand.
- The calla lilies outside Le Grand Colbert—I
  want to remember how the three sparks seemed
  to dance with each other.
- When Irène held my face—although those were
  more like baby filaments than sparks.
- Crying in front of the Madonna and Child
  which was, admittedly, so weird!
- Painting: The Mona Lisa.
- Painting: Titian's, The Woman in the Mirror—
  Oh, I just realized that the woman in the
  painting had red hair.

QUESTIONS FOR CONTEMPLATION

1. What do these things have in common?
2. Are these connections to my life as a human or a
   Helper or both? Could Nobu be right that it's
   not important which life the sparks belong to?
   No. This definitely matters. At least to me.
3. What am I not seeing?
4. What or who wants me not to know myself?

CHAPTER 21
IN WHICH IT SNOWS

n the courtyard of the Louvre, small bits of frozen rain fall gently from the sky. Nobu and I exchange an excited glance. Snow. An awareness of this arrives from the strange, secret place where my non-memories live until they're called forth.

"Come on. Let's check it out," says Nobu. There's already snow on the ground, and as we run, snowflakes fly up around our ankles. We walk above the Seine for a couple of minutes and then cross Pont Neuf to Île de la Cité. Although Notre Dame is still under construction, it looks magnificent from the outside, and we watch the snow fall on its roof and garden. Then, because we are already such creatures of habit, we cross the bridge at Notre Dame, pass Colette and Company, and enter the small park near the church of Saint-Julien-le-Pauvre. The snow has gathered like a blanket on top of the grass, and the streetlights, which are dimmer in the snow, cast long shadows across the park. Without warning, Nobu drops to the ground and flops over on his back.

"Are you okay?" I ask.

"Of course. Come down here with me." He's always so

very sane, so it must be okay. I clear the snow off one end of the bench and drop my bag there. Then I copy Nobu's position, falling into the snow right beside him. "Scoot over a bit," he says. We're going to need more space." Without getting up, I launch my body sideways by a few inches and then he begins moving his legs and his arms together, first away from his body and then back. I don't have any idea what he's doing, but it makes him laugh, so I do the same. I make three large triangles in the snow, one with each of my arms and one with my legs. As I move my arms and legs in unison, sparks shoot out my fingers and up into the night sky.

"It feels ... strange," I say. The snow is cold against my back and head. I'm glad not to be human at this moment.

"But good, right?" says Nobu.

"Yes. Sparks-good," I say smiling.

"Cool! Okay, now the next step is to get up without ruining the shape you've created in the snow." I sit and then hop up to a standing position. Nobu is struggling a bit, so I grab his hands and pull him up. We turn back towards the shapes we've created.

"Oh!" I say, finally getting it. "They're like angels."

"Exactly! They're called snow angels," says Nobu. "Kids make them."

At The Station, I asked Coach if we were angels. He said it was not the word he used, but in that infuriating way he has, he didn't exactly say that we're not. So maybe we are kind of angels, but I'm just not a very good one.

"What do you think?" Nobu grins and then laughs again. There's snow on his cheek. I reach out to remove it, but as my fingertips touch his face, I see another version of him that is two or three years younger. This Nobu is smiling at me, but there's something different about his eyes. They're softer and less focussed. My stomach flips, and I drop my hand.

"You okay?" Nobu asks. I tell him I'm cold, dismiss his reminder that technically, I can't possibly be, and lead the way inside.

There's no one in the bookshop, and no one staying in the apartment upstairs. We've learned, through trial and error, that it is often booked by visiting authors or young writers who work in the store, while writing the Great fill-in-the-nationality Novel. But even though I'm cynical about almost everything else, I don't want to be cynical about this desire. I can imagine that Paris inspires writers and fills them with hope and beauty, and that if you were going to write a Great Novel, this would be the place to do it. I have a theory that all great novels, regardless of where they are set or written, are really Parisian novels, due to the sparkly way they make the reader feel.

There's an ancient set of encyclopedias at the back of the store, and I grab the L volume and flip to the entry about love. I'm disappointed, but not surprised, to find there's nothing here that tells me what love IS. In our time on Earth, I have witnessed the humans of Paris demonstrate their love for family members, friends, pets, and even for communities of strangers, but this is also not helpful. I feel itchy with questions. I open my journal and write some of them down:

A LIST OF QUESTIONS ABOUT LOVE

What was happening under the stairs --
urgent, reckless and impolite?
Love or sex?
Both things at once?

How do you know?
How does romantic love differ
from all these other loves?
Is it a matter of intensity?
Is the love for a friend
less dramatic,
less demanding?
Can friendship become romantic love?
Suddenly or over time?
How does love arrive?
Where does it live in the body?
And where does love go when it's done?
What fills the space where love was?
How do you get over love?
Can you love a second time? A third?
Are subsequent loves less intense?
Less satisfying?
Can you love a person who is not good?
Do some people live their whole life without love?
Does that make them sad?
Is that what heartbreak is?

This word is inadequate for all the jobs it's been assigned. Too big or too little, I'm not sure which. This is followed by the bothersome thought that we need more names for the act of loving each another. I close my journal and tuck it back inside my bag, and then I slip this useless encyclopedia back into its spot.

I walk around the store looking for Nobu. For a moment, I stand in the darkness of the front room and watch the snow falling on Notre Dame. Snow has fallen on this church for approximately 760 years. I think about my own few years on

Earth and wonder about the people I loved, and how loving them has shaped me.

Nobu is seated on the floor of the Children's section with his back against a bookshelf.

He's reading a used copy of *Between the Stillness and the Grove* which he's been consuming, little by little, for weeks. "I wonder if you couldn't just borrow the book until you are finished and then we could return it to the store." He looks at me with complete shock.

"But it doesn't belong to me."

"It was just a thought. I'm headed upstairs." He doesn't look up from his book. Upstairs, I kick off my boots, stretch out on the wide window seat, upholstered in dusty pink velvet, and look out at the city. I imagine families eating dinner together, teenagers finishing their homework, and people who hate their jobs, calculating how many workdays remain until they can retire. The truth is that I'm a little tired of the humans at the moment, tired of their complaints and their mistakes. Is it too much to ask that they might clean up their own messes for a couple of weeks, so all the Helpers could have a break? Maybe we could all meet up in Reykjavík for a writing retreat and a quick visit to the fjords.

Based on observations and conversations I've witnessed over the past few weeks, I make a new list:

A LIST OF THINGS PEOPLE SHOULD QUIT AS SOON AS HUMANLY POSSIBLE

1. Unhappy relationships that can't be fixed
2. Jobs they hate
3. Littering

4. High heels
5. Gossiping on trains and other public spaces
6. Diets
7. Single use plastics
8. Not accepting things the way they are

I know this last one is about me. Why can't I accept myself the way that I am now and let go of the past version of me, Claire 1.0? I wonder what Coach would say if he were here, and my heart softens for a moment. Maybe he's not such a bad little dude, after all. Nope. Every single time I try to let Coach off the hook for what's happened to us, I realize I'm not ready to go down that road.

My eyes droop and there's no reason to fight this memory of needing sleep.

When I wake, I'm struck by the strength and intensity of the gold filaments that flow from my body and down the stairs to the spot where I'm guessing Nobu has fallen asleep, while reading the book he refuses to steal.

CHAPTER 22
IN WHICH THE WATANABES GET ROBBED

t's the space between the Musée d'Orsay and Notre Dame that has my heart. More human life has shifted and unfolded, more adventures have begun, more heads have been lost in these few square kilometres, than in the entire history of some countries. I'm becoming more skilled as a researcher and Paris is one of my favourite subjects.

Paris. Love. The behaviour of small children. Snow.

At night, while I research and write lists of noticings and questions and consider how these things might help me solve the mystery of myself, Nobu reads and sketches on scraps of paper. He peeks inside garbage cans, and when I ask what he's looking for, he looks down at his feet. "I'm looking for paper for drawing." I offer him some from my journal, but he declines. "I can manage," he says. It's a funny word. Manage. It feels like what I've been doing since we got here, but it's not a state of being I associate with Nobu. I want to ask him about it, but I don't. It feels like I shouldn't. We've been living, more or less, in harmony since the day he pointed out we're not tourists, and I'm working hard to preserve that peace, even though it might not be my natural state.

Thinking about my natural state both makes me laugh and saddens me.

This morning, Nobu suggests that we take the metro up to Sacré-Coeur.

"It's not safe," I say. "There are thieves."

"Claire, this is Paris. There are thieves everywhere. Also, and not to be insensitive about our current situation, but we're already dead, so they can't harm us. You're going to have to come up with a better reason than that."

"I'm not able to be rational about my fears. That's why they're called fears." Briefly, I feel proud of this argument. "I just don't want to go."

"But I'll be with you the whole time. We need to expand our area because I'm worried we're not helping enough."

"We help," I say, and when he raises his eyebrows, I amend that. "You help lots of people."

"I need to believe that I have more to offer than just directing tourists towards the *Mona Lisa*. Do you remember, back at The Station, when I doubted that I would be a good Helper?

I nod. "But I never doubted you, though."

"And I'm grateful for your confidence in me but I think there's a chance I could become skillful at this, not just because we were assigned this job, but because I want to make a difference in people's lives. But to find those humans, I need to explore new areas, even if they are less shiny and predictable than our immediate surroundings. Does that make sense?" Nobu places his hand on my arm, and out of the corner of my eye, I see a small spark rising.

A wave of sadness washes over me because I don't think I deserve this level of kindness and patience. To ground myself, I inhale and blow the breath out of my mouth like a sigh. The thing is that I am an anxious being. I'm genuinely afraid of things that don't seem dangerous or threatening to others. To Nobu. Why am I this way? Maybe this is left over from my human life, and that's all it takes, really, to convince me that Montmartre may hold clues for me, may plant some memory seeds, or knock something free in my strange mind-palace that will help me access my old life.

"Okay," I say.

"Really?" his face shines and I smile and feel guilty about not being more straightforward. But not that guilty. He knows what my mission is on Earth.

We're quiet on the metro ride. Although humans who aren't in need of help can't hear the actual words we say, a small percentage of very sensitive people perceive our speech on a kind of supernatural frequency, so we're meant to keep our public chatting to a minimum. We get off the metro at Abbesses and make our way up the narrow, winding streets of Montmartre. The snow has melted, the day is grey, and Sacré-Coeur rises above us, this huge Romano-Byzantine structure built in opposition to the opulence and excess of buildings like the Palais Garnier. Even so, it doesn't look very working class to me. We pass tourists struggling with the steep hill. It is one of the only benefits of being a Helper I've discerned thus far, our ability to do physical things without effort. I never struggle to keep up with Nobu even though he is taller and thinner than I am. We walk shoulder to shoulder without any effort on my part, although Nobu is still more likely to slip through a human in his path than I am.

The funicular to the church is crowded, so we opt to climb the stairs to Sacré-Coeur, and then we follow the tourists down a few steps to a large open space that overlooks the entire city. Nobu and I stand side by side, taking in the view, and although I know it's a cliché, I don't care. This city is breathtaking. The Eiffel Tower is as small as the souvenir key chains sold in shops all over the city. The sun breaks through the clouds and a patch of blue pushes itself through the greyness, asserting its right to be cheerful. I turn to share this thought with Nobu, but we are surrounded by a family.

"Do you speak Japanese?" a man asks. There are three of them: a father, a mother, and a teenage boy who looks about twelve. They are beautifully dressed, in clothes that actually fit them, which is also true of most French people and not true of most tourists. I'm not being a jerk about it. That's just a fact.

"Yes, we do. My name is Nobu. This is Claire. Is there something we can do for you?" The woman steps forward.

"Thank you. Our name is Watanabe. A few minutes ago, we were robbed and we're not sure how to report this to the police," she says. Her voice is controlled as she explains that they had just come out of the church, when a young man grabbed her purse and disappeared into the crowd. The bag contains most of their money and all three passports.

At this point, I can't help myself. I lean towards Nobu and whisper, "Hmmm. Thieves," and right on schedule, he glowers at me. I smile ever so slightly.

Nobu asks what the thief looked like, and the woman and man take turns describing him.

"What kind of purse is it?" I say. Nobu stares at me, but the woman answers immediately.

"It is a black Louis Vuitton Alma bag with red handles. About ten years old." Nobu gives a faint smile.

"We'd like you to wait right here," Nobu says. "We're going to have a quick look around and we'll be back in a few minutes." The couple and their son bow deeply. As we walk, I ask Nobu what he's smiling about.

"I read that thieves in Montmartre sell knock-offs of purses, as well as bags they've stolen from tourists. They pocket the money, passports and other valuables and then throw the rest in the trash. If this just happened a couple of minutes ago, we might have a shot at getting some of their stuff back."

After a few minutes, we see three men in black knit caps selling designer bags on a blue plastic tarp, and right in the centre of the tarp, there's a black Louis Vuitton bag with red handles. As we get closer, I see that the bag is not new. The men look nervous, their eyes constantly scanning the crowd.

I feel Nobu beside me. "The short one. He has a plastic bag in his pocket. It's thick. I'm guessing those are their passports and money. The tricky part here is to get the stuff without a hundred people noticing a designer purse and a plastic bag disappearing into thin air." He points to a small grove of trees about fifty metres away. "Let's get there first and see if the stuff in the guy's pocket belongs to the Watanabes. Then we can check the trash cans around this area and get this stuff back to the family. What we need is a diversion."

"I could knock over that garbage can," I say.

"That's good. I'll grab the package and the woman's bag," he says. "Meet you at the grove." He counts to three and I move towards the garbage can, but a loud whistle sounds. Four police officers run towards us, and the thieves grab three corners of the tarp. If we don't move now, we'll lose our chance. Nobu jumps into the centre of the tarp and grabs the black bag with the red handles, then he jumps again, reaching into the pocket of the shortest guy for the small plastic bag. The force of Nobu's jump pushes the man backwards. He loses his balance and some of the purses on the tarp fly up into the air. During the chaos created by sailing designer bags, escaping thieves, and police whistles, Nobu sprints to the grove. I shove my arm into the garbage can and rummage around until I find a white plastic bag with contents including a pink handkerchief with Madonna lilies stitched on it. I can't be sure this is Mrs. Watanabe's stuff, but it's worth a shot. I throw the plastic bag inside my messenger bag and head towards Nobu. The police officers are putting two of the men, including the shorter guy, in plastic cuffs. My non-heart is pounding. Then I hear Nobu's voice in my head, *It's okay, Claire. You're doing great.*

We sit on the grass between the trees. Nobu opens the plastic bag, and it contains three Japanese passports, two credit cards and almost a thousand euros. He checks one of the passports. Izumi Watanabe. He puts this bag inside the Louis Vuitton bag. The plastic bag I've plucked out of the garbage contains a package of tissues, hand sanitizer, a travel guide to Paris, a long, red leather wallet containing a photo of the Watanabes, and a pink handkerchief decorated with images of a white flower with six petals. As I touch the fabric, a spark shoots up and then a second and a third. This is the second time I've responded to lilies, and I promise myself to record this occurrence in my journal later today. I place the items in her purse and chuckle when more sparks are generated as I fold the handkerchief into her bag.

"What's funny?" says Nobu.

"Not funny so much as curious. Just some sparks," I say. He nods, but I can tell that his mind is on helping this family get their stuff back.

"Okay," says Nobu. "The safest, least public course of

action would be to bring the Watanabes here." I volunteer to get them. Back on the path, two officers are folding up the tarp with the bags, and the other officers and the thieves are gone. The Watanabes are waiting below Sacré-Coeur, exactly where we left them. They're happy to see me, happier still when I tell them we think we have their bag.

In the shade of the grove, Izumi confirms that this is her bag and that nothing is missing. This seems miraculous, even to me, and I was there to witness it. The man asks how we got the bag back, and Nobu says something between the truth and a lie. "The police showed up and caught the men, and we were able to identify your bag." For the first time, Izumi seems emotional. Mr. Watanabe wants to give us some money to thank us, but Nobu says that's not why we helped. The man bows deeply, and their son says, "Thanks, man. You two are really cool," and Nobu and I look at each other and laugh.

Nobu recommends that the Watanabes leave their passports in the safe in their hotel room, and that Izumi leaves her designer bag in the room as well. "Take photocopies of your passports and only carry what you need, what you can afford to lose," he says. Izumi agrees and takes my hand, into which she presses a twenty-euro note. I know exactly what to do with the money. We exchange a smile. Then Nobu and I watch them head off towards the funicular. The son turns back to wave, but we have disappeared from his sight.

As we walk down the hill towards the metro, I see a cyclist heading right towards me. Eager to skip the experience of having both a person and a bicycle zip through me, I step to the right into a tiny Citroën. Although I'm only inside the car for a moment, I emerge dizzy and nauseous. "Whoa," I say.

"Sparks?" asks Nobu.

"Kind of the opposite, I think. I just had this weird sensation. You know me!" I smile at him, but I feel shaken up and make a note to record this in my journal, too.

"You did great today," Nobu says.

"I didn't do anything."

"That's not true. You asked about her bag. If you hadn't asked that question, none of this would have worked. You helped." I'm not sure what to think of this. We sit quietly under the trees for a while.

"You were great with the Watanabes," I say.

"Thanks," he says, "it felt amazing to get their possessions back for them." He pauses. "I had a moment back there when I thought how nice it would be, if they were my family." I cover his hand with mine.

CHAPTER 23
IN WHICH I BUY NOBU
A SKETCHBOOK

We're a couple of weeks past the solstice, so the days are finally getting longer, but it's already dark as Nobu and I exit the metro at Concorde in Place Concorde, just after five o'clock. We pass the obelisk, and head through the Tuileries Gardens towards the Louvre. Although we stroll side by side, we are on very different walks this evening. While Nobu is actively scouting for people in need of our help, I'm foraging for things that remind me of me. Not a tourist, but still not a Helper.

The Tuileries Garden was created for Catherine de Medici in 1564, opened to the public in 1667, and became a public park after the French Revolution. Regular, non-Royal, humans have been enjoying this garden for 450 years, and I love that everyone feels welcome to drag the heavy green metal chairs into different configurations to suit their needs. There are pairs of chairs pulled close for two friends, and triangles and squares and pentagons of chairs around fountains, on the lawn, and under the trees. I stop beside a circle of five green chairs, close my eyes and imagine the people who sat here earlier today. Perhaps they shared a perfect baguette and some laughter. Maybe it was their first time in Paris, or their tenth. It's possible they were a family. I sit in one of the chairs and put my feet up on the concrete lip of the fountain. Nobu frowns.

"I'm quite certain I won't damage the fountain, Nobu. I've seen lots of people sit like this," I say.

"I just think we should get going."

"To where, exactly?"

"So people can find us if they need us," Nobu says.

"Dude, we went all the way to Sacré-Coeur today. There's no way in which we are slacking. Plus, we're right here in plain sight, so anyone who needs help in this part of the garden will see us." He shakes his head. "What's going on?" I ask.

Nobu drops into the chair beside me. It has a sloped back and was designed, I assume, to help people relax, to remind them to look up towards the sun and the sky. Nobu tries to sit up straight but the chair won't have it, and finally he surrenders to its sloped architecture. He closes his eyes. "I don't know. I guess I'm not feeling like myself tonight." If he were in a slightly better mood, I'd ask him which self, but he's already got a front row seat to my existential crisis.

"Is this about the Watanabes?" I ask.

"Is what about the Watanabes?"

"You. Not feeling like yourself. You said it would be nice if they were your family."

"I did?" he says.

"You did indeed. It was quite memorable, actually."

"I liked them a lot," he says. "There was a nice feeling between them, didn't you think?"

"I did," I say and then I leave a long pause for him to have a think.

"Yeah. It made me think about families," he says. "About having one. Being in one. You know?" I nod.

"Sorry this a hard day for you, Nobu." He reaches over to the place where the arms of our chairs meet, covers my hand with his, slides his fingers into the spaces between mine and squeezes gently. A small golden spark shoots up from our hands and explodes about ten feet above our heads, like one tiny firework cut off from the rest of the display. Nobu's eyes are closed. He doesn't see it, and I decide not to tell him. It's an error of omission more than a lie. At least that's what I tell myself.

"Thanks, Claire," he says. "I really appreciate our friendship."

As I watch the reflection of the falling spark in the water fountain, a tiny bird lands on the edge close to my feet. It must be so cold, and I wonder if it might not be happier in the south of France or Spain. Perhaps it thinks the same of me. As I'm chuckling to myself, I have the sense that the bird knows what I am. Although I'm not certain how I know this, I'm convinced that this bird's true nature recognizes mine. It sees that I am a creature that was once alive, but is no longer. The bird and I assess each other for a minute, and then it hops up onto the arm of my chair. From this close, I can see that it's shivering, and instinctively, I pull open the pocket of my leather jacket. The bird chirps and hops in. I could not be more surprised at this turn of events, yet it seems completely normal that a bird has taken refuge inside my coat.

"Let's go up to the Louvre for a bit," I say. "There's always someone there you can help." I have another errand in mind, but not one I'm ready to share with Nobu.

"Thanks for understanding, Claire. That would be

great," he says. Nobu pulls himself up to the front of his chair and sits up straight. "I'll do a bit of drawing when we get home."

Just as I hoped. Carefully, I pull myself out of my chair so as not to hurt my small bird-friend.

When we arrive, it's later than we realized, and the museum is closing for the day. Although we see a few people exiting the Louvre, they look right through us. I sense Nobu's disappointment, but this won't stop me from doing what I came to accomplish. In fact, it will make it easier.

At the glass pyramid, I sit on a bench and hold the pocket of my jacket open. The bird hops out and flutters down beside me. It chirps at me for a moment, I stroke its small head, then it flies away. Nobu mouths the word "Why?"

"It looked cold." He shrugs his shoulders.

It's dark and quiet inside the Louvre. There are always a few guards around after closing, but those who work this overnight shift are the least likely people on the planet to detect Nobu and me. They rely on a different set of senses.

We stop at a Vermeer painting that Nobu's obsessed with. It's called *The Lacemaker*. When I ask why he likes it, he thinks for a moment. "This work, the smallest one that Vermeer ever painted, provides a glimpse into domestic intimacy. I love the depiction of everyday objects like the bobbins, pins and needles. I'm also fascinated by the way he created several depths of field." He points at the centre of the painting. "You see, here? The woman's fingers are in focus and the farther we travel from this focal point, the blurrier the painting becomes, so that the white and red threads coming out of the cushion appear like dribbles of paint. I read that Vincent van Gogh was obsessed with the colours

Vermeer used in this painting: the yellows, greys, and blues. Sometimes, you see a thing that's so complete and masterful, you know it could not have been improved upon." He smiles shyly.

"You know what you sound like?" I ask.

"What?" he says.

"An art professor." Nobu laughs, but I mean it. I don't understand half the things he's said, but I can see how much this painting means to him. I tell him I'll meet him at the exit in about thirty minutes, and as soon as he moves on to the next room, I retrace my steps and slip through the glass doors of the museum's gift shop. There are lots of journals, which are not quite what I'm looking for, but at the end of the aisle, I find a small section of sketchbooks. They come in various sizes, and although I'm attracted to a large sketchbook, I know that's not a practical choice for a lovely undead, unhoused artist. I place it back on the shelf and examine the smaller sketchbooks. There is one that opens from the top, rather than the side, and this seems like a clever idea. It has a black cover, a black elastic to hold the cover in place, and it will fit easily in the inside pocket of our leather jackets. It's just eleven euros, so I decide to also buy a pencil and pen. I don't know anything about what makes a pen or pencil better than any other, so I choose inexpensive ones, and pick up a small plastic pencil sharpener and an eraser. The total is just under seventeen euros, so I have more than enough. There is a pad of sticky notes near the cash register, so I leave a note: "20 Euros in payment for a small sketchbook, pen, pencil, pencil sharpener and eraser." This feels incredibly responsible to me. I peel off the tags, stick them on the back of the sticky note, and leave it with the twenty euros on top of the register.

Outside the exit, Nobu is lying on a bench with his eyes closed. I put his gift on the bench near his head. He sits up.

"What are these?" he says.

"I got them for you from the museum shop. I thought this sketchbook would be a better solution than a bunch of scraps of paper. This way you can keep all your drawings in one place." I pick up the sketchbook. "See. It's small enough to keep in the inside pocket of your jacket."

Nobu sighs. "I can't accept something that was stolen," Nobu says. He looks so serious. My heart leaps up into my throat.

"What? They're not stolen!" I say. "Mrs. Watanabe, Izumi, she put a twenty-euro note in my hand as they were leaving Sacré-Coeur this afternoon. I would have been unkind not to take it. And I knew exactly what I would do with it. I added up the price of everything and I left a note with the money. It was more than enough, Nobu. Someone will find it when they open the shop in the morning."

Nobu stands. "I don't know which is worse. Stealing, or accepting money for something I expressly said we could not accept money for."

"Are you seriously angry at me, right now?" I say.

"Yes." He folds his arms across his body.

A wild sound escapes from my throat—something between a cry and a scream. Nobu's arms drop to his side and his eyes widen. He opens his mouth to say something, but I turn and then I'm running away from him, racing across the courtyard and straight through the stone wall that surrounds the Louvre, before crossing the street to the path that runs along the Seine. Part of me wants to take refuge in Colette and Company, but there's probably someone staying in the apartment upstairs, and it would be the very first place that Nobu would go, if he even cared enough to look.

Then I remember this church that Coach mentioned on our first day in Paris. Eglise Saint-Germain-des-Prés, in the sixth arrondissement. I've never been there or talked about it with Nobu. I cross the bridge and pass through the narrow streets of the Latin Quarter. Nobu doesn't follow me.

As I run, I start a new list in my head:

A LIST OF ALL THE WORDS I KNOW FOR UNGRATEFUL

1. Selfish
2. Oblivious
3. Self-centred
4. Unappreciative
5. Ungracious
6. Ingrate
7. Demanding
8. Rude
9. Dissatisfied
10. Faultfinding
11. Unmindful

The only problem is that the longer my list gets, the more it sounds like me and not Nobu, so I quit making it.

CHAPTER 24
IN WHICH I MEET ANAÏS

The plaque outside says the original church was built in the sixth century, and the exterior looks like a hodgepodge of structures from different eras. I slip through the outer doors and into a small vestibule. There's a door to the right and large double doors that lead straight ahead, and my best guess is that this is the way to the church. Inside, high vaulted ceilings are painted blue and covered with what look like golden stars. I slide into a wooden pew, and although my instinct is to look down, I lean against the back of the seat and gaze up towards the stars. I wonder how long these painted stars have been here, and how many people have sat in this seat, looking up, hoping for something better. I am such a new thing, compared to this ancient church. But perhaps I'm not new. Perhaps I was something, or someone, before I was Claire, and something else before that. Perhaps I have sat here before. I'm both intrigued and a bit frightened at this new thought, the possibility of this being one of many lives, even though the evidence of this is no longer in dispute.

Statues and paintings surround the nave of the church,

and at the back of the sanctuary, there are metal shelves with dozens of small candles, where you can light a candle and pray for something. It's hard to believe that outside these walls there is a modern city, fast asleep. A city that will wake and check their phones, use the Internet, ride the metro to work, and use many other technologies they take for granted, that could not have been conceived of, for most of the time this building has stood here. I remember reading that this church was robbed by the Vikings during the ninth century, at which time it had already stood here for four hundred years.

I hear a sound behind me. I spin around in my seat, which creaks as I move. A young woman is asleep on a bench at the back of the church, but the sound wakes her, and she sits up.

"Hello?" she calls. I hear the fear in her voice.

I stand and face her. "Hello," I say, although I'm not sure she will be able to see, or hear me. "Please don't be afraid. My name is Claire."

"How did you get in here?" she asks. I take a moment to consider how to answer this.

"I was here when the church closed." Note to my future self: try not to lie while standing in a church.

"Really? I didn't see you." She comes towards me. She's my age. Not yet twenty.

"Yup. I needed somewhere to stay tonight. This seemed like a safe place." The girl stops a few pews away. She's a little younger than I thought. I notice her sweatshirt is stretched over her stomach, but the rest of her is thin. Too thin. She's pregnant.

"A little cold though," she says. We both sit back down with a pew separating us. "What are you running away from?" I did not expect this question. The people who have asked Nobu and me for help have not shown interest in us, as they've been focussed on solving their own situations.

"Oh, you know. All the regular crap," I say.

"Yeah," she nods. "Are you from Paris?"

"No. I'm a long way from home. What's your ... situation?"

"Me? I'm okay. It wasn't working at home. My parents aren't too happy that I'm pregnant. They keep talking about how I've ruined my chances to have a good life, and what will I do without a high school diploma? You know, stuff like that." The girl is shivering, so I take off my jacket and drape it over the pew between us. "No. I can't take your jacket," she says.

"Just until the morning ... when it's warmer," I say. She bites her bottom lip for a moment then reaches out for the jacket and puts it on. She smiles shyly, and she reminds me of the sweetness that Botticelli depicted in his paintings.

"Thanks. That's really nice of you. I'm Anaïs."

"I'm Claire. No big deal about the jacket. So, what's your plan?"

She laughs. "Planning is not exactly my greatest strength. About a month ago, I just couldn't take it anymore, so I took off while my parents were asleep. My older brother is at university."

"Here in Paris?" I ask.

"No. In Segovia, in Spain."

"Do you have enough money to look after yourself?" I already know the answer.

"I had some cash saved up from babysitting and birthdays, but it's been gone for a while. I spent some on food and then one night, someone stole my purse while I was asleep. It was my own fault. At least my ID was in my pocket. And my library card. I tried sleeping there, but they're good at getting everyone out. Now I try to stay on my own in places like this, but I don't really have anything left to steal."

"But you do have something to protect," I say. She nods. "Is it okay … that I'm asking these questions?" She nods again. "Have you got a doctor? For the baby?"

"I went to our family's doctor a couple of times, but I know he'll rat me out if I go. He'll call them up and let them know where I am."

"Is there somewhere else you can go? Your grandparents?"

"Absolutely not. They're worse than my parents."

"Oh. I'm really sorry," I say.

Anaïs shrugs. "It's not your fault."

"What about your brother?" I ask. "Would he be willing to help?"

She hesitates. "He's great." Her face lights up for the first time since we started talking. "He studies at IE. He's super smart and hard-working."

"It sounds like you're close," I say, and she smiles again. "Could you call him?"

She rubs her hands together and blows on them. "Um, I don't want to distract him from his studies, you know? Also, I don't really have any way to contact him right now." She leans back in the pew. Maybe I've blown it with her, pushed too fast, too soon.

"I get it," I say. "Listen, I woke you up and now I'm talking your ear off. Why don't you go back to sleep?"

"Thanks. I am kind of tired, so I'm just going to shut my eyes for a bit." Anaïs lies down in the wooden pew. I hear my leather jacket rustling against the wood as she tries to get comfortable.

This girl is really in trouble. She needs good food and a warm place to sleep, and she needs regular medical check-ups. I don't know how I know this, but I do. I'm so pissed that she doesn't want to bother her brother, but then I realize that my anger is not even remotely helpful, and besides, he may not be aware of what's happening to her. There's a tiny part of me that wishes Nobu were here, but she might not have seen us if I'd been with Nobu. She chose me, and I need to figure this out.

While Anaïs sleeps, I explore the church. There must be an office of some kind, maybe a phone. There's an emergency exit at the front of the church, to the left of the altar, but no office. I return to the vestibule between the two sets of doors. I noticed the door on the right when I first entered the church, so I slip inside, but it's a small chapel. I return to the foyer and float through the door to my left, where I find a small shop and a church office. It's our lucky day, because there's a phone on one of the desks, and when I pick up the receiver, there's a dial tone. I open a donation box on a table, and I'm surprised to see it is quite full. While most of it is one and two-euro coins, there are some five and ten-euro notes and a few twenties mixed in.

I have a flash of how upset Nobu was with me earlier, for accepting the money from Izumi Watanabe. How he stood with his arms crossed. What I'm considering now is so much worse. As I close the lid of the wooden box, I notice what's written on the top: 'Donations for the most vulnerable people in Paris.' If that's not Anaïs, I do not know who it might be. I open the box a second time and count out enough for some food and a train ticket and a little contingency so that she has something between her and the worst-case scenario. I take an envelope from a small stack on the desk and place the bills inside, then fold the envelope in half and jam it in the back pocket of my jeans.

Back in the sanctuary, I wake Anaïs. "Hey. I found a phone. I thought maybe we could call your brother."

"But it's so late," she yawns.

"It's okay," I say. "I think he would want to know what you're going through."

She puts her head in her hands, and I can't tell if she is thinking, or if she has gone back to sleep. After a minute she sits up. "Okay. Yes. I think he would want me to call," she says.

I've already unlocked the big double doors and the office door, and Anaïs follows me to the desk with the phone. I point to it.

"Really? Do you think it's okay?"

I nod, and she dials her brother's number.

Someone answers the phone, and Anaïs apologizes and asks to speak to Maxime. She cries as she explains what's been happening. I hand her a box of tissues and leave the office to give her some privacy.

In the vestibule, I grab a red coat from the lost and found. It is an A-line coat with a hood, in surprisingly good shape, so I slip it on. It fits me well. I decide that I am, at this moment, also the needy of Paris, and that I will keep the coat.

When I hear Anaïs tell Maxime she doesn't have any money to get there, I pull the envelope out of my pocket, return to the office, and place the envelope in front of her. She cries again when she opens it. I hear her brother asking if she's okay. She tells him a friend has given her money for a train ticket, and that she will be there later today.

As we emerge from the office, we hear a key in the large wooden door a few feet from where we're standing. "Come on." I pull the double doors closed behind us to buy us more time, and dash to the front of the church. She can't move as quickly, so I hold the exit door open, and she pushes herself as much as she can. We descend the steps. She leads me down a path beside a park, then we turn right onto a narrow street.

We walk-run for about ten minutes, until we are both satisfied that no one is following. Anaïs laughs. "That was crazy." She sits on the steps of a shop selling fabric and pillows, and I drop down beside her. The sun is rising, and the sky is lit with light pinks and oranges. We sit in silence for a few moments.

"Your brother was happy to hear from you?" I say.

"He was. He didn't even know that I was pregnant, or that I had left home. My parents didn't tell him anything. He wants me to come to Segovia. He says we'll sort everything out and I can stay with him for as long as I want. I don't know why I didn't call him earlier."

"Maybe you felt stuck."

"Yes. That is the exact word. I felt stuck. Listen, I noticed a donation box in the office, and a pile of envelopes. You didn't steal this money, did you?" Her face is serious. "My family is kind of religious, and I can't take this money if you stole it from the church."

I think about her question for a moment. "Nothing was stolen," I say. It is true. She is the city's most vulnerable.

"Okay," she unzips the leather jacket.

"No, you keep it. I'm good." She shakes her head and

passes me the jacket. "Listen," I say, "I'm okay right now. I've got some things figured out. The jacket suits you. Keep it."

"This Little Red Riding Hood coat suits you, too, in a strange way," she says. We laugh. "Okay, I'm going to take the metro to Montparnasse, before I change my mind."

"Don't change your mind. It's not just you now. Please keep asking for help," I say.

She lowers her head. "Why have you been so nice to me?" I don't know how to respond so I stay silent, but she continues. "Really, you have taken a lot of risks to help me. Why?"

"I wanted to." I feel a goofy smile slide across my face.

Anaïs smiles back. "Thank you, Claire." She stands up and I stand with her.

"There's a pocket on the inside of the coat. It's a great spot to stash your money," I say.

She heads up the street towards the metro station. The leather jacket looks like it was made for her. She turns, as if to wave good-bye, but I am already gone.

CHAPTER 25
IN WHICH I LOSE NOBU

Shortly after Anaïs leaves, I pass a shop that is filled only with chandeliers, a fact that sort of blows my mind. I imagine what the store must look like when the lights are all turned on. That's when I see the glowing heart. I wonder which chandelier it belongs to, so I press my nose against the glass to get a better look, but the heart is growing and I notice that it's moving up and down with my movements. This is puzzling. It can't be responding to me in any way, as I'm invisible and don't even have a reflection to follow. But when I look down, I see that this gold, pulsating heart is inside me, and it does have a reflection. I wonder if anyone else can see it. Wow! This is new! After a couple of moments, the glowing heart begins to fade, and I watch as it slowly vanishes from view. The feeling of it doesn't vanish, though, and I know it's connected to how I'm feeling about helping Anaïs. I'm so happy that I could help her, that I knew what to do. Although I'm more determined than ever to discover who I was, I wonder if it's possible that helping might be part of my purpose, both in the present and in the past?

Although I don't feel the heat of the sun in the same way I would as a human, I feel my energy recharging, like a battery. I try to walk slowly, to pay attention to life in the sixth arrondissement, as people begin their day. Parents walk their kids to school. Commuters head for the metro station. In a small park, a group of older people are exercising through slow, intentional movements, and I watch for a while and then try to follow. It feels good to move my arms in such a slow, controlled way. An old woman waves. I look behind me, but there's nobody else here, so I wave and take a few steps towards her.

"Can I help you?" I ask.

"Oh, I don't need a thing," she says. But if she doesn't need anything, how can she see me? I'm well and truly stumped. Is there something I've missed from training? Some loophole in the invisibility clause?

"We are the same," she says, pointing first at me and then back at herself.

Oh! Another Helper. I'm not sure what the protocol is in this kind of situation.

"It's good to meet you," I say. She smiles and keeps exercising, so I stay quiet and finish my therapeutic arm movements, waving to her as I leave the park. After a few minutes, I stop at a small store and café with four metal tables and chairs nestled in the narrow space between the building and the sidewalk. I choose the one farthest away from the entrance. It's a health food store, which, given what I've seen of French cuisine so far, seems hilarious. Two women, possibly in their forties, emerge from the store and sit at the table closest to me. One carries a bowl of yoghurt and granola on a small green tray, and the other woman unfolds a small paper package to reveal a pain au chocolate, which she bites into, immediately.

The woman with the yoghurt says, "Ines, he's having an affair."

"How can you be sure, Miah?" asks Ines. She bites into her pastry.

"I found evidence this time. He had printed out some receipts for reimbursement from his company and I saw the hotel bills."

"But you said he was at a conference," says Ines.

"He was. In Brussels. That's what he was being reimbursed for. But there were three separate nights at a hotel here in Paris," says Miah.

"Ah," says Ines. She places her pain au chocolat carefully on the brown paper wrapper.

"When you add this to the late nights, the way he has been pulling away from me, and the scent of perfume ..."

"Yes." Ines sighs. "I see. What will you do?"

"The children are with their grandparents in the country this weekend. I will tell him to be more discreet, for the sake of the family, and that I also plan to start living my own life." She pauses and takes a deep breath. "I just never thought this would happen to us. To me."

Ines places her hand on her friend's hand. "I'm very sorry," she says. Miah nods and they sit quietly for a few minutes, while Miah cries. Then she wipes her tears away with a light blue cotton handkerchief.

"We should get going," says Miah. Ines wraps her half-eaten pain au chocolate in its wrapper and places it carefully at the bottom of her tote bag. The friends walk away together. It's only now that I register surprise that Miah didn't see me, that she didn't feel a need for help. It seems that she has everything she needs. Miah has her friend to listen to her, and she has already decided to ask her husband to conduct his affair more discreetly, rather than throwing him out of their apartment. If Miah had seen me and shared her story with me, I might have suggested that she talk with her husband about what she's observed rather than accusing him. But it's not a Helper's job to decide who needs help. I am reminded of what Coach said about free will.

Humans are surprising beings and perhaps their marriages are all different. I know that some are happy. Perhaps some marriages are also arrangements of different kinds. Financial, convenience, a place to raise children. I don't think I could live like that, as restraint doesn't seem to be one of my defining characteristics. Then again, there's a lot about life that I don't know. I pull out my journal and write:

A PARTIAL LIST OF THINGS I KNOW ABOUT MYSELF:

1. I was alive and now I am some other thing.
2. I'm nineteen. Ish.
3. I get anxious sometimes. I think that's pretty normal.
4. Anger seems to be my default emotion.
5. I'm more of a word-person than a people-person. I like to read and to write.
6. I see phenomena like filaments and sparks, and now, disembodied hearts which seems weird, even for a Helper. I want to believe that this is a superpower, but I don't yet understand the purpose of said power.

7. I'm a Helper. That's my job. Until very recently,
   however, I have not been able to help anyone.
   But I helped Anaïs and that's important.
8. I live in a bookstore with my best friend.

Nobu. I remember how angry he was that I used the money from Izumi Watanabe to buy him a sketchbook, and how infuriated I was at his lack of gratitude. But I don't feel that now. Then it dawns on me very slowly, that I have no idea how to find Nobu. It's not like my rage-bomb came with a plan to meet up for drinks after. I've been separated from the only person I know in the world, and this is entirely my fault.

The familiar feeling of anxiety cascades over me. My heart races, my hands tremble and I struggle to catch my breath. Here we go again. I put my head on the table and feel the cool of the metal on my cheek. "It's going to be okay," I repeat to myself. No. That's not quite right. That mantra is not going to get the job done. I search deeper inside my own mind, sit up, place my right hand over my heart and whisper, "I am okay." This feels better and true. After about a minute, a warmth begins to spread throughout my body. I lean back in the chair and tilt my head back so the sun can continue recharging me. I am okay.

Now, to find Nobu. I'll visit the places where we've spent time: the Louvre, the Tuileries, Colette and Company, the park beside it, Palais Garnier. I'll take my time and do a loop and then I'll repeat it. Nobu will be doing the same thing; I feel sure of it. At some point in our orbits, our paths will intersect.

I start where I last saw him, which was at the Louvre. I visit the Italian masters then make my way through the museum. I see some intriguing paintings I've not seen before and make a note to myself to return on a different kind of day. I walk the full length of the Tuileries, check outside and inside Notre Dame, cross the Seine, and then return to Colette and Company where I sit on a bench beside two young boys, who smoke cigarettes and talk about Nietzsche. They say something about no absolute values existing, but I don't have any idea what they're talking about. I smile with the realization that they probably don't either.

I go inside and search the store, then spend some time sitting on another green metal bench in the park next to the bookstore. Next, I head to the ninth arrondissement and walk through the Palais Garnier. On the grand staircase, I remember how I felt the night that I ran with the dancers, and how Nobu said it was irresponsible. If I could talk to him now, I would be more patient. I would try to listen carefully, rather than just getting mad and assuming he was trying to hurt me. He's not a perfect being, and neither am I. There's no sign of him in the opera house.

Think, Claire! How does a person find a lost friend in Paris? Wait, which one of us is lost? Focus. I try to remember what I'd heard a tour guide say, when her group was getting on the metro. 'If part of the group gets on the train but one or more of the party misses it, the people who got on the train will get off at the next station and wait. The left-behind people will take the next train and do the same.' They all nodded because they had a basic and unambiguous under-standing of the action to be taken to prevent anyone in their group from getting lost. Nobu and I have no rules about what to do under these circumstances. We've not established any basic and unambiguous understandings, although I do love that phrase. I sit on the steps of the opera house and remember that Coach is the one with all the rules, which reminds me that he wrote them in my manual. I pull out the book, but there's nothing here about getting separated, and I didn't ask because I hadn't been on Earth yet, well, not as a Helper, and I couldn't have imagined this situation. Coach. There's something about Coach that's niggling me. Something about the test run he made us do in the administrative building at the Louvre. The manual typewriter from which we could reach him. That's it. I can ask Coach to help me find Nobu.

I walk back through the Tuileries and although the sun is setting, I feel calm. Coach will help. It's literally his job description to help the Helpers. There's still a line to get into the Louvre, but it's very short which means it must be close to closing time, and the lights in the admin offices are off. I slip through ancient doors, descend into the basement, and head to the desk of the one woman on the planet, who still uses a manual typewriter. I'm hopeful.

As I approach her chair, I see the top of someone's head. Definitely not the white-haired head of the typewriter woman. My heart bangs in my chest as I back slowly away from the chair, but before I can get out of there, the person in the chair turns around to face me.

"Claire!" he says.

CHAPTER 26
IN WHICH BEST FRIENDS ARE REUNITED

"Nobu!" I jump towards him without thinking. At the same time, he steps closer to me with his arms extended. I wrap my arms around him, and with his hands on my back he pulls me tighter.

"You're crying," he says, without letting go.

"I'm happy. Relieved," I say. I'm not surprised to see sparks shooting into the air above us, and I lean back to take them in. Nobu looks up.

"Sparks?" he says.

"Yup. Fireworks," I say. We let go of each other.

"Claire, I am deeply sorry about the other night in the museum," he says. "You were incredibly generous towards me, and I acted like such a dick." I laugh and take a couple of steps back so I can see his face, but he grabs my hands and holds them.

"Hey! Where did you learn that phrase?" I ask.

"A couple of young philosophers on the bench outside Colette and Company."

"Were they talking about Nietzsche?" I ask. Something flutters in my stomach.

"Yes. Why?"

"I sat beside two kids talking about Nietzsche outside the bookstore this afternoon."

Nobu's eyes widen. "You think they were the same people? That we were there within minutes of each other, but missed meeting?"

"I think it's possible. Let's never lose each other again, okay?"

"Let's never lose each other again," he says. "I think we need a system."

"That's such a Nobu thing to say."

He laughs. "Nonetheless," he says, "Whenever we get separated, let's always wait for each other at Colette and Company. In the courtyard outside the store."

"Perfect," I say. He lets go of my hands, and as we move apart, a few small, golden sparks shoot straight up and disappear into the ceiling. We run back upstairs, slip through the large wooden door that leads to the courtyard, and sit on a bench facing the glass pyramid. "So, what have you done for the last couple of days?" I say.

"Mostly, I looked for you. I thought of all the places you really like and went there hoping to find you."

"Me too," I say.

"And I helped some people along the way. You know, the usual. A couple of lost kids. Someone fighting with their partner. I might have even talked to a dog."

"What?" I ask. He grins wildly.

"There was this dog, a Golden Retriever, I think, in the park near Colette and Company. It looked really sad, so I petted its head and said something like, 'It will be okay, buddy.' And it said, 'Do you really think so?' And I said, 'Yup. I'm sure of it.' And it thanked me and walked away."

"That's crazy," I say.

"What about you? Are you okay?" He turns towards me.

"Actually, I helped someone too." I tell him all about Anaïs and the baby she's expecting, how her parents were ashamed of her, and how she was living on the streets.

"People can be terrible to each other," says Nobu.

"But also, generous and compassionate. I encouraged her to call her brother and he was happy to take her in. There was a cash box for Paris's most vulnerable, so I gave her enough money for the train." I'm worried this fact will reopen the rift between us, but I'm not ashamed of anything I did to help Anaïs. I'm too tired not to be honest with Nobu.

"Hey! You helped someone. On your own. And it was a big one." He offers his hand for a handshake, and I squeeze it and remember how it felt to help her, what it was like to be certain that these were the right steps to take. My eyes fill with tears.

"Claire, this is such a big, good thing. Why are you crying?" says Nobu.

"I was remembering. She asked me why I helped her, why I took a risk for her. I said I wanted to help."

"Maybe you needed to do it on your own," says Nobu.

"Yeah. She might not have trusted the two of us. Some bad stuff happened to her while she was living on her own."

"No. I mean, maybe I've been stopping you from helping the humans. Maybe I've been standing in your way without realizing it." He looks down at his hands.

"Dude," I say. "That's totally not true. Don't blame yourself! I just wasn't ready because I was still heartbroken about everything that's happened. About not knowing what happened to me during my life. About being dumped here."

"Dumped here with me, you mean?" Nobu looks as though I've slapped him.

"No. That is definitely not what I mean. It's not like you to be so hard on yourself. You were helpful from the first moment we arrived, but I wasn't. I don't know why. That might be locked in my past, but I wasn't able to take what seemed to you like simple actions. Something about her triggered my helping instinct." His eyes brighten. He looks like he wants to believe me. I say, "Nobu, you are the best thing that's happened to me, you know, after everything."

As the words leave my mouth, I imagine that the individual letters fly up into the night sky and Nobu keeps reading them as they scroll away from us, disappearing, at some point, into nothingness. We sit quietly without looking at each other.

"That's an exceedingly kind thing to say." Nobu speaks quietly.

"It wasn't meant to be kind, in particular. Only true."

"Thank you, Claire," he says. I cover his hand with mine.

"Did you actually use the typewriter to contact Coach?" I say.

"Nope. I was about to start typing when you came into the office."

"Listen, I want to be inside tonight," I say. "Can we go to Colette and Company? We can read and maybe I'll write in the manual." I pat my bag as I do many times a day to make sure the journal is still there.

Nobu turns towards me. "Hey, you got a different coat."

"I gave the leather jacket to Anaïs. This one is from the church lost and found."

"It looks good on you. Not quite as angry."

I laugh. "You mean edgy," I say.

"Sure. Let's go with edgy." He grins as he unzips the top of his leather jacket and pulls something out of the inside pocket. It's the small sketchbook I gave him.

"You kept it," I say.

"Of course. I've been using it." He opens the sketchbook and shows me a drawing he's done across two pages. It's the church where I met Anaïs. Saint-Germain-des-Prés.

"When did you draw this?" I ask.

"This afternoon. While I was looking for you."

"Why did you draw this church?"

"I don't know. I felt close to you, which is weird because we've never been there before."

"Nobu! This is the church where I went after we fought at the Louvre. I chose it because we'd never been there. This is where I met Anaïs. Where we spent the night."

"That's a crazy coincidence." Nobu stands and extends his hands, and I allow him to pull me up. He can't help helping others. It's like it's in his DNA, or the ghost of his DNA. We walk towards the Seine.

"I don't know exactly how long it's going to take you to get this particular memo, Nobu. It is not a coincidence."

CHAPTER 27
IN WHICH WE SPEND THE DAY AT NOTRE DAME

There is someone staying in the apartment at the bookstore. There almost always is. But by the time we get there, we're both too tired from looking for each other all day to find another spot to shelter. This new person looks like she's in her early twenties, and she's placing books on the shelves when we arrive. Most of the people who work and stay here are more serious about partying with their friends after the store closes than they are about performing bookstore-related duties. Clearly, she's more of a Nobu kind of person. She's working in the front room of the shop, so Nobu and I sit on the floor of the children's book section. I'm so tired that I slide down to the floor like a raggedy doll.

"Do you suppose we'll ever just stay outside all night?" I ask.

"I'm ready. You?" Nobu says.

"Ah. I see. I'm the one holding us up," I say, as I pull off my bag and set it on the floor.

"Hey. I don't think of it as being held up. This book I was reading a few days ago asked the question, 'What if there is no there, there?' You know? Like humans are always pushing themselves to achieve or produce at the highest level because they believe, or somebody has convinced them, that meeting that goal will signify they are finally good enough. Since you and I have completed our round-trip journey on Earth, I feel confident in saying there isn't a magical achievement level we need to attain. It doesn't exist. As such, you, Claire, couldn't possibly be holding us up."

I lie down on my side and rest my head on my bag. "I want to follow your thinking, but I'm so wiped tonight that I can't."

"I'm just saying there's no race or competition. We don't ever need to sleep outside. I'm happy to sleep inside every day if that makes you happy." I smile at him. At least I try to smile, but I'm asleep before the message gets from my brain to the edges of my mouth.

In the morning, I wake to the sound of the young woman whistling. Nobu is sitting cross legged exactly where he was last night, and he is reading a book of poetry by Naomi Shihab Nye. A short rope of filaments connects us, the individual threads glittering as they move, and it seems as though the filaments are alive and fuelled by the two of us. The woman walks straight through Nobu's lap on her way to unlock the door. That's our cue to leave. Nobu carefully shelves the small book he's been reading back where he found it, I pull my bag on across my body, and we slip out the door as the first customers arrive.

As we cross the bridge to Notre Dame, Nobu asks, "You okay?"

"I will be," I say. I mostly believe this is true. "I'm starting to understand more about the weird things that are happening. The sparks seem to mean that I like or am attracted to something.”

“Like books and the Mona Lisa and the snow angels?” Nobu says. I nod. Neither of us mentions him.

“And the filaments represent a connection to you. Probably because we’re Helping partners.”

“That makes sense,” he says.

“But it’s weird you can’t see them.” Nobu nods his head vigorously. “Then, there’s a third thing. I saw it yesterday for the first time after Anaïs left for the train station. You know how we can’t see our reflection in mirrors or windows? I saw a golden heart beating in a window, and I realized the heart was coming from me.”

Nobu stops walking. “That’s a boatload of extraordinary phenomena.”

“Yup. Coach said I was highly sensitive or something.”

“Does it freak you out?”

“It doesn’t. I think they’re clues from the universe, about my identity.”

Nobu exhales heavily and looks at the ground.

“What?” I ask.

“I just don’t want you to get hurt if they’re not connected to your human life. It seems like whoever runs this place is pretty committed to us not learning about our former lives.”

“You’re right, but I don’t care,” I say. Nobu shrugs. “Hey. I appreciate that you don’t want me to get hurt. Listen, the good news is that I finally know that I’m constitutionally able to help the humans, so that’s something, right?”

“It is. I hope you feel proud of yourself, Claire.” Nobu’s voice is quiet, and his tone is sincere.

“I do ... but I’m going to keep looking for information about my past life, Nobu.”

"I know," he says. "I would never ask you to stop."

Notre Dame is closed to the public because it's too dangerous for humans to be close to the reconstruction work, but of course, we're not the public, or human. I assume we're going to wander the grounds where the chances of finding someone in need are high, but Nobu walks through the high construction fence and through the main entrance of the church. I follow him. He then looks around the construction site and his gaze rests on a beam far above our heads. I shake my head. "No way."

"It's okay. I'm going up on my own," he says.

"Be my guest," I say. I need my feet on the ground today. He climbs the metal scaffolding, fast and graceful, as if it's a task he's trained for all his life, and when he reaches the top, he sits with his back against the stone and his legs stretched out on the beam in front of him. I'm surprised again when he pulls his sketchbook and pencil out of his pocket and begins to draw.

I move through the thick stone wall of the church and emerge into the garden. Benches are arranged in the shade of the trees, and I watch two construction workers share a meal of bread, cheese, and salami. I choose a bench in the far corner of the garden, then realize that I've come outside without letting Nobu know. I look up and see Nobu lodged there on that beam in a church that is half open and half closed, like a doll's house. He draws intently and I consider calling out to him, but I stop myself and simply say his name.

"Nobu." He looks up and then looks around. "I'm outside. On a bench against the far wall of the garden." He sees me and waves for a moment, then goes back to his drawing.

Now this is a fascinating development. I don't know why

I'm surprised that sound works differently for us, but I am. We never asked Coach, and he didn't mention it. I wonder what happens if I just think his name. Nobu. He looks up and waves. I shake my head, and he returns to drawing in his sketchbook.

Why are we still discovering things this big, nine months after arriving?

I grab my journal and root around in the bottom of the bag for a pen. Nobu would have a system for keeping his pen in a place where it would be easy to retrieve. I write:

A LIST OF REASONS WHY THERE SHOULD BE A BETTER MANUAL FOR THIS

Shouldn't there be
a better manual for this?
Something more than
a list of ~~rules~~ guidelines
from Coach?

For just how long
will these surprises
continue?

Will we keep
discovering things
about ourselves,
the essence of us,
the way we are
and why we are,
for the rest of our lives?

For our Existence?
(Or whatever it's called
for Helpers.)

Oh Goddess!
Is this how humans feel?
Shit.

Claire, stop swearing. We're in a church. What? His mouth isn't moving at all.

Are you talking to me? I think these words at him rather than speaking them.

Yes. Clearly.

Without speaking out loud? I say inside my mind. He smiles. *When did you discover this?* I ask.

Just now, I think. That's unexpected, right? he says.

"Very," I say, out loud. He goes back to his drawing, so I return to my list, which is starting to feel more like a poem:

Yesterday I helped someone
on my own
for the first time.
I lost Nobu and I found him.
We spent the whole day moving
through the same locations,
sat beside the same teenagers,
like we were being pulled
towards each other
by some invisible force.

And now we've discovered
we can communicate

without speaking.
My mind,
or whatever allows me
to develop
and organize thoughts,
is going to explode
from the accumulation
of pressure
and pure crazy.

Yes.
This must be how humans feel.
Surprised,
delighted,
then crushed.
Perpetually overwhelmed
by their circumstances.
Bad luck or fate or destiny
or whatever they call it.

I look up at Nobu, whose head is bent towards his sketch-book, but I can't hear specific thoughts, just a humming sound. I can, however, feel the determination with which he's drawing. Maybe when one of us is concentrating very hard on something, we can't hear each other's thoughts. I'm reminded of a line of poetry by Mary Oliver, and keep writing:

What is the soft animal of my body?
Do I have one?
I'm not supposed to.
No Helper has ever felt romantic feelings.

Also, I don't like people very much.
Human and otherwise.
They're sometimes shallow
and kind of stupid.
Let's not forget annoying.
Except Nobu.
I never get tired of him.

Oh! I slam my journal closed and look up at Nobu, but he's lost in his sketchbook. I sigh with relief.

CHAPTER 28

IN WHICH BOYS ON BOATS NEED ASSISTANCE

Most of the snow has melted, and I'm starting to see small green signs of life pushing their way through the ground. I feel deep fondness for the spring, but I've noticed that regardless of the weather here on Earth, some humans are always unhappy. There isn't one season, one temperature, one kind of precipitation, or lack thereof, that suits everyone and although I'm sad for the complainers, I suspect I have this in me as well. A certain leaning towards grumpiness. I don't want that to be true, but whatever.

Then I remember the night that Nobu and I made snow angels in the small park. The memory contains no cynicism, whatsoever. Perhaps humans are not just one thing.

Today, I've suggested we take a boat trip down the Seine. Nobu thinks this is a brilliant way to expand our helping routine, but for me, the river is a new vantage point on the world I used to be alive in, an opportunity for me to get my Harriet-the-Spy on.

At the stop closest to the Eiffel Tower, as we wait for the boat to dock, we hear a French woman call this trip, "un mini-cruise," which makes me smile. We slip on board as the passengers on the boat disembark, and pass through the glassed-in cabin to the front of the boat, which is open to the elements and has the best view. From here, we'll be visible to anyone needing our help.

At the bow of the boat, I place my hand on the prow, as I look out over the river and am surprised by the appearance of the three small sparks that rise and move around each other in a familiar pattern. "Hello, dear sparks," I whisper, as they shimmer and then evanesce. Under my hand, I discover a brass plaque with the name of this vessel. Le Lys. The Lily.

"Hey! Are you seeing a thing, right now?" says Nobu who is now standing over my shoulder. Still buzzing with delight, I nod and point to the plaque.

All the passengers have boarded, and two small boys run onto the deck. They have dark brown hair and look so much alike that I wonder if they're twins, but one is a little bigger than his brother. They are perhaps seven and five. The little brother can't quite see over the side of the boat, so his sibling boosts him up by grasping him around the calves, and lifting. The smaller boy teeters dangerously close to the edge of the boat, and before I can speak or make a move, Nobu appears beside the boys, grabs the little one around his chest, and places him carefully on the deck of the boat. The boy looks up at Nobu and says, "Thanks, Mister. I almost oopsed right into the water." The boys' parents rush out onto the deck, and the mother picks up the smaller boy and asks who he was speaking to. "The man who caught me," he says, but when the parents look around, they see no one. They take the boys inside the heated cabin, and sit on the aisle end of the row, so their children can't escape.

We lean against the edge and watch the left and right

banks of the city go by. It's cool to see the places we frequent from the vantage point of this ancient river. Nobu pulls the sketchbook out of his jacket and makes lightning-fast sketches, with just a few quick strokes of his pencil. As we pass by Notre Dame on the left and Colette and Company on the right, a teenager in a navy coat comes out to the front deck and sits on one of the benches. He's not much younger than Nobu and me, and he's been sitting inside with an older man, whom I guess is his father. The boy takes in the view for a few moments, then turns towards us and says, "Hey!"

Nobu looks up for a moment and says, not unkindly, "You go ahead, Claire."

I move to the boy's bench. His name is David, but he's from Mexico City, so he pronounces it Da-veed. I tell him how cool that sounds and introduce myself. We might be speaking in Spanish. The language thing is so automatic that sometimes it's hard to keep track. David, who is in the mood to share, says his father suggested they travel to Paris for David's spring vacation from school. His parents are divorced, his mother has a new boyfriend and David suspects they're going to get married, because his mother seems much happier now. I nod, knowingly. He doesn't sound that upset about the divorce, though, so I wonder if there's even a problem.

"Is he your boyfriend?" David nods in Nobu's direction.

"Nobu? No. He's my best friend. Why?"

"I thought if he was your boyfriend, you know, if you had some experience with boyfriends, maybe you could give me some advice."

"Try me," I say.

David exhales and leans forward, resting his elbows on

his knees. "Nah. It's too complicated. Sorry to bother you." He goes to stand up and I place my hand on his shoulder.

"Really. You're not bothering me," I say. He settles back on the bench.

"So, I like this person. Like I really, really like them." He stops and looks up for a moment. "Okay, maybe I love them, but it's never going to work out, because they're in love with someone else."

"I'm sorry," I say. "That sucks." There's something so familiar about what he's saying. I close my eyes and hear a woman's voice saying my name. I think this is a memory. She sounds so sad, and I wonder if I was in love with her or if she was in love with me. David's voice jolts me back to this moment.

"Yeah. It really does. Also, this person is a guy so there's that."

"Why is that a problem?" I ask. I see all kinds of romantic partnerships in Paris, and the queer couples seem just as happy, and as unhappy, as the straight ones.

"People in my family." He flips up the hood of his coat. I look towards his father. "Not my dad. He's cool. So's my mother. But my grandparents ... you know, not so much. They say that no one can know what I am." I pat his arm and he goes quiet for a moment. "Like I know they love me and everything, but the way I am just doesn't line up with what they were expecting from their grandson." He pauses, waiting for me to respond.

"Do you think perhaps your grandparents need a bit more time?" I ask.

"Maybe," David says, flipping his hood back down. "That's what my mom and dad say. Just give them some time to get used to it."

"And the guy you like, does he know?"

"Yup. Told him just before the vacation. Last day of school. I wasn't planning on it or anything, but we were working out at the gym and all the other guys left, one by one, and it was finally just the two of us. I don't know what happened, but I kind of lost it and I went to kiss him, but he stopped me."

"Ouch! Sorry," I say.

David nods. "He was like 'I really want to kiss you, but I'm seeing this other guy right now, and that wouldn't be fair to either of you.' And I was like 'Yeah. Okay. I get it.'"

"Heartbreaking," I say.

"Definitely heartbreaking," he says. "I don't know what to do now. Like should I text him and pursue it or should I give him some space?"

I consider his question. "He understands that you're interested," I say, "so it seems like the next move is his, no?" David gets very quiet and looks out at the river and the city beyond it.

"I know you're right, but I just don't want you to be right." He lifts his head and looks directly into my eyes. "No offence."

"None taken. We don't always get what we want," I say.

David laughs. "But we get what we need. Stones. Good reference. What about your friend? Does he have any advice?" Nobu looks up from his sketchbook.

"Sure. Become the partner you want. But to yourself." Nobu smiles and goes back to drawing.

"Deep," says David.

"Yup," I say. "He's good like that. Hey, David, I'm sorry about what you're going through, but I have a hunch you'll be okay." The boat is pulling into a pier, and David's dad knocks on the glass. David gives his dad a thumbs up and thanks me for listening. As they disembark, I watch David's hands swoop and fly around as he talks, and I imagine he's telling his father about our conversation.

"You did really well," says Nobu. We're both leaning against the side of the boat, looking out at the Seine.

"Yeah?" I ask.

"Yeah. Humans don't always get what they want. He will be okay."

"That was perfect, what you said about being a good partner to yourself." Nobu smiles in my direction, but he seems lost in thought. I think again, of that Mary Oliver line about allowing the soft animal of your body to love what it loves, and I know, beyond all certainty, that I love Nobu. That I'm in love with Nobu, even though that's supposed to be impossible. There's nothing else that explains how I feel.

CHAPTER 29

IN WHICH CHARLES LOSES HIS WALLET

Outside the Musée D'Orsay, steps lead down to street level and musicians sometimes use this space as an amphitheatre to perform for tourists. There's a band I've seen a couple of times: three or sometimes four old men, who seem like they've been playing these old jazz standards together for a long time. Today, a woman joins them who might be eighty or even ninety. A tiny person, her white hair is cut in a bob, and she wears a long purple scarf around her neck. She stands about ten feet away from the band and when she is ready, she dances. I can't help but think she's not performing, but rather dancing with a partner who is no longer there. She's not even remotely shy about dancing in front of this crowd, but neither does she seem interested in the people watching her. Perhaps this is just something she does from time to time that makes her feel more alive. As she dances, she closes her eyes, and I feel her returning to the past, to the partner she loved, who was her equal.

The sky is bright blue and cloudless. Nobu and I sit on the amphitheatre stairs with ten or twelve humans, listen to the vintage jazz, and watch the old woman dance her sweet nostalgic waltz.

A man stands beside us. When he finally decides to sit down, he removes a white handkerchief from his pocket and lays it down on the cement before he sits carefully on top of it. I'm curious and turn to get a better look at him. He is elderly and wears a long cream-coloured coat with the collar popped up. An emerald green scarf is tied around his neck and tucked inside his coat. He's also wearing black leather gloves. He's French, I'm sure of it. He looks right through us, as if we are not there, which of course, is true for him. I turn my attention back to the band and the woman dancing below us.

A few minutes later, the man inhales abruptly. He's rummaging in the inside pocket of his coat. "My wallet," he says. "My wallet's been stolen."

Nobu leans towards the man, who sees us, surprised by our sudden appearance.

"When did you two get here? I didn't see you sit down."

"Sir," says Nobu, "we've been here for thirty minutes and were sitting here before you arrived. Is there something we can do to be of service to you?"

I imagine a scenario in which the man yells that these two young people have stolen his wallet, but of course, nobody else will be able to see us. I'm certain that's where we're headed when the man responds, "Yes. I would quite like some help. Thank you." The three of us stand and the man retrieves his handkerchief, which he folds and places in his front jacket pocket. We walk together towards the museum.

"When was the last time you saw your wallet?" Nobu asks.

"About three hours ago, when I bought my ticket to enter the museum. You hear about thieves and pickpockets around the museums, but I've lived here all my life. I thought I knew all the tricks and scams."

"Do you think you might have left the wallet at the cash register when you bought your ticket?" asks Nobu.

"Now that's an idea," the man says. He introduces himself as Charles. We tell him our names, and he says, "It's a pleasure to meet such fine, upstanding young people." I suppress a laugh. "Now, let's go inside and check." Nobu and I exchange a glance and decide to hang back, so Charles won't know we're invisible to the museum staff.

It's cool and quiet inside the museum. Charles approaches the woman from whom he bought a ticket, and asks if he's left his wallet. The woman shakes her head and points him towards the lost and found, which is attached to the coat check. We follow Charles to the second counter, but the person there reports that no wallets have been turned in.

Nobu asks Charles if he would like to retrace his steps inside the museum.

"That's a splendid idea," says Charles.

Charles is a retired art historian, so we end up getting a deluxe tour of the museum. As we retrace his steps, he tells us about his favourite paintings, the artists who made them, and the socio-political and economic times in which they lived. He smiles as he creates a tapestry for us, expertly weaving the threads of each of these works into a larger narrative about European art.

At one point, Nobu smiles at me, and I understand that for both of us, this is a gift. In addition to the impromptu art history class, I like Charles enormously. He is the very definition of a gentleman. Nobu proves an eager student and

Charles seems delighted at Nobu's questions and happy to share his knowledge. He is a professional, yet humble, guide.

We're leaving a section when Charles spots the entrance to the small cafeteria. "I came in here earlier," he says. "I got coffee and a croissant. Perhaps I left my wallet on the counter when I paid. Excuse me, I will go and inquire." We watch as Charles talks with the employee, but she shakes her head.

Charles returns to us. "I am afraid we're out of options, my friends. After I had my snack, I exited the building and sat down beside the two of you. I am simply out of ideas. I don't remember anyone bumping into me so, if I was pickpocketed, I was completely oblivious to it. You've been very kind to help an old man."

"Charles, are you sure you didn't put your wallet in another pocket?" I ask.

He pats the front pockets of his coat, then his hands go to the side pockets, then his trousers. "Oh," he says. "Oh dear." Out of his right-hand trouser pocket, he pulls a brown leather wallet and seems very surprised to see it.

Suddenly, his eyes well up with tears. "I don't know how that happened. I'm embarrassed to have wasted your time, when my wallet was right here all along." He opens the wallet as if he's going to offer us money, which reminds me of the family at Sacré-Coeur and the mess that came afterwards, but he doesn't. He removes a photograph of a woman and passes it to me.

"This is my wife, Celeste. She died six months ago. Sometimes I forget that she's gone and when I remember, it feels like I am losing her all over again."

"She looks very kind and wise," I say, passing the photo to Nobu.

"She was, indeed. She would have liked you very much, Claire. I can tell. Honestly, this photograph is the only thing I would have been sad to lose." Nobu passes the photo back to Charles, who slips it back inside his wallet. He then stores the wallet carefully in his inside coat pocket. "Thank you both for the time and care you've given me today. You've been exceptionally kind." Nobu bows and I wave as Charles walks away and I want to run after him, tell him where we stay at night, do something to stay connected to him, but I know there's no point. He won't be able to see us. That was all we are allowed to be to each other. Nobu slips his fingers between mine and squeezes.

Back outside, the old woman is still waltzing with her invisible partner. Her eyes are closed, and she smiles ever so slightly.

CHAPTER 30

IN WHICH A MAN IN A VELVET SUIT SEEKS THE PERFECT GRANDDAUGHTER GIFT

n the weeks since I discovered that I'm in love with Nobu, we've settled into a new routine. If you were to ask him, he'd say we established a routine for better helping. I would say, and not because I want to be difficult or anything, but simply because this is the way I see it, that we created a routine for living. No job, including being a Helper, is going to prevent me from searching for clues about my life on Earth, and making notes about the sparks and filaments, mind-reading, and other strange phenomena that show up on the regular.

In a surprising move, Nobu has begun sneaking into art classes around the city. I've worked hard not to suggest that this might be, just the tiniest bit, like stealing, but he's such a good being that I stay quiet. I find myself not needing the revenge. It also means I'm on my own more often and I spend most of this time exploring the city and putting objects, and the occasional small, domesticated animal, to the spark test.

If there's a better city on Earth in which to walk, I can't imagine it. At first, I felt anxious about getting lost. Where

Nobu always seems to know exactly where he is and how to get where he's going, I don't have a good sense of direction, but I compensate with a variety of maps I've found on buses and trains, likely discarded by tourists. I tuck this selection of maps inside my journal and consult them constantly, making little notes of places we have visited, so they are filled with annotations, small diagrams, quotes, and other tidbits from my travels. As time goes on, however, I relax more and rely less on my maps. I wander the narrow streets in the Latin Quarter and the Marais, and I choose to be okay with getting lost, knowing I have a map in my bag. Weirdly, having the maps helps me need them less, and it feels good to travel the city with greater confidence. Sometimes, in the evening, I'll suggest a walk in a new neighbourhood, and Nobu always tells me how impressed he is with my improved navigational skills.

This afternoon he is at an art class, and I head to the Eiffel Tower. Although some Parisians speak disdainfully about this landmark, it's one of the sights the tourists are most excited about visiting and taking creative selfies with. Something that makes so many people happy must be good, especially at night when it lights up the seventh arrondissement like a fairy tale.

I hop on one of the Bateaux Mouches at the stop near Notre Dame, and have the boat almost all to myself. As always, I stand on the bow and today, I pull my hood back and let the wind blow my hair out horizontally. The sensation of my hair flying all around me is so sublime that a giggle bubbles up inside me, followed by a full-blown laugh. Rather than suppressing the laughter, I let it out. I find that I am happy to be alive. Or whatever. A small girl on a boat travelling in the opposite direction catches me laughing and waves.

How can she see me given that she doesn't look one bit in need of help? She might be another Helper, but she's so young that this thought makes me sad. I wave back at her. At the Eiffel Tower, I let an older couple and a family leave the boat first, which must be a value left over from my time as a human. Perhaps waiting is a sign of respect, even if they can't see me to receive it.

Under the Tower, I pass the long lines of people waiting for the elevator. The wait for the stairs is always shorter; sometimes there's no line at all. I'm headed for the Champ de Mars, which means Field of Mars. Such a wonderful name for this large public park, where Parisians and visitors seem equally thrilled to hang out, to read, or enjoy a picnic. The trickiest aspect of a visit to this great green space is that you never know if you will be allowed on the lawn or not. Perhaps, when I finally figure out this system, I will feel like a real Parisian. Of course, the joke is that there probably isn't a system at all.

What there is, though, is a small squad of terrifying city employees, who seem to derive great pleasure from driving people off the lawn. They are led by a woman, as wide as she is tall. Her hair is pulled back into a bun that is only slightly less severe than her manner. My ability to sit on the lawn at the Champ de Mars, whenever I want, may be the biggest perk of my stylish, post-life invisibility cloak.

Although it's practically summer, it's chilly today and there aren't many people on the Champ de Mars. There's also no sign of Madame Getoff, as I've affectionately nick-named her, or the rest of her crew. Several people, including a couple drinking champagne out of pink plastic cups, have parked themselves on benches, while a few residents of the seventh arrondissement walk their dogs. I choose a bench and pull out my journal.

A LIST OF DELIGHTFUL BEINGS:

1. Two elderly women walked slowly on a side street. Each of them carried a designer bag and a baguette.
2. A concierge swept the sidewalk in front of her apartment building. She wore a burgundy sweater and her floral skirt fluttered in the wind.
3. A ginger coloured cat saw me from a window and identified me as its soul mate.
4. The small girl who waved to me on the bateau.
5. A young man in a red knitted beanie unloaded green bicycles from a van parked on the side of the street.
6. The couple with the pink cups. Perhaps they just got engaged.
7. The woman in the white coat and her poodle, who looked so much alike, it seemed impossible that they are different species.

Nobu says I'm pretty fascinated by the humans for a person who claims not to like them very much, and I suppose he's right. Mostly, I like them from a distance.

A middle-aged woman with perfectly bobbed hair sits on my bench. She is dressed in a caramel-coloured trench coat, leather boots and a fuchsia-coloured silk scarf that reminds me so much of my own, that I reach up and touch the soft fabric of the scarf wrapped around my neck. At first, she sits at the other end of the bench, but she fidgets as though she can't get comfortable so, she gets up and sits in me. Her well-dressed body squishes right through mine, swoosh, until her bottom lands on the green wood of the bench. I slide down to the other end of the bench, and as I scoot, I smell her scent. Jasmine. There's something so comforting and familiar about this scent. It creates a sense of peace in me, which is not exactly my go-to emotion. She pulls a book out of her bag. Of course, she's a reader. The book is about the Impressionist painters. She reads, and I write:

8. A woman with shiny black hair. She smells like jasmine and good things.

Grey clouds hover over the park, making the afternoon colder and darker. When the woman places a bookmark in her page, I catch a glimpse of something gold. Is it a bracelet? I lean in to take a closer look. No. It can't be! There's a slim filament running between us, more of a gossamer than the rope that connects me to Nobu. It is delicate and golden.

"I'm here," I say out loud. "It's me. Claire." My heart races with the possibility that this woman knows me. She furrows her brow for a moment, but she can't hear me. The sun comes out, the gossamer disintegrates, and the woman tucks her book inside her leather bag, stands up and heads for the end of the park.

I follow her. Like helping Anaïs, this is a decision. I need to know who she is and how we're connected. At the taxi stand, she waits patiently in line behind a man and his small daughter, both in matching red plaid scarves. I remind myself to add them to my list later. When the woman's taxi pulls up, I get in beside her as she buckles her seat belt.

Is this okay? WWNS? (What Would Nobu Say?)

She tells the driver the name of her hotel. Le Pavillon de la Reine at 28 Place des Vosges. She's either French, or she's a foreigner with perfect pronunciation, because the driver doesn't wince or correct her. As we drive through the Marais, I recognize the address as the square that Nobu and I stumbled upon a few months ago. When the driver pulls up in front of the hotel, the woman passes him thirty euros and tells him to keep the change, which leaves him with a six-euro tip. He almost smiles at her.

At the front desk, she chats cordially with the clerk, who passes her the key for room twenty-four. I follow her to the elevator, but a man dressed in a forest green velvet suit steps off and places his hand on my arm which prevents me from entering. The doors close behind the woman.

"Excuse me, young lady," he says. I just look at him, this annoying person who has interrupted my pursuit of the woman who smells of jasmine. "My name is Monsieur De La Tour, and I have a granddaughter who is about your age. She has a birthday coming up and I've had such a difficult time purchasing her a suitable gift. What do you suggest?" I look down at his hand on my arm, which he drops to his side.

I suggest that you don't call us young ladies. I suggest that you hire a personal shopper. I suggest that you examine why you feel entitled to hijack my day like this. "What does she like?" I ask.

"Well, that's just it. I haven't got a clue. We're all so busy and no one has any time to spend together, anymore." My heart softens towards this man in his silly green suit, which is quickly followed by the recognition that only artists and very wealthy humans dress however they'd like. I'm guessing this man falls into the latter category.

"What about spending a day together?" I suggest.

"Whatever do you mean?"

"Buy a beautiful card and write that the bearer of this card is entitled to one full day with her grandfather. The day's activities, their locations, and the menus for all meals should be chosen by her. I promise that by the end of the day, you'll know each other better." I expect him to protest, to say that he couldn't possibly get away from work for an entire day, but he doesn't say any of those things. He is blinking back tears. Oh dear.

"Yes. I think that is a marvellous idea. What did you say your name was?"

"You didn't ask for it, but I'm Claire."

"My apologies. Thank you, Claire. I appreciate this excellent idea." He smiles before he turns and approaches the front desk, demanding the location of a stationery store, oblivious to the fact that the concierge is in the midst of serving someone else.

I'm aware that I'm running short on time, as Nobu will return from his art class soon, but I can't leave the hotel without the woman's name. I'm hopeful that since I already know her room number, it will be easier to learn her identity. As soon as the clerk steps into the back room, I slip behind the counter. There's a computer which is useless to me, and a guest book where guests have written their names, but not their room numbers, so that's a dead-end.

Okay, what else can I try? As I stand behind the desk, the clerk walks through me several times as he performs his tasks, but I don't even care. I need a name. I watch the clerk drop several folded pieces of paper in a set of cubby holes painted in high gloss black. Each cubby has a number painted below it and that's when I understand that they're mailboxes. I'm delighted to see that there's a paper in the mailbox for room twenty-four, but I'll need to be careful about how I acquire it.

There's a small staff room behind the mailboxes and although I have never tried this before, I think I can reach through the wall and the back of the mailboxes to retrieve the paper meant for the woman in room twenty-four. Fortunately, the staff room is empty, but because there's no way to be sure exactly where my mailbox is, I need to just reach through and grab something to help me understand the placement of the boxes on the other side of the wall. The first envelope is for room sixteen. I set it on a table beside the coffee maker. My next attempt results in the mail for room thirty-two. I add it to the envelope on the table. I close my eyes and whisper, "Come on, room twenty-four," as if I'm in a casino, but what I'm really doing is asking the universe for some assistance. Gently, I reach my hand through the wall and when I pull it back, I see that the universe was happy to help. It's a copy of the registration for the woman staying in room twenty-four. Her name is Dr. Kano Takahashi, and she is booked to stay for two more nights. I place her booking on the top of the small stack of papers on the table and imagine the clerk frowning and shaking his head when he finds these papers out of place. Then I chuckle at the idea that some of the strange occurrences that humans grumble about—stacks of mail left in the wrong spot and missing socks and misplaced keys—may be the work of Helpers, trying to assist humans. But Kano Takahashi hasn't asked for my help. In this case, it's the other way around.

Relieved that no one saw me behind the desk or in the staff room, I saunter back into the foyer and through the front doors of the hotel. Although part of me wants to go directly to her room, Nobu will be concerned about my absence.

Kano Takahashi. She seems like a Kano.

I have two days to understand why a gossamer grows between us.

CHAPTER 31

IN WHICH EMILY FROM CANADA NEEDS HELP WITH WRITING AND DATING

"Hey. How was your afternoon?" Nobu asks. Colette and Company is now closed for the day and Nobu sits cross-legged in front of the poetry, like a cat returning to its favourite sun-filled window.

"We alone?" I sit on the floor beside him.

He nods and closes his sketchbook. "Yup. The tidy one ..."

"Emily," I say. "Her name is Emily and she's Canadian. You know this."

"Right. Emily. I'm astonished by her commitment to keeping this place clean. Anyway, she's gone out for dinner with friends, so it's just the two of us for the time being."

"Time being. That's an odd phrase, isn't it? I wonder ..." Nobu leans closer to me. "Ah, right. Stay on topic. My afternoon was good. I took the Bateaux Mouche, got off at the Eiffel Tower and spent the afternoon at the Champs de Mars. Wrote some stuff in my journal. You know, people I observed during the day. I saw this small girl. Like four or five. She was on a boat on the Seine. She looked right at me and waved. She didn't seem to need any help, so maybe she was a Helper. It would probably be good if there were a place that Helpers could get together. You know, hang out. Anyway, if my hunch was correct, she died so much younger than us. It kind of shook me up." Nobu nods but doesn't comment. He's good at just letting me be me. "Oh, and I helped a man in a green velvet suit come up with an idea for his granddaughter's birthday gift. He called me 'young lady'."

"Ooooh, I bet you loved that," he says, his eyes sparkling.

"I did not."

"Sounds like a good day," he says, and I smile. I want to tell him about Kano Takahashi, about the gossamer filament, but I don't. I choose not to.

"Hey, what about your art class? Anyone get naked?" I ask.

Nobu laughs and falls back against the bookshelf, knocking four books off the shelf. He sits up, reshelves the books, and opens his sketchbook. "No one took their clothes off, Claire. That's figure drawing. This was a still life class, where you draw or paint inanimate objects. You know, everyday commonplace things. This is from today." He passes me his sketchbook, which is open to a drawing of two pears sitting on a wooden bench, and although they're approximately the same size, colour, and shape, each has their own slight variations. I wonder if this is what a personality is. One is a bit greener towards the bottom. The pear on the right is slightly larger and bumpier. I feel like I could reach into his sketchbook, grab a piece of fruit, and take a bite.

"You're really good at this," I say. Nobu winces as if someone slapped him. "What?" I ask. "Can't you see how talented you are?"

"When I look at my sketches, all I see is what's wrong with them, what I need to improve," he says.

"Maybe you should take your own advice," I say. Nobu stares at me blankly. "Remember what you said to David, on the boat? You know, the thing about learning to be the partner you need, but to yourself." I pass the sketchbook back to him.

He closes the book. "Hm. I'll give that some consideration," he says.

I get up, ruffle his hair with my hand, and go to the back room, where I pull out my journal. I flip back to my entry from earlier today and add:

9. A man and his small daughter, both in matching red plaid scarves.

10. The man in the green velvet suit who wanted to choose the perfect gift for his granddaughter.

I choose not to write about him calling me 'young lady.' He was a pretty old dude, and he was probably doing his best and this thought chokes me up. After a few moments my eyes return to number eight:

8. *A woman with shiny black hair. She smells like jasmine and good things.*

I add 'Kano Takahashi,' in parentheses and picture the thin golden thread that joined us on the bench. But how? Our minds and all our memories have been wiped clean. A hard reset. It's not possible for me to recognize someone from my life before. A hot, angry flash tears through the centre of my body. Nobody asked my permission for any of this. They didn't ask me if I wanted this existence, or this job with this particular Helping partner, with whom I seem to be in love, even though that's supposed to be impossible. Who do I complain to? To whom would I address my letter of resignation, if I decided to quit? Coach? The only evidence that Coach ever existed is the guidelines written at the front of my journal. Does anyone even know we're here? Does anyone remember us at all? I inhale deeply and exhale. Getting angry doesn't help, Claire. This thought is a bit depressing, since I've been so reliant on that particular emotion.

Nobu calls me and I close my journal and tuck it inside my bag. Then I hear a second voice.

"How did you get in here?" It's Emily, and she can see Nobu, as plainly as we can see her. Ack! This was bound to happen, that one of these writers would need help when we were in the store. We've been too careless. Nobu scrambles up from a sitting position. I stand behind the door frame, where I can see the scene unfolding, but Emily can't see me.

"Uh. I guess the door was open. I wanted to buy a book of poetry and I've just been sitting here reading. Maybe I sort of zoned out." He's holding Andrea Gibson's *You Better Be Lightning* in his hand. Note to self: he's a very convincing liar.

"Shoot," says Emily. "I must have left the door unlocked. But you need to go." Nobu's mouth is slightly open, and he holds out the book with both hands. "Hey." Emily's voice softens. "Sorry. I can ring that book up for you, before you go."

"Um, I don't have quite enough money to buy it."

"Andrea Gibson. Their poetry is astonishing," she says,

looking at the book, but making no move to receive it. "Please, take it as a gift from me. I feel really bad about accusing you of trespassing, when this was clearly my fault." I'm witnessing the moment when Nobu meets a human as nice as he is. I swallow my laughter and stay out of sight behind the doorway.

"No, I can't take it. You've already been too kind. I totally should have noticed that no one else was here." Nobu tries to pass Emily the book again, but she keeps her hands at her side and shakes her head.

"Nope," she says. They stand there looking at each other.

"Only if you're absolutely sure," says Nobu. It's an epic battle of niceness.

"I am." She grabs a paper bag, takes the book from Nobu, places it in the bag, and passes it back to him. Nobu bows his head in thanks. "I'll walk you out," Emily says. Nobu opens the door. "You know, it's ironic," she says.

"What's that?" says Nobu, as the bell on the door jangles and the door closes behind them. They're standing just outside the shop, so I slip into the front room where I can watch them through the glass door.

"I came to Paris to write the Great Canadian Novel. I got this job, this apartment upstairs so I could earn a bit of money and still have lots of time to write. Every day I'm surrounded by the very best books, filled with the best words, and I can't write a thing. If it's possible to have a negative word count on a novel, that's where I'd be right now."

"That's a lot of pressure," says Nobu.

"How so?" says Emily.

"I don't know anything about writing a novel, but the idea of The Great Canadian Novel sounds like a pretty intimidating place to start."

Emily shrugs and shoves her hands in the pockets of her long black coat. "I guess so." She stares at her Chucks.

"What if you started with something smaller, like a short story. Like a very short story. Write about something that's interesting to you ... and because you love writing. You don't need to worry about publishing a great novel, yet. Life is long."

Emily looks up at Nobu. "I like that. Life is long."

"Yeah." says Nobu, "It is." A lump rises in my throat.

"I could start with short stories. I love sweet stories about people falling in love." Her cheeks turn red, and she looks back down at her shoes. "Or whatever."

"I think my best friend would like those stories," says Nobu, who seems not to have noticed her blushing. He holds up the paper bag. "Are you still sure about the book?"

Emily nods her head. "Yup. More sure than ever. Thanks, uh, I'm sorry. I didn't get your name."

"Nobu."

"Emily. So, are you just visiting Paris, or do you live here?"

"Um, yeah. I live quite close by, actually," he says. Poor Nobu.

"Cool," Her face lights up. "I really like talking to you, so if you'd ever like to get a meal or something, you know where I work." She places her hand on his arm. Wait? Is she asking him out? On a date? I'm suddenly feeling much less friendly towards Emily from Canada.

Nobu backs up and bows slightly. "It was good to meet you." He turns and walks away from Colette and Company, while Emily enters the store, pushes the door closed and turns the lock. By the time she looks back out the window, Nobu is gone. Except he's not. He's still there, looking at

Emily, and at me standing behind her. By now, I'm confident she can't see me as Nobu has already helped her, and although I try to dodge her, she slips right through me on her way upstairs. I pass through the door and join Nobu on the other side.

He pulls the small book of poetry out of the bag and tucks it in the pocket inside his jacket. Then he folds up the paper bag and places it in the paper recycling bin near the store.

"That was weird, right?" I say.

"For sure. I don't know anything about writing," he says.

"No, I mean her asking you on a date," I say.

"She did not," he says.

"She most certainly did. She asked you out for a meal. She said she enjoyed talking to you."

"Huh," says Nobu, as he finally understands Emily's intention and smiles. Despite my attempt to restrain myself, I punch him in the shoulder.

"Hey," he says, laughing. "I didn't do anything wrong. Also, as Helpers, we don't have romantic feelings, and even if I did, I will be invisible to her the next time we're in the store. Face it, Claire. You're stuck with me."

"How am I stuck?" I say.

"You know ... you're my best friend," he says.

"Best friend, eh?" I say and he grins and grabs my hand. How can we feel so differently about each other? My heart is sore with longing for something I can't describe. The reality is that his hand in mine, in this particular way, will have to be enough.

"Let's find another spot for tonight. Colette and Company is feeling a little crowded right now." We spend the night at an empty apartment, overlooking the Tuileries.

The owner, a man from Nobu's painting class, is having it renovated, so Nobu knows it's empty. We open the windows and let in the fresh air and the sounds of birds and Nobu sketches while I make a new list:

A LIST OF TRULY GREAT INVENTIONS:

1. Books. Bookstores. Libraries.
2. Hoodies. (Ah, the pocket and the hood!)
3. Electricity.
4. Birthday cakes. Candles on birthday cakes. That song people sing.
5. Ice skates.
6. Fireplaces.
7. Pumpkin soup.
8. Stop signs.
9. Musical instruments, especially the ones with strings. Also: pianos.
10. The heavy green chairs at The Tuileries.
11. Dogs.
12. Dogs as companions for humans.
13. Fireworks.
14. Chandeliers.
15. Tiny twinkle lights on trees and balconies.
16. Trees.
17. Handmade slippers.
18. Soap.
19. Beds.
20. Lilies.

Before closing my eyes, I think of Kano Takahashi.
Please don't leave early.

CHAPTER 32
IN WHICH A WOMAN DESCRIBES THE CIRCUMSTANCES BEHIND HER DIVORCE

Early in the morning, while the sky above the Tuileries is still in its pinks, I tell Nobu that I'm going for a walk and that I'll meet him at our park, around midday. Since Nobu is, without question, the moral centre of our little duo, I choose not to tell him that I'm going to spy on a stranger I followed home yesterday.

As I walk to the Marais on this sunny morning, I am practically alone on the streets, although I do provide a man with directions to the nearest metro station, and I help a woman catch her pug that got off its leash. Fortunately, I am faster than the pug and I'm able to catch her quite quickly. The dog's name is Florence, and she wears a tiny pink cashmere sweater, which strikes me as adorable. As I scoop her up, I can hear her thoughts. *I wasn't actually running away, you know. I just wanted to explore. We never go where I want to go.*

"I feel you, Flo," I whisper into her ear before passing her back to her person.

As I near the hotel, I pass a young couple kissing on a

bench, but I look away. I'm not in the mood for the kissing today.

Outside the hotel entrance, there's a small patio with six tables and chairs, where I wait for Kano Takahashi to leave her room. I've decided that I won't spy on her, but that I will snoop in her room and this distinction makes me feel less guilty. Although I'm intensely curious about who she is, I don't want to catch her in her pyjamas, even, or especially, when it's impossible for her to know that I'm there. I chuckle, recognizing that even I have my limits.

The sun has fully risen, and a young woman wearing a yellow beret arrives at the hotel. A few minutes later, an older man leaves pulling a suitcase. The wheels thunder over the cobblestone pathway. I smell coffee brewing and an older couple arrives on the patio with their breakfast on a tray. They are both tall, elegantly dressed, and white haired.

"Isn't it wonderful?" the woman says.

"What exactly?" says the man.

"Everything," she says. "The flakiness of the croissant, the bitterness of the coffee mixed with the sweetness of the sugar. The morning light. All of it. It's an exquisite day."

"As you wish, my dear," he says. He finishes his eggs quickly, pours his coffee down his throat and sets his cup down, a bit too loudly. "Listen, I'm glad you're enjoying your-self, but if we're telling the truth, it's too breezy out here for me. I'll be inside. Let me know when you're ready to go." He stands and goes back into the hotel, and she continues to look out at the trees and gardens surrounding the patio. She reaches into her bag and retrieves a tissue with which she dabs each eye.

"I'm very sorry you had to hear that." She looks directly at me.

"Pardon me?" I say.

"My husband just now. I'm sorry you had to hear us fighting." She pulls out the chair beside her.

I say to myself, 'This is your job, Claire. This is your job,' and I get up and join her.

"Shall I pour you a cup of coffee?" she asks, and before I have a chance to respond, she's already poured it. She places the bowl of sugar and the small pitcher of cream carefully next to my cup. I am careful not to touch anything; right now, she's just a person talking to herself and not a floating coffee cup.

"Of course, it hasn't always been this way, she says."

"What hasn't?" I ask.

"Us, of course. My husband and me. Back at the beginning of everything, when we were your age, it was wonderful between us. So romantic. I suppose it always is, at first. You'd never guess it, to look at us now, but we used to be very much in love. He was a very attentive lover." She pauses.

"I see." It's the only thing I can think to say. Is this really happening? Did she just tell me that her husband was a sensitive lover? This seems like way too much information to share with a stranger before 9 a.m.

"And then came the children and the house and our work and all this mad proving ourselves to the world. We have six grandchildren. Isn't that amazing?"

"Congratulations." I smile, though I suspect this story is not about her grandchildren.

"But somewhere along the way, we lost each other." She dabs the tissue below her eyes again, although I don't see any tears. "I suppose I've seen it coming for years." She pauses and stares at me.

"I'm sorry, but I don't understand," I say. "What's been coming for years?"

"A divorce." I'm completely out of my element here. I contemplate thanking her for the coffee and getting out of here as fast as I can. Then I hear Nobu's voice in my head. *Exhale*, he says. *Trust your instincts.*

"Listen," I say. "I don't know anything about marriage, but I wonder if your husband wasn't just a bit cold and grumpy this morning."

The woman puts down her coffee cup and leans towards me with an intense look on her face, but I can't quite put my finger on the kind of intensity this is. Anger? Surprise? Curiosity? Then she laughs. She laughs so uproariously that her chair tips back on its hind legs for a moment, and then she wraps her arms around her rib cage.

"Oh, dear. That is delicious." She sits up straight and laughs again. "And very likely true." She sighs and finishes her coffee. "Well, then. I suppose I best go up to the room so we can plan the day. Perhaps this would be a good day for a boat ride on the Seine."

"Every day is a good day for a boat ride on the Seine," I say. The woman thanks me for the conversation, which I find hilarious, as there hasn't been a conversation, at all. She piles the plates and cups on her tray, and as she approaches the door of the hotel, Kano Takahashi holds it open for her. After Kano passes the table where I'm sitting, I wait for a few minutes, then I beeline through the main entrance and onto the empty elevator.

It's easy to find room twenty-four. When I pass through the door, the scent of jasmine greets me. The room is, just as I expected, meticulously tidy. Most of her clothes are folded up into perfect little rectangles, like envelopes, inside the dresser drawers. A couple of silk blouses, a skirt, and a pair of trousers hang in the wardrobe. I check the tag on her suitcase. It says Kano Takahashi and then an address in London, which I record in my journal.

On the desk is the book she was reading the other day, the one about the Impressionists. There's a paper folder from The European Conference on Humanities & Arts, a conference she seems to be attending. On the outside of the folder, someone has written "Professor Kano Takahashi" in black marker, so there's another mystery solved. A university professor. Inside the folder is a programme for the conference, and Kano has circled the sessions she wants to attend. One of them has a star beside it, and then I notice that she's presenting that session. It's called, 'On Making and Teaching Art in Response to Loss.' I set down the booklet. Is that what Nobu is doing? Making art to cope with loss? I haven't spent much time considering how he might be feeling about everything we've gone through. He always seems fine, but maybe he's not as okay as he appears. I make a mental note to ask him.

Her session is at ten, tomorrow morning. Immediately, I decide to attend her talk and record the name and address of the venue, along with the name of her talk and the room number listed.

That's enough. I should go. As I stand, however, I notice a brown leather tote bag sitting on a chair. The contents include slippers, a sleep mask, headphones, hand sanitizer and a novel, and everything is organized neatly inside small pouches. I admire her relationship with the physical world. There's nothing surprising here, but I do find, tucked inside a pocket, a photograph of a little kid, maybe two years old, with black hair and a huge smile. A spark shoots up and my heart skips. They look so much like Kano. Is this her child? I place the photo back inside its pocket, pop the tote back on the chair, slip out of the room, and return to the lobby, where the couple I saw earlier are finally setting out for the day. The man helps his wife pull on her cashmere cardigan, and she pats his arm in appreciation. I slip through the main doors of the hotel, out into the sun. She was right, the elegant woman who seems to have decided not to divorce her husband after all. It is an exquisite day.

A LIST OF WHAT I WAS LOOKING FOR IN THE ROOM OF KANO TAKAHASHI

I want to protest here.

I want to say I don't know
EXACTLY
what I was looking for.

Something to explain
the warm, familiar feeling
I have in her presence.
Why I feel more comfortable
with her
than I do with myself.
Why I react so strongly
to the smell of her perfume
and what about that filament,
that whisper of connection?
The single spark
in response
to a photo of a child.

Might Kano Takahashi
carry
inside her
some knowledge of me?

Or is she simply
what she appears?
A well-organized
Art professor from London
who deserves better
than having some dead kid
go through her stuff.

I'm looking for a way
to reconcile
my right to glimpse,
to understand
my life
and hers to be left alone.

CHAPTER 33
IN WHICH GUS HAS LOST HIS WAY

t's early evening when I meet Nobu at the Tuileries. When we first arrived on Earth and were making plans to meet up, I would ask him exactly what time. "Tell me. Two o'clock or two-thirty?" Now it feels as though time matters less. We said we'd meet up sometime after his art class. I know exactly where he'll be, and I find him sitting in a green chair with his feet up on a large stone fountain, closer to the Louvre than to the obelisk. Of course he's drawing, as I slip into the chair beside his. I hope he can't see how heavy my heart is.

"How was class?"

"Good," he says. "Really good. On the walk here, I met a woman whose daughter died recently."

"That's heavy. You okay?"

"Sure. She just needed to talk about her, you know?" I nod. "How was your walk?"

"Yeah, good. I helped a couple of people in the Marais," I say. He looks up from his sketchbook and smiles. "Three actually. Nothing big. Directions. Then I caught a runaway pug named Florence." Nobu laughs. "A little later, I listened to a woman who thought her marriage was ending."

"Was it? Ending?"

"Nope. Her husband was just a little grumpy, I think." I notice there's a young guy with light brown hair a few seats away, wearing a khaki jacket and jeans. "Is that guy staring at us?"

"Yeah. That's Gus. He's been hanging out," says Nobu.

"And he can see you?"

"Oh yeah. We've been talking, on and off, all day. In fact, he came to art class with me."

"Wasn't that a little awkward given the fact that everyone else there could see him but not you?"

"Um, not really. Artists are tolerant people and I guess he just looked like a guy talking to himself. Gus is ... I'll just invite him to join us." Nobu waves him over and Gus drags his chair across the stones to where we're sitting. "Gus, this is Claire. I told you about her earlier. Claire, this is Gus."

"Claire. You're the angel!" Gus says. I frown at Nobu who shrugs and goes back to his sketchbook.

"It's good to meet you, Gus, but I'm definitely not an angel."

"Oh, I know. Nobu said you would say that. He explained that you're called Helpers, but if we're telling the truth about what you do all day, we'd have to call you angels."

I lean over and close Nobu's sketchbook. "We need to talk. NOW." We walk about ten feet away from the chairs. Gus waves at us before leaning back in his chair, crossing his legs, and resting his feet on the edge of the fountain. "Nobu, what is going on with this guy?"

"I don't know how this is possible, but Gus knew what I

was, without me saying anything. I think he can read my mind. He might be able to read yours as well. I've asked him how I can help, but he says he's fine. He says he's just looking for some company."

"Well, he's freaking me out. Do you know anything about him ... like where he's from?"

"He doesn't know where he's from. He doesn't know where he lives. He doesn't know how he got here. He just knows that his name is Gus," says Nobu.

"Wait a minute. He doesn't remember any details of his life, but he knows his name is Gus?" I say. Nobu nods. "Doesn't that remind you of anyone?"

Nobu shakes his head, then stops. "Us. The day we woke up in the field."

"Can the humans see him?"

"Pretty sure they can. Do you think that's even possible, that he's a Helper, but something went wrong?"

"I don't know. I'm starting to think that anything is possible, but we're not going to be able to look after this guy, Nobu. This is way above our pay grade."

"You're right, Claire. I thought about contacting Coach, but I'd like to try to solve this on our own," Nobu says.

"How?" I ask.

"I'm not sure yet, but I'm working on it," says Nobu. We return to our green chairs and Nobu pops his sketchbook into his pocket.

"You're right, Claire," says Gus. "It's a real pickle."

"Gus, I'm sorry this is happening to you. We're going to figure out how to get you some help," I say.

"But you are the Helpers," says Gus. He sounds a lot younger than he looks. More like thirteen than twenty.

"We are, Gus, but you may need a different kind of help

than what we can provide." Gus nods his head slowly and my heart feels sore for him. At least I know what I'm doing down here. At least I have Nobu.

As the three of us watch the sun set over the gardens, Nobu says he has an idea of how to help Gus. He suggests I head home, and says he'll meet me at the bookstore later.

Evidently, Emily has taken Nobu's advice and begun writing short stories and she goes directly to her room after work, so I have the shop to myself. I grab my journal and write:

A LIST OF PROS AND CONS FOR TELLING NOBU ABOUT KANO TAKAHASHI

Pros:

1. I would feel less guilty.
2. I could be less secretive.
3. I could tell Nobu about the filaments between Kano and me.

Cons:

1. Nobu will know that I followed Kano back to her hotel.
2. He'll know that I took unnecessary risks to learn her name.
3. He'll know that I snooped in her room, rummaged through her tote bag, and read the documents on her desk.

4. He'll know that I kept all of this from him for at
   least two days.
5. He'll think I've been reckless and selfish.
6. For sure, he will be disappointed in me.
7. Depending on what I learn at the conference
   tomorrow, there may be nothing to tell him.

I read the list over several times. It's not just about the
number of items on each list, but about their weight, their
significance, and as of tonight, I don't know if all of this adds
up to anything. I decide that, for tonight, I will say nothing
and tomorrow, no matter what I learn, I will come
completely clean with Nobu. The thought of that conversation makes my stomach flip.

I'm reading *Anne of Green Gables,* when Nobu returns.

"Hey! Is Gus okay?" I ask.

"I think so. There's no way to know for sure, but I think
it went okay." I close my novel. "I wrote a note explaining
that this was Gus, and that he doesn't remember who he is or
where he lives. I gave Gus the note and escorted him to a
police station in the Marais staffed by Camille, a police-
woman I trust. She's good at her job and she's kind and she
knows everybody in the neighbourhood. Like she knows
them, by name."

"Was she on duty tonight?" I ask.

"Yeah. I marched Gus right up to the front door of the
station, opened the door and sort of pushed him inside."

"Gently though, right?" I feel so scared for Gus, in this
story.

"Of course. Everything went smoothly. Gus gave
Camille the note and she read it and asked Gus how he got
there, and he said 'My friend Nobu brought me. He's

standing right on the other side of that door.' It was a glass door." I nod.

"You knew he would point to you, but that the police officers wouldn't see anyone there." Nobu's eyelids droop and the corners of his mouth turn down. "You had to make them believe he was unwell, to get them to help." Nobu nods, but doesn't look at me. "The thing is, in some way we don't yet understand, he is unwell. Poor Gus." I place my hand over Nobu's, and we sit quietly for a moment.

"Camille brought Gus a bowl of soup, a baguette, and some water," Nobu says, "and while he was eating, I slipped through the door to listen. Camille called social services to explain that Gus needed shelter and psychological assistance. While she was on the phone, I knelt beside Gus and told him what was happening, but Gus was so busy gulping down his meal that he didn't even look up. Then, as I was leaving, Gus called out, 'Nobu, man. You did what you said. You helped me. Thanks, dude.'" Nobu starts to cry, and I wrap my arms around him.

"Hey, I know that was hard, but you didn't have any choice. You did what was necessary to help Gus. I would never have thought of that in a million years," I say.

"I feel like I should have done more, you know?"

"There was nothing more you could have done."

Nobu is quiet for the rest of the evening, and I tell myself I've made the right decision, not telling him about the woman I've been trailing. We sleep curled up beside each other in the children's book section until we hear Emily's footsteps on the stairs in the morning.

CHAPTER 34
IN WHICH I ATTEND A CONFERENCE

Nobu feels better about Gus in the morning, and he goes off to one of his art classes. I'm deliberately vague about my plans, as I don't want to add lying to the long list of transgressions I feel guilty about. We agree to meet back at the book shop around sunset.

The Paris Convention Centre is in the fifteenth arrondissement and the most sensible way to get there is probably the bus, although people are much chattier on the bus than on the train. I wonder why that is. It's not that I don't want to help, but that my bandwidth for helping right now is low. Whatever I learn about Kano Takahashi, and hopefully about myself, this morning will help me move forward in this life. More than anything else, I would like to be unstuck, to feel like a being with free will.

I keep a low profile on the bus by slouching down in my seat, and looking out the window. People sit in me a couple of times, so I'm forced to move seats, but I'm happy that no one seems to notice me.

At the Convention Centre, I wait until the very last moment to enter the room where Kano is speaking. I'm probably a tad more visible than normal in a room full of people interested in the topic of grief, so I head to a dark corner at the very back of the room. There's a hand-out on the chair and I pick it up and hold it in my hands, as Kano begins speaking, "Good morning. My name is Dr. Kano Takahashi, and I would like to thank you for joining me for this session entitled, 'On Making and Teaching Art in Response to Loss.'" I'm struck by how melodious her voice is, clear but also sweet-sounding. The way she pronounces her words reminds me of someone.

Kano continues, "For many years I have worked as an art professor within the Bachelor of Fine Arts program at Central St. Polina's School of Fine Arts, in London. As an artist and as a teacher, I have always been aware of the power of art-making, to help us make sense of our lives. But it was not until I experienced tragedy within my own family that I began to understand how deeply a person's art practice can support them when nothing else seems to make sense."

Kano is projecting slides on an enormous screen at the front of the room, but the screen remains black to me. Ah yes. I am an emitter of light.

"There are events so disorienting, losses so devastating that we feel as though we've lost the ground beneath us. Some people turn to religion at such a time, while others, unfortunately, fall into the abyss of substance abuse. My salvation, however, has been art. Not with the intention of creating anything particularly good, whatever that means." The audience chuckles at this comment. "I wasn't making art around a particular theme or looking to exhibit this work. Promoting myself as an artist was quite literally the last thing on my mind. But the physical act of making things, the process of applying colour and texture and line to a canvas, has helped rebuild the ground beneath me. I was drawing the walls of a room in which I could bear to continue to exist. Once I had one room, I could create a second room and then a small house, a place for my husband and I to be together in our grief and to wake up every morning and have a cup of tea and a slice of toast. So, we could turn towards the beautiful, heartbreaking task of raising our granddaughter, Lily. That we might be hopeful, and possibly joyful again, someday."

As she speaks, I imagine the rooms she paints into existence, imagine her painting herself into them. Her husband, her granddaughter. But not her daughter. I wonder if this is the loss she's speaking of.

"I was aware, when I took my proposal forward to Central St. Polina's that the answer might be no, but I was determined to find a way to provide for regular people, not just those privileged enough to be able to afford a posh education, but anyone who had suffered a loss, an opportunity to experience art as therapy. Not only did my university say 'yes,' but they also approved a substantial grant to provide art supplies for all participants."

Audience members applaud. As Kano describes the project, I realize who she sounds like. Nobu. She looks like Nobu. She moves her hands like Nobu. How is that possible, though? I open the hand-out I'm holding and read the sentence, 'This project was prompted by the loss of her son and daughter-in-law, in a tragic car accident.' My hands begin to shake. On the back cover of the pamphlet, there's a photograph of Kano, and she is holding a framed photograph of three people: a young man, a young woman, and a baby. It's Nobu and me. In my mind, I see an image of three tiny sparks dancing around each other. The sparks that came from the lilies. Lily. Our Lily.

"I want to be clear," Kano says, "that there is not a single day that I don't miss Nobu and Claire, that I don't long to hear their voices again. They were just eighteen when they died, and Claire had had a very tough life, before she and Nobu found each other. But they did find each other, and my husband and I adored her, and when Lily was born, my heart was full."

I sit back in my chair and close my eyes for a moment. Thoughts fall and splatter like raindrops. I was a mother. Nobu was my husband. This poised and gracious woman was my mother-in-law. On Earth, my life was big and full of love. And I am missed.

"There is no art I can make that will give us back our beloved children, but I am more alive now than I was when they died, and that feels like a good goal: to live as fully as possible, for as long as we're here." People are on their feet applauding for Kano. Some people are crying. She bows to the audience, a gesture I've seen Nobu make a hundred times. Even though she's just described a personal loss to hundreds of strangers, she appears calm and composed, and now I understand where Nobu gets it. It's not so much that I am a turbulent mess, although maybe I am, as that he has been raised and loved by this woman. This force of nature.

Yesterday—could it be only yesterday that I read the description of Kano's talk?—I wondered if Nobu was making art to cope with his loss. Even though he can't remember his life, perhaps some small part of him knows.

So many things make sense. The strength of my connection with Nobu. The filaments between us. But how will I tell him, how will I tell him, how will I tell him?

Audience members line up to ask Kano questions. I want to slip into the queue, throw my arms around her, smell her jasmine perfume one more time, but I know I can't. I tuck the hand-out inside my journal and slip out of the room. Although I don't know this neighbourhood, I walk home without consulting a map. I just keep walking towards the place where I know the bookshop will be. It occurs to me that I'm in shock, but none of the human treatments will work. I don't get cold. I cannot hydrate. I just keep walking.

Nobu. We were married. This is not the first time I have loved him.

Lily. She is the child in the photo in Kano's purse.

No. I push the thought of Lily away.

I can't yet. I can't.

CHAPTER 35
IN WHICH I CHANGE NOBU'S LIFE

'm sitting in the dark under the computer desk in the back room when Nobu gets back, but that's not so uncommon, since we don't need light to see. Nobu sits beside me and begins telling me about something that happened at his art class. I try to listen, but my mind is all jumbled and I'm exhausted from crying.

"Claire, what's going on? Is this about Gus?"

"It's not about Gus."

"Okay. Whatever it is, you can tell me. There's nothing you can't tell me."

I think about this for a moment. Is this true? Can I really tell him anything? I take the leap. "There is no way for me to tell you about this without making you angry, so I'm just going to tell you. A few days ago, I encountered a woman named Kano Takahashi, and I saw a filament connecting us."

"A filament? Like the ones you see between us?"

"Yes. But not nearly as big. Listen, I'll answer all of your questions, but I need you to let me tell you this." He nods. "I followed her to her hotel and learned that she's an art professor from London, and that she was giving a talk at a conference this morning, so I went to hear it. Her presentation was about how making art can help people deal with loss. Her son and daughter-in-law died in a car accident a year ago. They had a baby. Her name was Lily."

"Claire, I don't get what this woman has to do with us." His voice is shaking as if part of him has begun to understand. I pull the hand-out from my journal and pass it to Nobu who begins reading.

"There's a photograph on the back," I say, but he's gone silent. He's seen the photograph of the two of us with Lily. I hear him gasping for breath, for words.

"Where? Where is she staying?"

"I think she's checked out, Nobu. Last night was her last night. And even if she's still there, she won't be able to see you. She will never be able to see you." His hands are shaking as he stares at the photograph of Kano, holding the photograph of us, and the paper makes a rattling sound.

"Claire, please." I write down the name and address of the hotel and tear the page out of my journal, but before I can pass it to him, Nobu has ripped the page from my hand and he's running so quickly I half expect to hear shattered glass as he launches himself through the front door. But there's nothing. A vacuum where Nobu used to be.

I stuff my Little Red Riding Hood coat inside my bag, pull the bag across my body, and run after him. He shouldn't be alone.

This is my fault. I should have told him about Kano that first day when I followed her back to her hotel. I should have described the scent of jasmine, the feeling of home, the strange sense that everything was going to be okay. Perhaps, in a way, I was prepared for this revelation, but he's been blindsided by the news. In my mind, I try to make A List of

Things I Could Have Done Differently, but nothing comes to me. I did my best with what I knew at the time, as the Claire I was at the time. Now I am both Claires. I'd hoped knowing who I was would feel better than it does.

The sun has set by the time I reach the hotel at Place des Vosges, and I'm surprised that Nobu's not already there. I check the closet and dresser drawers for confirmation, but as I suspected, she's gone. Fortunately, no one else has checked in yet and when Nobu comes through the door, I break the news to him.

"Are you certain this is the right room?" he says. "Room twenty-four?"

"I'm sure, Nobu. This was her room, but she was due to check out this morning. She must have gone straight back to London after the conference."

Nobu crumples onto the floor and wails as though he's injured. I kneel, wrap my arms around him, and hold him until he eventually quiets down.

"She was here," he says.

"Yes."

"My mother."

"Yes."

"How could they not have told us we were parents?" he says. "It's too much, Claire." His voice is desperate, ragged with emotion. He doesn't seem like the Nobu I know, as though he's been taken over by someone else. Maybe this is what grief looks like.

"I'll help you," I say.

"But this is happening to you too." Nobu wraps his arms around me, and I press myself against his body and release the stress of all the complicated things I've been hiding for the past few days. "Thank you for finding her, Claire. Everything adds up now. You and me." He leans in, closes his eyes, and rests his lips against mine. I have so much wanted this kiss, but not like this. Gently, I move my lips away from his. He touches my face. Ropes of golden tendrils pile up in the space between our bodies. Nobu gasps. "The filaments," he says, and my body vibrates with the knowledge that he finally sees them.

"Lily," I say. "I think the filaments are because of Lily. Because we're her parents." Nobu groans and begins to cry.

CHAPTER 36
IN WHICH NOBU AND I MAKE A PLAN

ack at the bookshop, we stay up all night talking.

"I don't know how I'm supposed to feel about all of this," says Nobu. He sits with his back against the wall and my head on his lap.

"I think we can safely say, screw how you're supposed to feel." Nobu places his hand in my hair. "How do you feel? That's the only question, really," I say, as I sit up and cross my legs in front of me.

"I feel ... I feel ... so many things. Surprised to be part of a family. With parents and you and a kid," says Nobu.

"Only surprised?"

"Happy. But then again, heartbroken." We sit quietly for a couple of minutes. Nobu places a hand on my knee.

"I guess this is why we aren't meant to remember our lives as humans," I say.

"Yeah. But you did remember us," he says. "You told me about the filaments and the sparks, and the golden heart you saw after you helped Anaïs, and it's not that I didn't believe you, but I couldn't see them for myself. I didn't get that you were remembering your life." He gasps. "You saw

sparks when you saw that plaque on the boat. The Lily."
I nod.

"My theory is that I wasn't so much remembering as I was experiencing a connection to moments from my life, and to you ... and to Lily. The filaments were a pretty good clue that we were something more than helping partners, randomly assigned at The Station."

"Claire, I regret not taking your phenomena more seriously. I should have stopped everything, and helped you discover your identity," says Nobu.

I close my eyes and feel what is between us. "There's nothing to apologize for. You did your best. You always do."

He takes my hands in his. "Is this okay, Claire?" I nod my head. "I think we need to consider the consequences of finding my mother." This sounds like the Nobu I know.

"I've done some big trespassing, for sure, and whoever they are, the Seers and the Station Masters or whoever else there might be, they can probably see us. I don't think it's possible for us to hide anything we do," I say and squeeze his fingers.

"But where's Coach? Really, where the hell is he?" Nobu asks.

"Is that where you went? Why I got to the hotel before you?" I ask. He nods.

"It made sense at the time. To send an emergency message from the typewriter at the Louvre. But I don't think he's coming." We sit in silence for a moment, with what that might mean.

"Maybe he can't," I say.

"You're not suddenly defending Coach, are you?" Nobu asks.

"Not exactly. Listen, there's no way for us to know the

consequences of my snooping around. Maybe they fired Coach."

"Or worse ... what if we're sent away from each other?" says Nobu. This possibility has never occurred to me.

"They wouldn't," I say.

"Maybe not, but this will definitely get us demoted," he says.

"I could not care less if we can't become angels, or whatever. Don't care."

"But what if getting demoted is what we used to think death was? What if we lose everything, now that we've just got it back?" Nobu says. I shiver. Think, Claire. Think. We are in a mess of epic proportions. Part of me wants to find Coach, confess everything, and ask for his protection. But we're so close to understanding everything about ourselves, our whole lives. And then there's Lily. I'd like to see her. Just once.

"What are you thinking about?" Nobu asks.

"Next steps. Pros and cons."

"You said you have my parents' address in London?"

"Yes. I got it from Kano's luggage tag. Not my shiniest moment."

"Not true. You were brilliant." He touches my cheek, then drops his hand. "Screw it. Let's go to London."

"That's what I want, too, but there are ramifications," I say. "We're definitely not supposed to see the people from our old life."

"I thought you didn't care about the rules," says Nobu.

"I don't. I care about finding out about our lives," I say. "I care about you," I add quietly.

"You know I've always followed the rules, but serving humanity as a Helper was based on the assumption that I'd been dealt with fairly." His voice is loud and determined. "That's not the case, is it?" I shake my head.

"It seems not," I say.

His eyes flash with determination. "Come on then, let's go!" He grabs my hand, and as we cross the front room, I notice that our filaments aren't fading the way they normally do. If anything, they're growing brighter and thicker. I feel like I'm vibrating, like I'm going to come right out of my skin. Nobu and I sail through the front of the bookstore and right through a couple of teenagers making out against the door. It doesn't even bother me.

We're going to London.

We're going to meet Lily.

CHAPTER 37
IN WHICH WE RIDE A TRAIN UNDER THE OCEAN

At the Gare du Nord train station, Nobu leads us to the big board with all the upcoming departures. It's analog, with a cascade of flipping letters, and normally I would find this romantic, but today I'm just grateful it's not digital, because it means we can read it. There's a train to London in fifteen minutes.

"Wait. Wait just a minute," I say. "We can't take the train to London."

"Of course, we can," Nobu is moving towards a train, sitting at platform four.

I stop following him. "No. Nobu. The sea. There's an ocean between France and England."

He turns to face me. "It's okay, the train goes under the sea."

"Nope."

"Claire, it's perfectly safe. There's a tunnel under the sea. It's not that long. Like fifty kilometres or something." He takes my hands. "You can do this. I know you can."

"No. I don't think I can ride a train that goes under the ocean. I can do a lot of things. Dying, for example. I can die.

I can write lists of questions and tiny, beautiful things. I can help pregnant girls. I can even find your mother, but I don't think I can cope on a train passing under all that water. If something happens, we'll be crushed."

Nobu places his hands on my shoulder. "Claire, we're already dead. We're not real. These are not bodies." His voice is quiet and calm. I know that what he's saying is completely rational.

"I'm afraid," I say. It's just that simple. I know I'm more of a supernatural hologram than I am a person, but I still experience fear. I'm relieved to tell Nobu how I feel.

"I'll be with you the entire time. Right beside you. The whole trip is just two and a half hours long."

"That's not very long, is it?" I say.

"Not very long at all. And if we have to ride on a plane, it will end up taking much longer."

"Oh, I'm not flying," I say. "There's no need for a discussion about that."

"Okay, then. That's settled. We're not flying. Shall we board the train?" he says, and I nod and let him pull me along. He chooses car seven, which looks empty, and we sit down. A few minutes later, a young couple sits in us, and we roll our eyes as if to say, 'With all the empty seats on this car, why did they need to sit here? In us?' We move up a couple of rows and the train pulls slowly out of the station.

Nobu has given me the window seat to try and butter me up, and I watch the view like humans watch their pocket screens. The sky is more grey than blue, which makes me think a storm is coming. Quickly, we are out of the city, past the suburbs, and racing through the French countryside, and as we travel north, rain begins to fall on the fields and villages. It starts as a light mist, but grows heavier and more insistent, until I can hear the drops pelting the metal roof over the noise of the train. Mesmerized by the storm, I forget, for a few minutes, why we're on this train.

Then I remember.

I've never seen Nobu like this. Never seen him angry or impatient or undone the way he's been today. It feels like I've been aware of everything for days, when, in truth, I've only known for a few hours longer than him. Why am I so calm, when he's not?

Because somewhere deep inside me, I already knew. I was right to wonder if there was something big left over from my life. I was right to suspect that I loved Nobu as more than a friend. At long last, it's such a relief to feel less crazy.

The day I woke up in the green field with Nobu, I had the feeling that I was supposed to be somewhere else. I'm not crazy to feel that. I'm supposed to be with Lily.

Nobu's eyes are closed.

"What are you thinking?" I ask.

"I'm trying not to think," he says.

"How's that going?"

"Not very well." The edge of his voice is sharp, but there's something else there that sounds like pain. I look back out the window.

The people behind us are talking excitedly about entering the tunnel. I grab Nobu's hand, and he laces his fingers through mine and squeezes tight.

"Breathe," he says. I laugh a little, which is as much as I can do, given how terrified I am. As I exhale, my shoulders descend. That's better. I rest back against my chair. *You're doing great,* he says inside my head, and somehow, the words sound different than when he speaks to me out loud.

Do you think this is the reason we can communicate this

way? Like in our heads? Because we knew each other before? I say.

Possibly, he says, and squeezes my hand again. I close my eyes and try to relax, try to turn my mind off, try not to think about the pressure of the sea pushing against the tunnel. *Or maybe it's just a Helper thing. It doesn't always work, though.*

"Really?" I ask.

"Yeah. Like if you're focussed on something else and I try to speak to you inside your mind, I can't. It's like the message won't go through. I think there needs to be a clear intention to communicate on the part of both people."

"That sounds right to me," I say. The train shudders and I squeeze his hand.

"Claire, maybe it would help to remember that night, the first snowfall, when we made snow angels."

"The city was so quiet," I say. *It felt magical.* My body is starting to relax.

Yes. Magical, says Nobu. I sneak a quick peek. His eyes are closed and he's leaning against the back of his chair and although I'm not sure how it's possible, I think the two of us are in this memory together. I wipe a snowflake off his cheek. We laugh. I pull him out of his snow angel. But in this memory, we don't return to the bookstore. We flop down and create two new snow angels and we sing *Frosty the Snowman* and then *Silent Night,* and while I'm not sure which past we're in, I feel safe.

"Okay, Claire. We're almost there." Then the train is out of the tunnel, and I can breathe on my own again. The south of England looks very much like the north of France, which is interesting, given the cultural differences. For however long I exist, I will never stop being fascinated by the humans. I rest for a while and open my eyes as our train approaches

London's St. Pancras station. It's still raining. As the train enters the platform, I see a man wearing a camel-coloured trench coat and hat right outside the window. He stares at me as the train slowly passes him. There's a look of sadness in his eyes, but nothing about him seems to be asking for help. That's odd.

Despite his initial hurry to get here, Nobu does not jump out of his seat.

"You okay?" I say.

"Yes." He pauses. "No. I'm also afraid."

"Of what? Do you know?" I say.

"Not sure. What we'll find. What we won't find. That it will be too much or perhaps not enough. You know?"

"I do. I know exactly."

CHAPTER 38

IN WHICH WE ARRIVE IN LONDON

Outside the station, we are swallowed up by a sea of umbrellas, but I spot the taxi stand, where a man in a dark grey suit says the name of Kano's street. I have no idea if his destination is near her house, but it's a start. We run towards the taxi, and I pull Nobu into the back seat just as the man closes the door. The passenger tells the driver exactly what route to take and in the rear-view mirror I see the driver roll his eyes, but he says nothing.

I look out the window at London, remembering the glimpses I had of it through the Training Room door at the Station. The door that takes you where you most want to go. London is different from Paris. If Paris is dressed up for a romantic night out, London looks like it's ready to roll up its sleeves and get to work. It feels sensible to me. Reliable. All the things that Nobu is, which makes sense, since this is where he's from. We're stopped at a red light, when a young woman in a yellow raincoat leans in against the passenger window. Neither the cab's actual passenger nor the driver seems to notice her, but she can definitely see Nobu and me. She stares at us with a look of disappointment. Or worry. It occurs to me that she must be a Helper. Maybe the man on the platform too. If that's the case, we're really in trouble. As the light turns green, we pull away and the woman's fingertips leave streaks along the window. Nobu's eyes are wide and my heart lodges itself in my throat.

The fare ends in front of a house that is just two doors down from Kano's address. What are the chances of this? We're learning that where Nobu and I are involved, the chances are much higher than one might guess. The opposite of random.

We tumble out of the car without waiting for the man to open the door, and I point. "Two doors down. With the red door," I say. Nobu stares at me wide-eyed. I meet his gaze and squeeze his hand.

In half a minute we're standing outside the Takahashi family home. Two formerly live people, two rogue Helpers. Are we still Helpers?

"Do we just go in?" Nobu asks.

"Wait! We haven't thought this through yet. Will they be able to see us?" I say.

"No. Coach was emphatic about this ... that no one from our lives would ever be able to recognize us," Nobu says.

"Sure, but will they see someone? Like if they need a Helper, will they be able to see two young people floating through the door?" I say.

"Oh. I don't know."

"Nobu, we need to slow down, so we don't scare the life out of anyone. There's probably a garden at the back," I say. We slip through the tall, wooden fence and find a small, immaculately groomed garden, where we sit on the ground, with our backs against the house.

"Okay. What is it that you hope to get here?" I say.

"I'd like to see my parents and Lily. I'd like a little information about my life. Like maybe there's a yearbook or something like that."

"Is that even possible? Wanting just a little information?" I say. Nobu looks confused. "I mean, don't you want to know everything?"

"I know that's not possible, Claire. Look, I know what you're saying, that once I find out one thing about my life, I'll have more and more questions, but the thing I'm after is like … it's more like a feeling." He closes his eyes and rests the back of his head against the stones of his parents' home.

"What's the feeling you're after?" I say.

"A feeling of belonging. You know? Like I fit, here. Like I am part of the life that happens in this house. Like these people miss me. Like it matters that I'm gone."

I nod, but the thought that Nobu doesn't believe that he belongs with me, feels like being stabbed.

"Claire, I love you." He's heard my thoughts. Of course, he has. "And I don't yet understand all of the ways I love you. But these are my parents. I come from them. I need that." His voice is kind and filled with certainty.

"I know," I say, "It's okay."

"Is it?" he says. I nod. "What about you? What do you want here?"

"I want to see our kid," I say. Nobu nods. "That's all I really want. I think maybe the me who was alive was not so different from this me, so I don't really care about the details."

"Really? That surprises me," says Nobu.

"Me too, actually. Now, we need a plan that doesn't blow up your family," I say.

"The most responsible thing would be to wait until

everyone has gone to sleep," he says. That way we can see them, but there's no chance they will see us. One night only. We learn what we can and then that's it. We leave and we don't come back. Agreed?"

"Agreed." I nod my head. As we wait, I take the risk and pull out my journal even though I'm aware that Nobu can enter the wide foyer of my mind at any time, and hear what I'm thinking or writing:

A LIST OF THOUGHTS ABOUT LOVE SCHOOL

i
Today
I understand,
for the first time,
that all these months on Earth,
I've been in Love School.

My teachers:
David from Mexico,
who loved a boy
who didn't love him.
Charles from the museum,
whose wife was at the centre
of everything.
The woman
whose husband
was having an affair.
The woman at Kano's hotel
on the verge of divorce
while her husband

was just having
a bad morning.
Anaïs who loved her unborn kid
and the brother who took her in.
So many loves.

Including my own.

In this past day,
so crammed with life
and travelling under the sea,
there's been no time
to stop
to breathe
to feel.

To notice who
and how
I am
knowing that Nobu and I
made a person
together.

Every day,
the filaments glowed
and hummed me
into remembering
I am a mother.
I was a mother.
There is a Lily.

ii

Still, I can feel his lips on my lips
but that moment
was all grief
and desperation.

The wrong time.
Every part of me
knows this.

I hope
and I hope
and I hope
for a time that's right.

CHAPTER 39
IN WHICH WE ENTER THE HOUSE

think time works differently for Nobu and me than it does for humans. Although we spend the afternoon and the evening in his parents' backyard, it feels more like a few minutes. Nobu is quiet now. Calmer.

When the lights upstairs go out, we wait a few minutes then slip through the back door and into the kitchen. "Let's see if we still have a room," whispers Nobu. Now that we're inside the house, the thought of seeing our daughter overwhelms me. My stomach churns and I feel shaky, like I did on my first day at The Station. We climb the stairs to a hallway with four doors. The only open door is the one to the bathroom. In one of these rooms there is a two-year-old girl named Lily. In one of these rooms Nobu's parents are sleeping. Hopefully, the bedroom that we shared still contains some clues about our lives. But which one is it? Nobu stands in the middle of the hall and closes his eyes. "I think it's the one at the end of the hall on the left. I'll check." He disappears into the room.

I stand uneasily in the hallway. This is the first time I've been worried that we're doing something very wrong. When

I accepted the twenty Euros from the Watanabe family at Sacré-Coeur, it felt right. When I took the money and the coat from the church at Saint Germain-des-Prés to help Anaïs, I was completely at peace with my decision. Even following and finding Kano was the right thing to do. Now, I'm not so sure. Shouldn't a person have access to the facts about her life without having to sneak around the home of her in-laws in the middle of the night? And then I remember. Not a person. Nobu reappears in the hallway and he's smiling. "Come in," he says. "It's our room."

This room looks different from the rest of the house, which is tastefully decorated. Restrained. In stark contrast, every square inch of wall space in this room is covered with Star Wars posters, poems, quotations and photographs. On one wall, two large bookshelves are loaded with books and small toys, and on the other three walls, from the floor to the bottoms of the window frames, someone has taped up hundreds of photographs. Without even opening a drawer or a yearbook, we can read the story of Nobu's life. Here he is with his mom and dad as a baby. He's smiling and waving at the camera. There's a photo of him holding a trophy under a sign that says Science Fair. He looks at me and raises his eyebrows. "Of course, you won the Science Fair," I say.

"Fair. That doesn't come entirely as a surprise," he smiles. There are so many versions of young Nobu, with his parents and other adults, perhaps aunts and uncles or friends of the family. Guessing by the number of candles on the cakes, it seems like all his birthday parties are represented here. Nobu is seated at the centre of a table with his cake, his friends are crowded around him, and there are always girls at his parties. I suspect his mother oversaw the invitations, and thought it was healthy for Nobu to have lots of girls as friends. We both stop in front of a photo, taken at his sixteenth birthday party. There are candles in the shape of a one and a six on the cake. It's the first photograph that I'm in. I feel like I've been punched in the gut. The face staring back is me, but not me. My hair is long and black and I'm wearing a lot of dark eye make-up. Unlike the other kids in the photograph, I'm not smiling, but I'm standing next to Nobu. Sixteen. How long ago was this, I wonder.

"You look so different," Nobu says.

"Kind of scary, right?"

"I must not have thought so. Look how close I'm standing to you." Nobu bumps into my shoulder with his.

"How are you doing?" I ask.

"I'm okay. It's pretty trippy." We continue making our way around the room, moving through the flow of our lives. After the photograph of his sixteenth birthday, there are a lot more photos with friends, and I'm in most of them. There's another guy and a girl that turn up a lot. The girl is shorter than me, and the boy is blonde and wears glasses. They both look kind and smart, which is exactly the kind of person I'd guess that Nobu would choose as a friend. As we move through the photos, I notice that I'm smiling more and there's less eye make-up. Then there's a picture of just me. I'm wearing a light blue sweater and my hair is blonde, which must be my natural colour since that's the colour it is now. I'm looking directly at the camera which, my intuition tells me, was held by Nobu, and I'm smiling. It's not a crazy, gigantic smile or anything. It's the smile of a person who feels safe and loved. I find myself smiling back at her. I have such compassion for this younger version of me, who has no idea what's coming, but of course, we're not allowed to know. You can only find out what happens at the end of the story, by living it. By waking up every day and saying, "Okay, Life. Let's do this." I realize that's what I'm doing even now. Every day, Nobu and I enter into the relentless flow of things as Helpers, never knowing how it will turn out. This uncertainty seems to be a prerequisite of all existence.

"You look happy," Nobu says. He's standing beside me.

"Which one? The girl in the photo or actual me?"

"Both," he says.

"Yes. I think that's true. It looks like our relationship was really good for me." He nods. Then there's a bunch of photos of the two of us. Goofy ones. A selfie with us kissing. Then there's a photo of the two of us standing with Nobu's parents. Kano and I are dressed in kimono, and Nobu and his father are in suits, and we're in front of an official looking stone building. "Our wedding?" I ask. Nobu nods. Nobu, his parents and I, all look really happy, like we didn't have to get married, but we're still so young. There haven't been any high school graduation photos yet and I haven't seen any photos with my parents. I wonder where they are?

There are a few photos of me pregnant. In one of them, my shirt is tied just below my breasts, and someone has drawn a smiley face on my huge belly. Nobu is crouching beside my belly waving at our kid. In another, I'm hugely pregnant and standing with my arm around a red-headed girl who looks alarmingly like the girl from Tokyo, who smelled like oranges. Beside it, there's a polaroid of Nobu and the girl laughing. When I run my fingertips over the photos of the redheaded girl, sparks fly up. The next photo appears to have been taken from the second floor of this house. Nobu and I are making snow angels in the back garden.

I'm not prepared for the next photo, even though I know it's coming. We're sitting on a hospital bed. I'm holding Lily, who is still tiny, red, and wrinkly, and Nobu is on the other side of the bed beaming at us. He looks surprisingly like he did the day he won first place at the Science Fair. I feel Nobu standing behind me. He lets out a sound. An "Ohhhh-hhhhh." I can't respond. He steps closer and wraps his arms around me. I place my hand on top of his hands, where they are folded against my stomach. He rests his head on my shoulder, and we allow ourselves to cry for these sweet kids and everything they've lost.

After a few moments of taking it all in, we move to the last section of the photo gallery. These are primarily photos of Lily. There's a photo of Nobu and me at what I assume is our high school graduation and a second shot of our family taken on the same day: Nobu's parents, Nobu, and me, holding Lily. She's very small, but I look completely comfortable holding her. In the next one, she's sitting in a highchair, and Nobu is trying to get her to eat from a tiny spoon. There are so many photos of her just being adorable. Lying on the carpet. Dressed up as a tiny grinning pirate for Halloween. Strapped onto Nobu's chest for a walk in the woods. Here's a copy of the photo that Kano carries in the side pocket of her bag: a closeup of Lily looking directly at the camera. Weirdly, she looks like both of us. She has dark shiny hair like Nobu, but she has light skin and freckles like me. Her eyes are light blue. She looks happy and curious. There are loads of photos of Lily with Nobu's parents. Then we get to the last photograph that we're in. Lily's first birthday party. She's wearing a red and blue striped paper hat, and she's staring at the candle on her cake. I'm standing on one side of her highchair and Nobu is on the other. We're looking over the top of her head and smiling at each other as if to say, "Can you believe we made this tiny, exquisite person!"

There are a few more photos of Lily on her own, and Lily with her grandparents, but that's the last photograph of us. I sit down on Nobu's bed, which is covered by a soft, navy-blue duvet cover.

"How are you doing, Claire?" Nobu asks. I don't know how to answer this, so I say nothing.

He sits cross-legged in front of the bookshelf and examines the contents. I listen to my intuition telling me to open the drawer of the bedside table, and I find a black Moleskine journal with my name on it. There's also a sticker that says, 'Don't open this. I warn you. I know where you live.' That makes me smile. I get up and drop the journal in Nobu's lap. He looks up.

"It's mine, but I don't think I can read it. Feel free to give me the highlights."

"You sure you want me to?" he asks.

"Yup. I can't. I don't want to know who I was pissed off at when I was sixteen, or how much I hated my hair or my body or my lab partner, or whatever stupid stuff I was obsessed with. I just want to know where I came from, and how you and I met." I take a deep breath and look at all the goodness captured on the photo wall.

"I totally get that, Claire." He opens the journal to the first page.

"Hey, you," I say. "It looks like we had a good life together." I place my hands on his face, just like Irène did to me, that day she thought she had lost her mother.

"No. We had an amazing life. But part of you already knew that."

CHAPTER 40
IN WHICH NOBU
READS MY JOURNAL

While Nobu reads my journal, which he says is much better than a yearbook because literally every page is about us, I study this amazing gallery of photographs. After an hour or so, I look over at him and the rope of filaments between us is as thick as my arm and is sending tiny sparks into the darkness of the room.

"Nobu," I say. "Can you see that?"

"Yeah. I've been able to see them since you told me about Kano in the bookshop. Is this how they normally look?" he asks.

"Um, this is a little more intense than normal. I'm happy you can finally see them, because it makes me feel like less of a freak." I cross the room and sit on the edge of the bed. He scoots over to make more space for me.

"You were never a freak, Claire." His voice is quiet and serious. "You've been connected to Lily and me this whole time, even though they tried to wipe your mind. What you are is a freaking miracle." He holds the journal, but doesn't open it. "You ready?" I nod.

"Just the highlights, please," I say.

"I understand," he says. I scoot around on my butt so we're facing each other, and he begins. "You were born and raised in Paris. We met in eleventh grade. My family lived there for a year, while my mother was on a sabbatical from her university. You had a really hard time as a kid. Your mother was a deeply unhappy person who never wanted children. Although you don't say this in your journal, it seems like maybe she was emotionally abusive towards you. At the beginning of the year we met, your best friend moved to Japan, and things were weird between you. She'd been the only person you could depend on, since middle school, and you felt lost without her. Robbed, maybe." I inhale, and he places his hand on my knee.

"What was her name?" I say.

"Skye."

I close my eyes. "That's a good name," I say, and nod for him to continue.

"We met on my first day of school, in Paris. We both volunteered at the food bank, and we became friends, and then more than friends. One of the first things you told me about yourself was that you couldn't wait to get away from your parents." For some reason, that tracks. "When you turned sixteen, you applied for legal emancipation from your parents, which was granted, but my parents loved you and couldn't bear the idea of you living in some sketchy little flat in Paris, so we asked you to move back to London with us."

"And Lily?"

"You got pregnant that summer, so we decided to get married. Apparently, that was my idea. Lily was born in March of our final year of school and my parents helped with the baby so we could finish high school, and then attend university. All four of us arranged our schedules around caring for Lily." I try to take in what he's saying.

"How old were we ... when Lily was born?"

"Eighteen," he says. "Still in high school. You wrote about how lucky we were to be supported by my parents, how you loved being a mom, how this life would not have been possible had you not left your family in Paris. You said my parents never let us feel ashamed."

"I can feel that from these photos with your family." Nobu nods. "Learning how this unfolded for us makes me think about Anaïs. I hope things are working out for her." My stomach feels tight.

"You did everything you could, Claire. By the way, you're an excellent writer. The way you describe your life, our lives ... it's like reading a great novel, the kind you don't want to end."

"Thanks for the writing critique on my diary." Nobu smiles. "What else?"

"My full name is Nobuhiro."

"It suits you," I say.

"Yeah, I like it. It sounds noble. You also wrote that our names together mean, 'trust the light.'"

"Oh. That's a surprisingly cheesy entry," I say.

"You got cheesier as a person, Claire. The happier you were, the cheesier you got. You started using the word 'lovely.'"

"I'm quite certain I did not," I say. Nobu flashes me a big grin. "Okay, what else should I know?"

"We had these really close friends, named Oliver and Sadie. We had lots of great adventures. I'm afraid we were all a bit nerdy. You too, Claire. You were a right brainiac." I snort and he rolls his eyes. "You wrote a lot about Skye. She was in love with you, and you said it would have been a lot easier if you'd felt the same way, because she was your favourite person in the world. You had a falling out when she first moved to Tokyo, but you made up. There's a letter from her, and a bunch of photos taken here in London. She must have visited us here." He passes me one of the photos.

"Nobu, this is the girl with red hair that I saw, at Shibuya Crossing. There are a couple more photos of her on the wall."

"No way! From our training day in Tokyo?"

"Yup! Have you not yet accepted that nothing is impossible?" He chuckles. In the photo, four of us stand smiling in front of the London Eye, with our arms around each other's shoulders and waists. There's Nobu, then me, then Skye and a Japanese girl who looks about our age. I flip the photo over, where I suspect an earlier version of me has written our names: Nobu, Claire, Skye, and Akari. I wonder if this is Skye's new love. I want Skye to have that, even though I can't quite remember her. What I do remember, is the feeling of her.

"Claire, you and I were happy together. Like legit in love. We made each other better people. You know?" I nod. "When we were at The Station, you told me you had this feeling that you were just starting to figure some things out, before you died." I cover his hand with mine. "You were right." His words settle inside me. I remember my anger at having been ripped out of my life, just as it was getting good. There was no way for me to know, but I knew. Our eyes are filled with tears.

"And you belonged, Nobu. You were part of something," I say.

"I was," Nobu sighs. "I still am, Claire. I know that."

Nobu lies down facing me. I recline, push my left arm between the pillow and his neck, and rest the other hand on his shoulder. For a few minutes, we're silent, both of us floating in our own little past-life pods, but still connected. In the sweetness of this moment, I imagine Nobu touching my face and kissing me. I close my eyes and take a few deep breaths. It's impossible to know whether this is a memory or a prediction.

When I look up, I'm startled to see that the shining rope of filaments between Nobu and me has sprouted two tendrils that are growing quickly towards the door where, I suspect, one golden thread will head for Lily's nursery while the other will connect us to Nobu's parents.

"Whoa!" says Nobu. "That's new." I nod. "Shall we go meet her?"

"Yes. I know it's time but I'm scared, Nobu," I say as I sit up.

"Me too," he says. I take his hand.

CHAPTER 41
IN WHICH WE DEVELOP A FILAMENT PROBLEM

The sun is rising, and in Lily's nursery, the light through the window is soft and pink as it illuminates her face. She's even more glorious than in the photographs in our room. We stand at the crib, and as we gaze down at her, she opens her eyes and looks directly at us.

"There you are!" says Nobu.

I don't know how, or if this is possible, but Lily seems to remember us. She reaches her hands out towards us and laughs. She's part Nobu, part me, and part something entirely herself. Out of her belly button, two strands of filaments gently unfold and unbraid and connect themselves to the golden ropes coming from each of us. All three of us are now attached to each other via these glimmering cables. Lily pulls herself up to a standing position and reaches for her father. "Daddy, pick up," Nobu's mouth falls open, and I feel giddy. Not only does she know us, but she's speaking. Of course, we don't know what age kids do things.

As soon as he recovers, Nobu reaches down and picks her up. He carries her over to the rocking chair, where he sits and holds her in his lap. She laughs and puts her fingers in his ears and his mouth. Then she turns towards me, extends her arms, and says, "Mama, hug."

Suddenly, my stomach is in knots. "Nobu, something about this doesn't feel right."

He looks up. "What do you mean? She's not even frightened, Claire. Don't you want to hold her?" I desperately want to hold her. Lily's filaments tug at me, but I don't think I should. I shake my head. "Okay," Nobu says. "But we agreed. One night. I'm going to hold her until my parents wake up. And then we'll go. I promise."

I sit across from them in a leather chair. I think back to how angry I was at The Station, how I felt robbed of a beautiful life. A hard won, beautiful life. And I feel happy and relieved to learn that I turned things around and was loved by friends, by Nobu, and his parents, after being neglected by my own family. I was studying at university. I gave birth to this small miracle. Lily wrinkles her nose and giggles, as if she can hear my thoughts. But I exist as a Helper now, and I'm loved by Nobu, although differently, and Lily lives here with her grandparents. She is safe and thriving. I will always be alive in her, and in her children, if she has them. I feel strangely peaceful as I let go of the story that was feeding my anger.

As it turns out, I lived a whole, beautiful life and then I died. Humans die.

This chair must be where Nobu's parents sit, when they're getting Lily ready for bed at night. She's such a happy baby, and she's already walking and talking in phrases. After a few minutes, Nobu and Lily grow quiet, but they're still staring at each other intently.

"You're reading her thoughts?" I say.

"Sure. Aren't you?" he says.

"No."

"Hm. That's strange," Nobu shakes his head.

"What's she saying?" I ask.

"Simple things. Mostly she's happy to see us. She knows who we are. Just now she asked me to read her a book." Nobu picks up three books off the bookshelf and holds them up. Lily points to the one in the centre, and Nobu opens it and begins to read. Lily giggles at the funny bits, which makes Nobu laugh. He asks her to help him turn the page and she reaches up and mimics his gesture. Every part of me wants to relax and enjoy this reunion, but something is definitely off. No, more wrong than off. The hairs on my arm stand up.

As Nobu and Lily fall more deeply in love with each other, I notice that the thick rope of filaments between Nobu and me, and the smaller one between Lily and me, have begun to fade, while the new set of filaments that has sprouted between Nobu and Lily is growing rapidly, like seaweed being pushed forward by the tide, creating a golden cocoon around the two of them.

I shake my head. Wake up, Claire. Clear your mind. The sun is up now, and I can't understand why Nobu's parents haven't come into the nursery, especially as Lily is laughing and burbling away. I creep out of the nursery and cross the hall, into Nobu's parents' room, but they're still asleep. I can see the gentle rise and fall of their bodies under the blanket, so they are definitely breathing.

What was it that Coach said? Think, Claire. Think. We must never make contact with people from our old lives. No, he said it was not possible. That the people from our old life would never recognize us. It was part of the design of the afterlife. But Lily sees us. She knows us. My knees buckle.

Back in the nursery, I kneel in front of the rocking chair, where Nobu, who seems not to have noticed I was gone, is still reading. Lily reaches out to touch me, but something in me knows I cannot allow her to. I move back a bit, just out of her reach. "Nobu, I need you to listen to me." He doesn't look up from the book, so I raise my voice. "Something very wrong is happening here." Nothing.

Think, Claire. I try communicating with him without speaking. *Your parents are still asleep. They shouldn't be. They should be in here, getting Lily dressed, changing her diaper.* He looks as though there's a mosquito flying around his head that he's trying to ignore. "Nobu," I say in as loud a voice as I can, without scaring Lily, but he doesn't see or hear me.

We've been with Lily for hours now, and I know she needs to eat and have her diaper changed. I lay out a small blanket on the floor and place a diaper there along with an undershirt, and a tiny burgundy velvet shirt and leggings. I grab the container of wipes and place them on the blanket as well. Nobu sees the items I've laid out.

"Oh. Shall we change your diaper, then?" says Nobu. He rises carefully from the rocking chair and places Lily on the blanket, changes her diaper, and then dresses her. If the circumstances were different, I'd be impressed with the deftness with which he accomplishes these tasks. I run downstairs and grab a jug of milk out of the fridge and fill a sippy cup I find in the cupboard. There are a couple of jars of what looks like homemade baby food in the fridge, and I grab a small spoon and sample one. Carrots, green peas, and chicken. Oh, Lily, your grandparents are absolute saints! I drop the jar and small spoon, a bib and a roll of paper towels into a canvas bag, grab the sippy cup and run back upstairs.

Back in the nursery, Lily and Nobu are dancing in the centre of the room, both lifting their fingers towards the sky as if they are touching the stars. Lily is stepping on her tiptoes which is both adorable and heartbreaking. I place the contents of my bag on the table, beside the rocking chair. Lily squeals, picks up the sippy-cup and starts drinking immediately. Poor kid—she must have been so thirsty. Nobu scoops her up and rocks her, while she drinks. When she's done, he places the empty cup on the table and picks up the jar of chicken and vegetables, the bib, and the spoon. I can't tell if he knows I am there, but he's committed to caring for Lily.

As Nobu feeds Lily, I return to Nobu's parents' room. They're still asleep in the same positions they were in when I was last here. When I glance out the window, I don't see anyone. I'm not sure how much time has passed. Everything feels surreal. Is it noon? I run down the stairs and out the front door. There's no one on the streets. No cars, no one walking their dog. Not a soul.

It seems that everyone on Earth is in a coma. I shiver and wonder if we've caused this, but I already know the answer.

CHAPTER 42
IN WHICH THERE ARE SEVERAL VERSIONS

As I return to the second floor of the house, a girl runs out of the bathroom and down the hall. Her black hair is pulled back in a ponytail and she's wearing an avocado onesie pyjama, with a hood. She is both familiar and unfamiliar at the same time. Surprised, I inhale sharply, and she stops and looks around, but can't see me. This girl has blue eyes. Lily's eyes. When she doesn't see anything in the hallway, this twelve-year-old version of our daughter runs into our old room and slams the door. "Lily?" It looks like being twelve is challenging for our girl, which she probably comes by honestly, and I place my right hand over my heart and send her love. Then, because I'm unable to stop myself, I follow her through the door.

But it isn't our room anymore. Someone with much better taste than Nobu or me has redecorated. A quick scan of the room reveals sage green walls and a ceiling that's wallpapered with tiny birds flying against a white sky. A headboard has been covered with plaid fabric and a portrait of Jane Austen hangs above the bed. The photo walls are gone, but three of the photographs have been blown up and framed in white mats and black gallery frames: Nobu and me at his 16th birthday party, us with his parents on our wedding day, and the one of Lily, Nobu and me on her first birthday. There's an open suitcase on the bed and standing over it, there's Lily. Only she's not wearing an avocado onesie, and she's not twelve. She's my age. And she's looking right at me.

"Mom?" she says, quietly. She's wearing a navy, Central St. Polina's t-shirt, tucked into jeans. Gone is the ponytail from a few moments ago and in its place, a cool bob that swings as she moves. She looks like the little girl from the photo in Kano's purse, but also not. I can't find a single word, so I just nod like a dork.

"Hi," she says. All the questions in my mind race to my mouth at the same time and tumble over each other. "There are so many things I want to ask you," she says. I nod my understanding.

"Me too! Where are you going?" I ask, glancing at the suitcase. Of all the questions, that's the one that makes it to my lips. "Also, Hi Lily."

She smiles and says, "Tokyo. I'm taking a year off."

I hear myself repeat, 'Tokyo,' and then I remember the girl with red hair who smelled like oranges. "Skye," I say quietly.

"Your best friend!" Lily nods. "She moved there before I was born. You wrote about her in your diaries." She looks sheepish for a moment. "I hope you don't mind that I read them. I held out until I was twelve, but I needed to know everything I could about you."

I nod again. "Nobu and I were just reading them." I say.

"Dad?" she says. And suddenly I remember Nobu, in the next room with two-year-old Lily, and the potentially world-ending mess I've gotten us into. "I keep Dad's letter with me all the time," says Lily. I'm not sure what she's talking about, but we can't get into that now.

"I don't have much time, Lily. I just want you to know that we love you, your Dad and me, and we're so sorry we left you alone."

"I've never been alone, Mom. I have Baa-chan—Grandma Kano and Jiji-Hiro. I feel loved. Like all the time." I smile because I believe her, and because my own kid is trying to cheer me up, to reassure me.

"You know, baa-chan told me stories about you. She says you're a badass."

"Really?"

"Really!" she says. Tears stream down my face, and I don't wipe them away. I want to grab her, to hug her, to place my hands on her exquisite face, but I know I can't do any of that, so I close my eyes and try to lock in this memory, so I can retrieve this feeling of complete love, whenever I want. When I open my eyes, I see that Lily is reading my thoughts, and I am reading hers.

"You are infinitely loved, Claire." That's when I get the memo the Universe has been trying to deliver for a year. I AM loved, and so is Lily, and nothing can change that. Not even dying. I find myself wishing there were something I could give her, something that could stand in for me, in my absence from her life ... I flip open my bag and take out the journal that Coach gave me. I don't want to risk touching her, so I place it in her open suitcase.

"You can read my diaries, anytime you want," I say. "I

love you, Lily. Your father does too. I don't want to leave you, but I need to get back inside that nursery, before your father ruins time." The last thing I see is a slightly confused expression on Lily's sweet face, as I turn and dash into the hallway.

CHAPTER 43
IN WHICH THINGS GO, AS THEY DO, FROM BAD TO WORSE

nside the nursery, I wonder if my vision was affected by the bright light outdoors. No, I can see baby Lily, perfectly. Only Nobu has begun to fade from sight.

The golden cocoon around Nobu and Lily is brighter than when I left, but Nobu is disappearing. Becoming a shadow. For a moment, I wonder if this is the next plane of his existence, if he's moving from being a Helper to the next thing. Oh, what's that thing called? I can't remember.

No, nothing about this is natural. Nobu is disappearing right in front of my eyes, and if I don't do something, he will cease to exist. There is a good chance that Lily will not have a chance to grow up to become an angry twelve-year-old, or a young person embarking on a great adventure.

But this is about way more than us. Without irony, I realize that I need to save the world, which our actions have endangered, and to do so, I must get Nobu out of here.

My mind races, and my hands shake, and I can't think, but I don't have the luxury of not thinking right now. Focus Claire! There's nobody here to help you, so you'll need to do this on your own. You can do this!

Because I'm no longer concerned about waking his parents, I yell Nobu's name and wave my arms in front of him, but he can't see or hear me, anymore. He does, however, continue to be finely tuned to what Lily needs. He's singing her the spider song he sang to Irène, when her mother went briefly missing. Poor Lily-girl. She must need a nap by now. Oh! If I can get him to put her down for a nap, maybe I can work out a way to get him out of here.

There's a blue blanket and a toy giraffe in Lily's crib. I place them on our impromptu changing station on the floor, along with a fresh diaper, and a onesie with tiny sheep jumping over fences. Lily sees the blanket, toddles over and picks it up. She holds the blanket against her face, pops a thumb in her mouth, and sits down on the floor with a bump. Nobu sees what's happening and says, "Are you tired, Lily? Is it time for a nap?" She nods her head. "All right, my girl. Let's get you changed into these cute jammies and get you into bed." She falls asleep several times, while he's changing her. "Sorry, boo. It looks like I've kept you up too long." He picks her up, carries her to the crib and lays her down on the mattress. Without Lily in his arms, it is even more difficult to see him, and I realize I have just seconds left. He turns to retrieve the giraffe from the floor. Behind him, daylight pours through the window, and he's faded so much that in some places, the sun shines right through him. He's disintegrating in front of me.

"Nobu, thank you for taking such good care of Lily. I'm happy you were able to hold her." I take a step towards him and Nobu looks around, as if he hears something, but he appears confused and scared.

"Nobu, there was a family of refugees we met when we first got to Paris. You helped them find their son, who was lost." I'm speaking more loudly now, trying to get his attention and he leans towards me, straining to hear. He bends down and picks up the giraffe, and his brow wrinkles. "They can't go home because the city they're from doesn't exist anymore. Ours doesn't either, at least not the way we want it to." His eyes open wider as if he's finally heard me, and at that moment, I take three quick steps and fly against Nobu with all my might, tackling him the way I've seen kids tackle each other in parks, and we fly backwards through the open window, sliding down the shingles of the roof and over, falling to the ground below. I'm still wrapped around his torso, as we land in a pile of our own limbs in the driveway between Nobu's parents' house and the house next door. I imagine that this fall has killed us, and then I remember that's not possible. There's no pain anywhere, I haven't even had the wind knocked out of me. I hold Nobu down by his shoulders, terrified that he'll get up and run back upstairs to be with Lily.

After a few moments, Nobu opens his eyes. "Claire? What's happening? Where are we?" He's becoming himself again, and appears more solid with each passing second. Whatever was happening to make him fade is reversing itself, so I release my grip on his shoulders. When Nobu sits up, I lose my balance and land on my back in the gravel. Finally, I let the tears come and Nobu kneels beside me and looks at me with concern. "Why are you crying? Please tell me so I can help." Then he looks at the stuffed giraffe in his hand and places it gently on the grass beside us.

My sobbing slows until I sound like a machine that's still whirring, even after the engine's been turned off. Finally, I'm able to catch my breath, and I wipe the tears from my cheeks. Somewhere, not too far away, a bird sings and another bird replies. A small boy rides his bike on the sidewalk in front of the house. Two cars drive down the street, then a third. A person in a paisley dress, and their small dog, pass the boy on the bike. Although none of them seem to notice us, the day has finally begun for them. Phew! We did not break the world. I sit up and place my hands over Nobu's.

"Claire, what's happening? You're really freaking me out. The last thing I remember, we were entering Lily's room."

"You don't remember anything after that?" I say. He shakes his head. "As soon as you picked Lily up, you went into a kind of a trance, and you couldn't focus on anything or anyone, but her. You said you could read her mind, but then you stopped being able to see or hear me. Your parents didn't wake up and there was no one outside—no commuters, no little kids, no dogs. Then I saw two older versions of Lily, which confirmed that we were, in fact, breaking the space-time continuum, or whatever. Then you started to fade from view and that was the very scariest part."

"You met an older Lily? As a teenager?" I nod. "What was she like?"

"The twelve-year old was very angry about something. The second Lily was our age. Poised. Funny. They were both amazing," I say.

"Of course, she was. Wait. What do you mean, I was fading?"

"The filaments disconnected from me and formed a cocoon around you and Lily. I think it's because you held her, but inside the cocoon, you were becoming invisible."

"What? I don't understand."

"I think it was because we weren't supposed to touch Lily," I say.

"I'm sorry. I can't remember any of this. It must have been so frightening for you, Claire." he says.

My thoughts turn to Lily. I make Nobu promise to stay exactly where he is for a few minutes. I pick up Lily's giraffe and run back into the house, and look inside his parents' bedroom, where the bed covers are pushed back, but his parents aren't there. In the nursery, Nobu's father holds Lily in his lap, and Kano sits in the leather chair across from him. I'm unbearably happy to see them both, awake and well. I have so much I want to say to them, which is, of course, entirely impossible, so I push my thoughts from my heart to theirs. *Thank you for being such amazing grandparents to Lily. Thank you for raising Nobu to be such a kind, intelligent man. Thank you for loving me and for saving my life.*

"Why did you leave these diapers and clothes on the floor, when you changed Lily for bed last night?" Kano sounds mildly annoyed with her husband, but not really angry.

"I assure you I did no such thing," he says, "And I am going to forget this absurd accusation, which is obviously a desperate attempt to cover up your own forgetfulness." They both laugh, and I realize that each of them genuinely believes the other has left these items on the floor. I gently lay the giraffe on the floor under Kano's chair, where they won't notice it suddenly appear, and where I'm sure they'll find it before too long.

"Let's go downstairs and have breakfast. It's a brand new day. Let's make it a good one, Lily-Bear," Kano says. She gathers up the items from the floor and heads downstairs. Nobu's father follows her, holding Lily by the hand. As they pass me, Lily reaches out her other hand and waves. Lily. Our Lily. *It was lovely to see you again.* I blow her a kiss and she blows one back, as she and her grandfather round the corner into the hallway.

I wait a moment for the family to enter the kitchen before I run downstairs and slip out the front door. Thankfully, Nobu is at the side of the house where I left him. "She's okay," I say. "Your parents are awake and they're making breakfast with Lily. I think that whatever terrible thing we triggered is over."

Nobu wraps his arms around me. "Sorry I messed up, Claire. Thank you for getting me out of the house, and for making sure that Lily and my parents are safe." He squeezes me tighter, and I lose it. I cry so hard I start to shake. Maybe I'm feeling the fear from before, from when we were in Lily's room, and I didn't have the luxury of feeling afraid. Lines from that poem I love pop into my mind. Fine! I will let the soft animal of my body love what it wants. I do tell Nobu about my despair. And yes, apparently, the world does go on.

"Okay, Mary Oliver. Message received."

"What are you talking about?" says Nobu.

"I'm remembering this poem called 'Wild Geese.' The last line is about announcing your place in the family of things."

"The family of things," says Nobu. "I like that. Our family got a lot bigger today."

"Yes. Infinitely. We need a plan, my love," I say.

"Back to Paris?" says Nobu.

"We can't stay here."

CHAPTER 44
IN WHICH I YELL AT COACH

"Claire? Nobu?"

We hear someone calling our names, but that's impossible. Whoever it is, I can tell they're getting closer, and then a small boy runs into view, sees us, and runs straight towards us. The kid is wearing a white T-shirt, khaki shorts, running shoes, and white athletic socks pulled up to his knees. He's wearing a whistle around his neck and holding a compass.

It's Coach and he's smiling. The unbelievable nerve.

Nobu runs to Coach and hugs him.

"What in the actual hell?" I yell.

"Claire, it is lovely to see you," says Coach. He steps towards me, but I back away and hold up a hand.

"Oh no. There's no way you get to show up here, after everything we've been through, after we saved ourselves. No way!" I'm yelling even louder than before. "You abandoned us. Nobu wrote to you for help. You never answered. You don't get to show up now and pretend that you care about us, because it's pretty clear you don't!"

Nobu grabs my hand. "Hey. We're okay. I don't think yelling at him is going to help," says Nobu.

"Maybe not, but it sure is making me feel better!" I yell.

"Don't you want to know what happened?" Nobu says gently.

"You are managing me right now, Nobuhiro, and it is pissing me off."

He laughs. "Fair enough, but I'm not wrong. Can we please just let him talk?"

"Fine. Back garden," I say. We ghost through the fence and into the small, shaded space between the house and the garden shed. I look directly at Coach. "Talk!"

"Claire, you have every right to be angry. You both do."

"We know! But why didn't you come when Nobu wrote to you?"

"After I dropped you off in Paris, I wrote up your intake and training report, and sent it to Admin."

"Admin? What is Admin?" I say.

"They're my line managers."

"How can you have line managers in heaven?" I say.

"This is not heaven," says Coach.

"You can say that again," I say.

"Claire," Nobu says gently. He nods at Coach to continue.

"Almost immediately, I was called to a tribunal regarding your demotion, as Helpers." Nobu and I exchange glances.

"Coach, didn't you say that never happens, that Helpers are never demoted," says Nobu.

"Yes. Up until that point, it had never happened," says Coach. Nobu leans back against the stone wall of his parents' house and closes his eyes.

"Did you see the filaments and the sparks? When we

were at The Station?" I say. Coach nods his head. "Did you put them in your stupid report?" He nods again. "So, two dead barely-adult beings are being punished for being exceptional, in a situation that was completely beyond our control?"

"Yes. That is the gist of the case I made to Admin on your behalf," says Coach.

"Claire, we're not exactly blameless in all of this. We broke the rules. We found my mother. We came to London and met Lily, even though we knew we weren't meant to," says Nobu.

"We were also not supposed to have any memories of our life before. Of each other. But I did remember." The word 'remember' catches in my throat, and I'm afraid I'm going to cry. I will not cry in front of Coach.

"If you would be so kind as to give me a few moments, I would like to explain where I have been and why I did not respond to Nobu's recent message," says Coach quietly.

"Please do," says Nobu.

"By all means," I mutter.

"Let's sit down." Nobu and I drop to the ground and Coach sits cross-legged in front of us. "Claire, there is no precedent for your gifts, at least none of which I am aware. In our short time together at The Station, I observed your extraordinarily strong empathic skills, along with the evidence of residual memories from your life. While this was undoubtedly connected to the strength of your ties to Nobu, the child you share, and the fact that you died together, the death process normally wipes the slate clean. You, however, arrived at The Station with a strong sense of self and a fierce desire to know who you were when you were alive. Although I could see your discomfort, I knew there had to be a reason for it, something to be learned or explored." I'm about to explode with snarkiness, when Nobu squeezes my hand a little tighter than is strictly necessary.

"Keep going, Coach," says Nobu.

"But Admin did not see Claire's gifts as an opportunity, so they called for your demotion. Of course, since this has never happened before, there was no method in place for making such a decision, so we've been simultaneously creating a process, while also hearing the case."

"But it's been months," I say, moving my hand out of Nobu's reach.

"Yes. For months, I have argued that we should allow the two of you to become Helpers in your own, unique way. I asked that we empower Claire to reimagine the way that Helpers live and help on Earth. To make the process more humane, if you will." Coach smiles at his own pun.

"You've been fighting for us for months?" says Nobu.

"Yes. Since you left The Station," says Coach.

"And?" I say.

"Oh yes, quite right. We won."

"We won?" Nobu and I say in unison.

"Yes. Just this morning. We watched what's happened in Nobu's family home, as if we were watching the World Cup Finals."

"Really? A sports metaphor?" I say.

"Claire, you know what he means," says Nobu. "Coach, please continue."

"The decision was made at the precise moment when Claire understood that saving Nobu was not just about saving him, but about saving the world. You showed the tribunal what Helpers are capable of when we get out of your way."

"So, we are definitely not demoted," says Nobu. I frown at him.

"No, far from it. You are free to move on to your next state of being, however you define that," says Coach. Our next state of being? My head is spinning. I close my eyes and lean against the cool stone of the house for a few moments, and then I open my eyes and make eye contact with our clever Station Master.

"Coach," I say. "There was this night when I was freaking out and a voice told me to breathe. Like inside my head. Was that you?" Coach nods and smiles. "And what about our filaments?"

"They are gone, Claire. It seems that they served their purpose." Although I had guessed that was the case, the confirmation blows a hole through my heart.

"A lot has happened here, Coach," says Nobu. "Claire has done a lot of heavy lifting on her own. We're going to need some time to recover, before we return to helping."

"Of course. Let's head back to your new Station where you can rest, and you can choose what comes next," says Coach.

"Claire?" Nobu says quietly.

For a few moments, I flash back to my encounter with teenage Lily, and the feeling of unconditional love. Of course, Coach is telling the truth. He's had our backs this whole time and I've been such a jerk to him. "Yes," I say. "Some time at our new Station would be good. I would welcome animal-shaped pancakes and mint tea, served in a small green cup with peonies in the bottom."

CHAPTER 45
IN WHICH I IMAGINE STANDING AT THE EDGE OF THE OCEAN

"Imagine you're standing at the edge of the ocean. It's summer, your feet are bare, and your trousers are rolled up. Got it?" Coach has introduced me to Ms. Van Den Borne, a Seer and wise woman, who lives in a small village in the Netherlands. Twice a week, I use the WHEREVER door from our new Station to visit her in her snug little office, where she makes me a café latte before we begin.

I close my eyes and visualize this scene. "Yup," I say. "I'm standing on the beach."

"Good. Now observe the waves come in."

"Okay. I'm watching them," I say and take a sip of my coffee.

"Good. Now what happens next?"

"They go out. This is not a very difficult quiz," I say.

"And what happens after the waves go out?" Ms. Van Den Borne asks.

"They come back in. Listen, I know this must be an analogy for something."

"Clever girl. This is grief, Claire. The waves are grief, and they will arrive on their own schedule. They will come and then they will go. You can allow them to come, or you can fight against them. The choice is yours."

"That sucks," I say.

"Yes, it does. Eventually, though, you will feel less sad and less angry. Coffee will taste better, and the sky will look bluer, and you will be ready to think about what you want next."

"But I'm not exactly alive, am I? Isn't the grief you're describing for humans?" I ask.

"Excellent point. You have, however, been very recently human. You have memories and evidence of your life as a human woman. You are entitled to that grief, and to deny those feelings will cause other problems." I love that she calls me a woman.

"An interesting thing happened when I encountered the young adult Lily. I heard her or someone say, 'You are infinitely loved' and I knew that message wasn't just for me and Lily."

"How so, Claire?"

"At that moment, I understood that there's no separation between beings, and love is never lost, not even when people die," I say. The tears come as they wish, and I let them, and Ms. Van Den Borne does not shush me, or hurry me, or try to cheer me up.

After a bit, she repeats what I've said, "'There's no separation between beings, and love is never lost.' It's the best description of interbeingness I have ever heard. If you made that into a bumper sticker, Claire, it would be so popular, you would never be able to keep it in stock." We laugh.

"But there's this weird tension," I say, "between the grief I'm experiencing as a former human, and the peace and connection I feel as a Helper, or whatever I am now."

"Yes," she says. "And it's up to you to decide whether you want to call this a tension or understand it as a both/and situation."

"Like the way that Lily exists in my mind as a two-year old, a twelve-year-old and a young woman?"

"Yes. Just like that. Here's the really good news," she says. "Whatever you choose to do next, the love inside you, the love that you're made of, will continue to grow." Suddenly there's a lump in my throat. At first, it's Lily-sized, then Nobu-sized, then it's a smaller Coach-sized lump. "That's enough for today, darling girl. You are doing splendidly."

After our session, I write two new lists in the new journal Coach left on my desk:

AN INCOMPLETE LIST OF THINGS I LOVE ABOUT LILY

1. The way she trusted us so quickly in London.
2. How easily and how much she laughs.
3. With every part of her body, she expresses her emotions and needs.
4. How she knew exactly what book she wanted to hear.
5. She reminds me of Nobu.
6. The avocado onesie and the passionate door-slamming of Lily, the twelve-year-old.
7. The poise, confidence and style of Lily, the young woman.
8. That no version of her lives in fear.
9. That she feels loved.
10. That she exists in the world.

A SMALL BUT IMPORTANT LIST OF THINGS I'M READY TO LET GO:

1. All the things I don't know about my former life.
2. Being angry all the time.
3. The dream of hugging Lily.
4. My resentment towards Coach.
5. Being in love with Nobu who is not in love with me.

CHAPTER 46
IN WHICH I APOLOGIZE

Of course, I find Coach in the kitchen.

At first it was a bit hard to get used to the new Station, but I have to admit, Coach did a smashing job with the design. The ceilings are high, Georgian, I think, and there's a feeling of elegant spaciousness. Nobu and I have our own rooms across the hall from each other and mine is connected to a cosy study with a large wooden desk and a wingback chair, covered in plaid fabric that looks very much like the one from our old kitchen. A floor to ceiling bookshelf holds hundreds of volumes, including all my sparky books from the old Station, as well as those I discovered at Colette and Company. My desk faces a large, tall window, from which I have an astonishing view of a blue-grey sea. Coach laughs when I ask him if the new Station is close to Lunenburg.

Nobu's bedroom is connected to an art studio with enough canvasses, sketchbooks, and paints to last a lifetime. Whatever that means now. Each time Nobu completes a new painting from a drawing in his sketchbook, Coach produces an extraordinary frame and hangs the new work in

Nobu's studio. I suspect this impromptu exhibit fills Nobu with embarrassment and delight. Canvas by canvas, Nobu is calling back our life in Paris, breathing life back into those beautiful and difficult days. He's just begun a painting of Lily, and although I haven't said this to him, it's clear that his art-making is the equivalent of my time with Ms. Van Den Borne. Nobu is so much like his mother, a fact for which, I will be eternally grateful.

There isn't a room of puppies here, but there is a Golden Retriever named Sam, who is entirely devoted to Coach, and who is quickly becoming friends with Nobu and me.

"Good morning, Coach," I say. Sam brushes up against my leg and I scratch his head between his ears.

"Hello, Claire. I just put on a pot of tea. Can I offer you a cup?" I nod. Genuinely, I did not think it was possible for Coach to surpass the cosiness of the kitchen in the old Station, but he has. There's a small bistro table with three cane-covered chairs beside a tall window that is identical to the one in my study, and shares the same sea view. In stark contrast to the cream-coloured walls, moldings and base-boards, the wide wooden floor planks have been painted black as have the cabinets. In the place of a kitchen island, there's a long counter that looks like a bar and three stools have been tucked under the outside of the counter so we can chat with Coach while he cooks. Coach has made us a café, not exactly like the one at the Paris departure gate, but similar in style and feeling.

When I arrive today, there's a fire burning in the wood stove, and a plate of brownies on the counter. Coach knows all my love languages. He uses a wooden footstool to reach the green cup and saucer with the peonies in the bottom.

"You remembered," I say.

"Oh, I did not simply remember. I had this one made for you the day you and Nobu arrived at the old Station." He jumps down to the kitchen floor and places the cup in front of me. He pours from a bright orange teapot, and we sit quietly together for a few minutes sipping our mint tea.

"I'm curious, Coach. Is this the same teacup? Or a new one in its image?"

"Are you familiar with the law of conservation of energy?" he asks

"I think it means that energy can't be created or destroyed. It can only be converted from one form to another."

"Exactly right, Claire. This cup then, the one with the peonies in the bottom, is both old and new."

It's going to take me some time to solve this energy puzzle. "Okay, regardless of its age, the fact of this cup is extraordinarily kind, Coach. And not just the teacup, but all of it. The pink scarf and the copy of *Heidi* and the manual and advocating for us and coming to London and making this new Station and introducing me to Ms. Van Den Borne, and for always being patient with me, even though I've been so mean to you." I stop to think if I've missed anything. "Thank you for all of it." Coach nods, and I realize that for the very first time in our relationship, he's speechless. I wait for everything to kick back in for him.

"That means a great deal to me, Claire."

"Coach, I'd like to try something new. It's called an apology."

He smiles. "Truly, there is no need," he says.

"But there is. Maybe you're so highly evolved that you don't need to hear it, but I need to become more skillful at making amends." He nods. "Coach, I now understand that you've always done what you believed was best for me and Nobu. You saw me, like really saw me, and you advocated for the two of us when nobody else would. I'm sorry I wasn't able to trust you, and that I said hateful things to you. You deserved much better and I will do that, from now on."

"Thank you, Claire. That was one of the best apologies I have ever received," he says, wiping tears from the corners of his eyes.

"Top ten, would you say?"

"Top five, at least." He grins and then we sit quietly for a few moments. "None of this has been fair for you," he says.

"Nor for you, Coach." I don't know how long he has been a Station Master, and I'm not sure he'll ever tell me, but I know how old he was when he died, and that thought always makes me feel a little melancholy.

"Don't be sad for me, Claire. I have a happy and meaningful existence."

"I'm not sad for you, Coach. Not really." Next to him, I place a small package wrapped in red crepe paper from Nobu's studio, and tied with a wide gold ribbon. Coach carefully unties the enormous bow and eases the paper off.

"They're slippers!" he says and within thirty seconds, he's peeled off his socks and dropped them and his spotless white runners on the floor and is pulling on his new, navy, knitted slippers.

"Oh!" I say. "They're a little longer than I intended them to be." They're almost at his knees.

"And you sewed leather onto the soles?"

"To make them last longer. Nobu helped me with that."

Coach jumps down, spins around twice and then dances around the kitchen. As he hops and slides from one slippered foot to the other, he puts his hands up in the air and shakes them. I laugh, not at him, but as way of releasing the delight building inside of me.

"So, I'm guessing you like them?"

"No." He stops dancing and faces me. "I don't like them. I LOVE them!" And then he laughs at his own joke, and I can see Coach as he would have been, as a six-and-a-half-year-old. A small human without a care in the world, and the gift of cosy new slippers, hand-knitted by someone who loves him.

"Are we becoming friends, Coach?" I say.

He hops back up beside me. "That would make me immeasurably happy, dear girl."

CHAPTER 47
IN WHICH WE WALK TO THE GREEN FIELD WHERE WE MET

Nobu is rinsing paintbrushes in the sink in his studio, and it's still strange to see him in different clothes.

We've both ditched our Paris uniforms: his black leather jacket, and my Little Red Riding Hood coat. I'm teaching myself how to sew, out of a book in my study, and I'm looking forward to making my own clothes. What I want to wear most right now are simple garments made from soft materials, and I'm giving head-to-toe black a rest and experimenting with some soft greys and light blues and even a bit of white. Coach says these clothes suit me. I remind him that he's not even seven years old. I suppose the more things change, the more they stay the same.

Today, Nobu is wearing a navy and white plaid shirt, a pair of jeans, and the slippers Coach made him, which he says he prefers after so many months of walking around Paris in big clunky boots.

"You look lovely, Nobu. Entirely yourself," I say. He smiles, but his energy is quiet today. When I ask him about

it, he shrugs. "No problem, if you don't want to talk about it,"
I say.

"I don't mind. It's that I miss Lily and my parents. I
know that sounds absurd because you and I have each other,
for which I feel deep gratitude, and until very recently, I
didn't even know I had parents and a Lily."

"But ..." I say.

"Sometimes, during round two on Earth," he says raising
two fingers, "I would imagine belonging to a family."

"Like when you met the Watanabes," I say.

"Exactly," he says.

"Okay," I say.

"Okay what?"

"I mean, okay. Go ahead and miss Lily and your parents
and our friends. Don't try to convince yourself that you're
okay when you're not." I pause. "You've lost so much. We
both have." I can feel my tears springing up.

He lowers his head for a moment and then makes eye
contact again. "Wow! Where did that come from?" Nobu
says.

"Therapy. We're talking about grief. It turns out that it's
okay to feel your feelings. Beneficial, even," I say.

"Ah," he says. "That's good stuff, Claire. I admire the
work you're doing for yourself." I place my hand on his back.
"Do you want to walk with me?" he says. I nod and accom-
pany him across the hallway, through the doorway and into
the green field, where we arrived. I wonder why Coach
included this field.

"So, I've been thinking about writing a letter to Lily,"
says Nobu.

"A letter?" I say, and there's an echo in my head of my
conversation with young adult Lily. *I keep dad's letter with*

me all the time. I wonder if it's possible that the letter she's held onto for her whole life is one he hasn't written yet.

"I know you'll think it's a terrible idea, in terms of the space-time continuum," Nobu says, "but I've talked it over with Coach, you know, the ramifications of such a letter. He says it's fine if it's dated before we died."

"Hmm," I say. I'm trying to decide if I should tell him what Lily said.

"What do you think?"

I realize this is a question that's already been answered. But he needs to get there on his own. "I understand why you want to send a letter that she'll appreciate later in life," I say, "but Lily feels loved by us." A wave of something powerful moves through me, and I remember that we grieve because we loved. "She's okay, Nobu." I say. He nods and bites his bottom lip lightly. "But I'm in full support of whatever you decide." It's all the push he needs.

"This is a sensible and measured response. Both kind and logical. What have you done with Claire?"

"I know, right? Now that I'm not in crisis all the time, I'm really settling into myself." Nobu smiles at me with his whole being and the quality of the air and the light in the field changes. Everything is sweeter and more saturated, I sit down in the spot where we woke up the day of the car accident, and Nobu sits beside me. "Shall we now, at long last, speak of that about which we never speak?" I say. I expect him to laugh but he doesn't.

"I'd like to, but I don't want to ruin things," says Nobu.

"How could we ruin it?"

"What if we don't feel the same way? What if we're not able to stay friends?"

I cover one of his hands with mine. "There's no world in

which we're not friends, Nobuhiro. It doesn't exist. Let's just tell the truth, and every other thing will sort itself out."

"You're sure?" I nod. "Okay. I've attended to this question with my heart, and I know that I love you deeply, Claire. You're my best friend and the mother of my child. Having read your journal—"

"With my permission," I say. It's a lame joke made because my heart is pounding, because I'm so afraid of what he'll say.

"—with your permission. Now let me finish, because I'm really nervous. Having read your journal, I know that what we shared as humans was amazing and real, and that our connection was strengthened by Lily's birth. But the Nobu I am now, here at this Station and in Paris, well, I'm not the same Nobu as the one whose bedroom we were in."

"I understand, Nobu. I know you don't have the romantic feelings you had when we were human." I have not dared to hope.

"No. You don't understand. Please let me finish." I'm not sure if I can keep quiet, but I nod. "Something has been happening that feels new, like how I imagine the filaments and sparks felt for you when you first experienced them." I nod. "Every morning, just as I'm floating up from sleep, I remember you, I imagine your face, and I have this feeling that I want to be with you all the time, and talk with you, and touch you." He places his hands on my face. "I'm in love with you, Claire. Like really, properly in love." My stomach flips over.

"But you haven't said anything. We've been back for weeks," I say. He drops his hands from my face and rests them on my knees.

"I didn't mean to keep it from you, but I needed time to

understand my feelings and to be sure of what I wanted. Coach has been my, uh, Coach in this regard and he's been great at just letting me talk things through. If I'm perfectly honest, I'm afraid that what I put you through in Lily's nursery, the day you had to save the world by yourself, that it might have been too much. That I might have made it impossible for you to love me, again." His voice is soft, and his eyes are wide. I lean towards him and brush my lips across his. It's the briefest of kisses, but it holds the ghosts of all the kisses we've ever shared, and a hope-filled green field, for those to come.

"I love you, Nobuhiro Takahashi," I say.

"Just like that?" he says.

"Sure. Let's see what happens between the beings we are now."

"Can it really be that easy? Can we just choose to be with each other, as this Claire and this Nobu?" he asks.

"Pretty sure." I smile at him. We sit quietly for a few minutes, and I become aware of the smallness of us and the bigness of this strange, wonderful universe.

"You're really changing, Claire."

"Yes, I think that's true. Do you remember when I wasn't able to help anyone, when I was so determined to discover who I was?"

"Of course."

"I was obsessed with the idea that if I could just find out who I'd been when I was alive, I would know who to be now, and how to be her. But the truth of who I am doesn't exist in the facts of my old life. This life is about Irène, who held my face in her hands when her mother was lost to her. Anaïs, the most vulnerable girl in Paris. Gus. The Watanabes. David and his broken heart on the bateau. All the people looking for the *Mona Lisa*. Charles at the museum and the woman dancing in the ampitheatre outside. Books. Snow Angels. Walks through the Tuileries. Coach. You. This is my life now. These are the people in my life now. This is the work I get to do now." My voice wobbles with emotion.

"Nothing is wrong, Claire."

"I know." I pause for a moment and look around the field, where we're seated. "Hey, Nobu. I see you attending, with your whole heart, to the questions of your life, and your place in the family of things. I'm inspired by your goodness."

As this sweet man and I wrap our arms around each other, I hear a soft sizzling sound and we look up to see a canopy of golden sparks exploding above our heads.

CHAPTER 48
IN WHICH NOBU WRITES A LETTER

Dear Lily,

This is the day on which you are expected to arrive on earth, but you won't read this until you are twelve. While we wait for you, your mom and I have played several games of Scrabble, watched the first (fourth) Star Wars film, and danced, somewhat awkwardly, to 'Coffee,' by Sylvan Esso. Although I am, admittedly, not much of a dancer, your mom's moves are glorious. She's writing in her journal now, so while I have the chance, I've decided to write a letter to you, at twelve years old.

You must be thinking 'Why twelve?' (You might also be thinking that your parents are such dorks. Listen, we own this.) We both remember twelve as being quite a tricky age. People didn't take us seriously, or understand what we were saying, and they had definitely forgotten what it was like to be twelve. At least, that's how it felt at the time. Your mom says she was quite an angry person at that age, but she and I didn't meet until she was sixteen, so we'll just have to take her word for it. I'm writing this letter now, because we suspect you might be feeling that life isn't always fair, and we hear you.

On the momentous occasion of your twelfth birthday, it is our wish that you live your teenage and adult years as though life were fair. As if you've been heard and understood. We hope that you will stay open to the possibility that things will get better. We say this because there is so much goodness in the universe and in you.

We hope you will spend time outdoors every day, befriending trees, plants, and animals; that you will walk barefoot in tall grass and on sandy beaches; that you will take time to watch and marvel at sunsets and other ordinary miracles. We hope you will always remember that your hardware is ancient and that you are part of nature, not something separate from it.

Stay curious about the world and everything in it and choose your own adventures. There's so much cool stuff to try—music, meditation, dancing, rock climbing, advocacy, sports. You might love to cook like your grandfather, experiment with visual art like your grandmother and me, or write lists, observations, and stories, like your mom.

We urge you to fiercely pursue your interests and ignore anyone who declares them weird or a waste of time. They are not you, Lily, so they don't get to decide what is a waste of time for you. Every second matters, as does every second after.

Please don't get discouraged if someone makes a critical remark about something you create. Some people are quite fearful and risk-averse, and they may not understand how vulnerable we are, the ones who try. Keep going for it, kiddo. Discover a million ways to express your essential Lilyness to the world. Dress in a way that brings you joy. Dance as often as possible. Learn how to hand knit socks for your best friend.

Someday you may fall in love with some very lucky person. We're confident about two things:

1. You will know how to love and support your friends and romantic partner.
2. Because you will feel worthy as a person, you will never abandon yourself by accepting disrespectful words or actions from others.

If you choose a partner, we hope that you will enjoy and cherish each day with your person.

When it's time, you will figure out what to study and do for a living, and although it would be cool to be in love with that work, it's completely fine if you're not. Many people find a nice, stable job and keep their passions for other parts of their life. Always remember that your job is only a rental agreement for your time; your life is your own.

Think critically, dear one, about the ways in which the world is broken, and use your voice and your freedom to advocate for change. At the same time, we urge you to practice gratitude with your entire being, to notice what is beautiful, and to celebrate the happiness of others. We invite you to steadfastly develop your capacity for delight. This balance will not be easy, but we promise it will improve the quality of your life.

Your mom wants me to say that there's not just one path to a lovely and meaningful life, but many. She says that only you will know what's right and that you should trust yourself. She also thinks this letter is long enough already, and I'm smart enough to recognize that she's right.

We know twelve can be challenging, but we also believe you already have everything you need inside of you.

Your mom and I are always on your side. We are always watching out for you, even if you don't see us doing it.

You are infinitely loved, Lily. Happy 12th Birthday!

Your dad,
Nobuhiro Takahashi

AFTER EVERYTHING

ACKNOWLEDGMENTS

Thank you to the Readers of The 38 Impossible Loves of Naoko Nishizawa

Thank you to the readers of my first book, *The 38 Impossible Loves of Naoko Nishizawa*. Thank you for purchasing it, for checking it out of the library, and for giving it to your friends. I will always be grateful for the wave of book-love which encouraged me and helped me write the second book.

Thank you to my Editorial Team

Damien Pitter, Developmental Editor. While I recognize that most writers would not willingly employ their partner as their developmental editor, our work together has shaped this manuscript into a novel. Other writers told me that second books are challenging and now I believe them. Thank you for giving me the critical feedback I needed to hear in the kindest possible manner. Claire and I are filled with gratitude for your fierce editing game.

Catriona Turner, Copy Editor. You are amazing, Catriona. You made my prose richer and stronger. *After Everything* is a better story, thanks to your dedication to the authors with whom you work.

Caitlin B. Alexander, Cover Illustrator and Designer. You design my covers as though you're inside my brain, as though you've met Claire, Nobu and Coach. Thank you for creating this beautiful illustration of Claire.

Thank you to the Generous Friends of After Everything

To my friend and teacher Rachael Herron and my fellow writers in her Grads Masterclass; Mindy Owen, my unexpected proofreading fairy godmother; the intrepid Edward Giordano; Irina Bryan, Nada Honjo and Elaine Yandeau; Jun Sekiya; Ann, Jaya and Cary; my sister Megan Sunstrum; my steadfast partner in crime and all things, Damien Pitter; and the ARC readers of this novel.

Thank you to the Universe

Claire makes lists of questions and observations in her journal and some of those impressions are also mine.

In particular, I am grateful for:
sunsets, bookstores and roast chicken,
dogs of all kinds,
mint tea served in green cups,
for Lunenburg, Barcelona and Tokyo
all of which we've called home,
and Paris, a home of my heart,
for the shimmering love of friends,
and the filaments connecting me
to good people
and to stories.

ABOUT THE AUTHOR

Monna McDiarmid is a writer, life coach and educator. She and her partner live in a tiny apartment in Yokohama, Japan and an old, wooden house in Nova Scotia, Canada.

For updates about new novels and courses, sign up for Monna's newsletter, The Sunday Reader at:

monnamcdiarmid.com

Claire experiences mysterious phenomena that point towards her hidden past. As she pulls the threads that lead back to her life, Claire and Nobu unravel the seams between death and life, time and space. What will Claire sacrifice to save the world?